D0943202

To my children - Andrew, Steven, Benjamin, and Naomi

And, to the REAL Gabe — you know who you are.

Contents

Chapter 1

"To remain loyal to Jehovah, we need to avoid associating with those who are disloyal to him. We also need to separate ourselves completely from false religion." Truth Book

I am the invisible girl. In History class, I fade into the background in my gray and brown dress, the color of dirt. The only way to survive Armageddon and join Jehovah in Paradise is to stay hidden and apart from the World. Armageddon is coming soon; that's what the Brothers say. I need Jehovah to see my faithfulness to Him. I'm fifteen, and I've been baptized one year— one year of serving Jehovah every waking moment. I can't slip up, not once, or Jehovah will leave me.

Rubbing my thumb, its nail chewed to the quick, over the worn edge of my sketchbook, I try to drown out the hum of voices around me. My classmates are excited about spring break. Mr. Cooper gave up trying to teach a while ago, throwing his hands up in surrender, saying History can wait. It's not going anywhere, and he still has us for a few more months of ninth grade. He can cram a lot of history in those few months. Which makes the class groan.

Val shifts in her chair to face me. Her perfectly rounded bubblegum-pink fingernails, the same color as her lip gloss, press gently on the edge of my desk. Sometimes, I wish my nails were as nice as hers. Or that I could wear lip gloss. I'd wear dark pink or red. When I start talking to myself this way, I know it's true— Satan is doing everything he can to ensure I don't follow the Truth.

"That's pretty," Val says, looking down at the page in my sketchbook littered with butterflies. "You've always been good at drawing. Remember fifth grade, Ms. Shannon's class?" Before I can answer or stop her, she flips the page.

I sit taller, holding my breath while she stares at my pencil sketch of Armageddon. It was one of my best drawings. I'd based it on one I'd seen in my Truth books. It was hard to copy, but I'd captured everything, even the smallest details.

Jehovah's loyal people, the Brothers and Sisters, those in the Truth like me, stand shoulder to shoulder in the foreground. Their upturned faces glow with happiness. They're safe during Armageddon and on their way to Paradise. Behind them, jagged bolts of lightning shoot down from the darkening sky. Smoke and flames billow from cars and buildings as the Worldly run in all directions, their faces frozen in silent screams.

Val's mouth opens like she wants to say something, then closes again. She glances up at me and says, "This is really dark, Sara."

Bailey leans around Val. "It is dark. You drew that? I like it." She runs her fingers through her purple hair, pulling it up into spikes.

Heat prickles across my cheeks. "You shouldn't."

I drop my pencil into my sketchbook and close it. My picture is good enough for her to see what will happen during Armageddon. She should be scared, not excited. She doesn't have the Truth. She will be one of the people running for her life, wishing she had listened to me when I told her about Jehovah.

"We're having a pool party after school. You're invited," Bailey's lips curve up in a half-smile. "Dark girl."

Val mouths for Baily to stop. Val knows I would never go to a party. But she doesn't know why. Armageddon can happen at any moment. If it came while I was at the party, I'd be toast – just like them. Jehovah would never save me, unlike when I'm at school. School is school. It's not a party. Some places are safe.

"Did you see what she drew? Her cult is dark," Bailey says.

"It's not a cult," I whisper down to my chest.

"Bailey cut it," Val says.

"Whatever," Bailey says.

"I'm sorry, Sara, for my friend," Val says, her face pinched with sadness.

I feel a little sad too, not because of what Bailey said, but because I miss Val. We were friends through grade school, up until sixth grade. Sliding my sketchbook into my backpack, I assure Val I'm fine. With a flash of white teeth, she shifts back to Bailey. Their heads pressed together, making plans for later.

I sink low in my seat, wishing I were more like Neena, my best friend and Sister in the Truth. She's so confident in Jehovah and herself; it beams out her fingertips. If I were like Neena, I wouldn't be afraid to tell Bailey why I am not going or would never go to one of her pool parties.

The final bell startles me—the class cheers. Chairs screech back on the gray vinyl floor. Mr. Cooper cups his hands around his mouth and tells us to have a fun Spring break and stay safe. My head down, I tuck a strand of my painfully straight brown hair behind my ears and remain in my seat, not wanting to be caught in the jumble.

"Sara Stephens," Mr. Cooper eyeballs me as he gathers a stack of papers. "You better hurry. Spring break is starting without you."

"I guess," I mumble.

Hugging my books tighter, I walk to the door, pausing before stepping into the swarm of students filling the hallway. Val stands at her locker in a tight circle with Bailey and Zoe, her best friends. Except for Bailey, they all look the same. Jeans, tight t-shirts, and flannels tied around their waists. They are immodest and show their bodies to the boys, begging for sexual attention. I'm glad I'm not like them, in my dress that falls almost to my knees.

Sucking in a breath, I weave through the turquoise-colored hallway heading to the doors leading to safety outside. I pass Gabe standing at his locker with some of the jocks from the soccer team. When someone pushes me from behind, I can't tell if it's by accident or on purpose. I stumble, and my sketchbook falls to the ground at his feet.

"Hey!" He yells, his face softening when he sees me. "Oh, Sara. Sorry, I didn't mean to yell at you. I thought it was my jerk brother."

"Sorry," I say, my breath catching in my chest. I feel the heat rising on my cheeks.

He bends and gets my sketchbook. "Here," he hands it to me, and our fingers touch.

I yank my hand back like it burns and hurry away. I round the corner and lean against the cold metal of a locker. I try to breathe but can't—the air unmoving as if caught somewhere far away. Jehovah had seen Gabe and me. I'd sinned. *Please forgive me*, I beg. It *was an accident. I didn't mean to touch his hand.*

"You okay?" Val asks, making me jump. Where had she come from?

"I'm fine," I say, my voice catching. I wipe the sweat from my hands on the coarse fabric of my dress.

"You sure? You want a ride home? Bailey's mom is taking us," Val says.

Her face has a look of concern, not pity, unlike when Zoe asked me why I couldn't come to her Halloween Party last year. I'd told her about Jehovah and the Truth. She'd just stared at me, her mouth open, and then hurried away from me like I was contagious.

"I'm fine. I'll walk." I move to go around her, the fire in my stomach so hot it burns into my throat. I reach into my pocket and unroll two antacids from their silvery tube. Popping them into my mouth, I chew them until they are minty dust.

"Are you coming or what?" Bailey yells across the hall over the top of Zoe's head.

Val shakes her head, and I see it's pointless to fight it. Val is walking home with me. I follow her toward the double doors passing Mr. Balentine, the art teacher.

"Sara, I'm happy you entered the Art Show. I was hoping you would. You have so much talent." Pushing the door open, he smiles at me like a proud father.

"What? I didn't--" I start to say, and Val pulls me away, looking as if she'd swallowed something whole.

"See ya, Mr. Balentine," she calls over her shoulder.

What was that about?

Val pulls me to a stop and faces me. "Sara, I have to tell you something. You have to promise me you won't get upset," she says.

"Sure, I guess. I mean, I don't know," I stumble over my words again, wishing I could be more like Neena.

Val's gaze is off to the green hills in the distance. "I entered you in the art contest," she blurts out.

The words hit me like a brick wall. Why would she do that? Art contest. It's wrong on so many levels. It's a competition. The Brothers warn us about competition and how it can take my focus from Jehovah. Losing focus lets Worldly thoughts and images slip into my art. Any of my art not centered on Jehovah and the Truth has to stay a secret, like all my sketchbooks stored in the tiny cupboard in the back of my closet.

"That's what Mr. B. was talking about?" I ask. Somehow, my words come out smoothly and without a squeak. Is this what Worldly friends do to each other, go behind each other's backs? "You shouldn't have done that."

"I know. It was wrong. I should've asked you. But I knew you," she stops, her lips twisting as she forms the words. "I knew you wouldn't enter it on your own. You're good, really good. And the awards are art supplies and classes." She waves her hands.

The prizes sound nice. I could use the art supplies. But the classes? A ribbon of fear runs through me. I cannot go, even if I want to. Saturday is Meeting Day. Jehovah will never forgive me if I put my art before Him.

"Forgive me?" She asks sheepishly.

Val is Worldly; she doesn't understand Jehovah and his ways. In her own strange way, I realize she is trying to be my friend and help me. What picture had she entered? The only drawings I have are in my sketchbook tucked deep into my backpack and the place no one else knows about. How did she even get something to submit?

"I forgive you. But what did you enter?" I ask.

"It was one that you gave me, don't you remember? Your sister, Kaylee," she says, and I cringe. Not that one. The shadows are all wrong.

"Ya, I remember that one," I say. Mr. Balantine won't be upset when I tell him to withdraw my entry. He'll see it was a mistake.

"Remember when we used to walk home every day, back when we were at Sutter?" Val asks.

I nod, remembering how we used to walk home together. It seems so long ago, like a different me. She was the only Worldly person who didn't stare at me like they felt sorry for me when I told her about Jehovah and the Truth. Momma used to let me go to Val's house after school sometimes. It all stopped when Val came over one day during the summer with a new dress and a book she'd gotten for her birthday the night before.

Birthdays are a pagan celebration, and Val is Worldly. She doesn't want to learn about Jehovah and the Truth. Worldly friends will take me away from Jehovah. Momma's words and the words of the Elders echo in my head. They're right.

My stomach sours as we pass the lime-green house with spindly palm trees lining the yard's edge. The house where the lady yelled at me that she had her own religion, and I could take my Jehovah and shove it.

We get to Val's corner, and I say, "Thanks for walking with me. I feel better."

I move to go. Val grabs my arm, and my fingers tingle from when I touched Gabe. "Hold on." She reaches into her back pocket, pulling out her phone. As she taps at the screen, I glance over my shoulder; I have to get home.

She holds up her phone for me to see, "I'm going to be a counselor at this camp, Camp Horizon. It's up in the mountains."

"That's nice," I say, trying to sound interested.

"All my friends say I'm weird for doing this church camp thing. You get it, though. You should come too. It will be fun. Plus,

I miss hanging out with you," she says, and I believe her for a second. But then I remember the truth about church camp, how it's riddled with the lies of Satan. It's one of his tricks to lead everyone away from Jehovah to die in Armageddon.

"Thanks, but I can't," I say. Now more than ever, I want to get away.

"I'm leaving on Sunday afternoon. You can still come if you change your mind, but not as a counselor. There's room, I know for sure." She rifles through her backpack and pulls out a glossy flyer, Camp Horizon, printed in bold yellow letters across the front, and pushes it into my hands.

"Sara, there's something else. Please, don't take this the wrong way," she pauses and tucks a strand of hair behind her ear, "try and have a fun time over break. Don't be so...miserable."

I force myself to take the paper from her, hiding the shock at what she said. I push the corners of my lips up, curving them into a smile. *I'm not miserable*, I think, because I can't find the words to say it out loud.

"Uhm, okay," I manage to say. I fold the flyer in half, slip it into the pocket of my dress, and walk away.

I am *not* miserable. I have something none of them have: the Truth. I am going to be saved when Jehovah destroys the World during Armageddon. They made their choice, and I've made mine.

A flit of blue, a flutter of wings, catches the corner of my eye. A bright blue butterfly dances over a bed of bright yellow daffodils, jumping from flower to flower. A faded memory scratches at the back of my brain, something I'd once found, a question I'd asked.

In a flash, the butterfly darts away, and I shake my head, continuing to walk home.

Chapter 2

Walking the rest of the way home alone, I feel Val's eyes on my back. She's wrong about me. I lift my chin and push my lips to a smile. I am not miserable. Shoulders back, I head toward the safety of home,

At the corner is the gnarled walnut tree, a remnant from the orchards and farmlands which once spread across the valley before being replaced by rows of houses and streets. I turn like usual. And there it is, our house, sitting in the bend of the road, like the crook of an elbow, where it can be seen from all directions. Its' bright coral pink paint, weathered white trim, and patchy brown grass are all out of place among the other houses with their neatly trimmed lawns and paint colors like toasted almond and creamy butter.

We've lived in this house the longest of all, two years. For the first time, I have my own room. There's no sharing with Kaylee and Pearl, my younger half-sisters. I know none of this will last. Momma will get the urge to move, or the rent will go up, and we'll pack up and move again.

As I near home, Kaylee, the youngest, runs toward me. "Guess what? Guess what? Guess what!" She bounces around me, the doll in her arms flapping.

"You're not supposed to tell her. Why are you so dumb?" Pearl, who's a few years older than Kaylee, says.

"Pearl, that's not a very nice thing to say. How do you believe Jehovah feels about your words?" I ask.

Pearl frowns.

"Well?"

"Sorry," Pearl says in a sing-song voice.

Shifting my books to hide my sketchbook, I kneel and take one of Kaylee's tiny hands in mine. It's so small and pale, the blue veins visible underneath the surface.

I finger the hem of the doll's dress. "Is this the surprise? A new doll?" I ask.

"No, silly, the doll is from Sister Wilson," she holds up the doll, and I see the dirt smudges on its face, the one blue eye faded to nothing, and the tattered hem. Another gift from one of the Sisters, something they didn't want anymore. "It's something else. I'm not supposed to tell, but..." Kaylee twists the toe of her shoe into the grass.

"You might as well tell her now. You blew the whole surprise," Pearl sighs, her forehead crinkled, eyebrows forming an angry V.

"Well, what is it then?" I ask. I want to go inside.

"Momma's bible student Rachel is moving in. Her family won't let her serve Jehovah. They say the Truth is a cult. But that's not true. They don't want Rachel to live in Paradise," Kaylee blurts out in one long breath.

"Oh," I stand, dropping Kaylee's hand. "I knew she was moving in, but not so soon. I like Rachel. She's not a bible student anymore; she's a Sister like Momma and me. Part of being a Sister is obeying Jehovah, no matter what. A bible student is studying to learn the Truth, to get to know Jehovah as a friend," I remind. Kaylee nods, her eyes wide.

Pearl crosses her arms over her chest and says matter-of-factly, "Yah, but did you know she was going to take over your room?"

"You mean sharing my room?" I correct.

"No, I mean, Momma packed your room while you were at school. Rachel's stuff is in your closet. And you're moving into our room." Pearl spins, her ponytail flying with her.

Kaylee hugs me around my waist before taking my hand. She pulls me to follow. Something inside me feels cheated. I suck in a deep breath. I can do this. I can. Jehovah will love me more if I do this. He has to. I've already done so much to displease him.

What about my closet, though? My secret. Is it safe? Has anyone found it?

I let go of Kaylee and hurry up the threadbare stairs, taking them two at a time.

I push the door to my room open. Momma faces me, wiping her hands on the front of her apron. Rachel, her long auburn hair hanging in waves around her shoulders, stands behind her, a pained expression on her face. Like she'd been caught doing something wrong.

For a moment I don't understand what I'm seeing. My room is emptied. My drawings of Paradise on Earth taken off the walls, leaving behind bright squares where the paint faded around them. All my books, gone. My yellow comforter, the color of weak lemonade, and the mounds of pillows on my bed —everything gone. My stomach rolls and I stop myself from reaching for an antacid.

Momma fastens a box closed with clear tape. She prints my name on the side in big black letters. "There, that's the last of your books," she says. "You don't need to have these."

I'm fifteen. Why does she treat me like I'm six? I start to say something and stop when Momma glares at me with the look that says not to question.

"Jehovah is going to reward you," Momma says to me. "You're making such a big sacrifice for Rachel."

Rachel mouths, "I'm sorry." And I know she is. "Sister Michaels, I don't need to have this room all to myself. It's too much."

"Nonsense. You are used to having your own space. And you need a place to study Jehovah's word."

While the two discuss what Rachel needs and doesn't need, I peer into the closet. I touch the soft fabric of the sleeve on one of Rachel's dresses, definitely silk. Her parents work and aren't in the Truth, so Rachel has nice things. She's so kind; she'd share with me if I were as tall as her. But her clothes would hang on me, and besides, Momma would put a stop to it. Momma doesn't like pretty things, especially on me.

I don't care about Rachel's clothes; I want to know if what's in the back, behind the plastic bags stuffed full of old clothes and boxes of old Truth books Momma couldn't throw away, is still undiscovered. My secret, hidden in the little cabinet under the eaves behind Momma's junk.

Silently, I slide a hanger over and glance down, trying to act like I'm not looking and draw attention. Momma's always watching, always suspicious. The bags and boxes are still there. A surge of relief rushes through me, along with sadness. My secret is safe, but all my belongings are gone. Not a trace of me left. I bite back the tears.

It's wrong—all wrong. But what does Jehovah say? What does he require of me? I wipe the corner of my eye. I know what he requires—my thankfulness. Jehovah has chosen me to make this sacrifice for Rachel. I need to be a good example for Pearl and

Kaylee and show them what it means to be one of His true believers. The more I do for Him, the more He loves me.

"Your stuff is in the garage," Pearl announces, her nose pointed in the air.

"Not all of it. Some stuff is in our room. We already put up some of your paintings," Kaylee adds. Her dress flutters up around her as she spins with her doll.

Momma glares at the two of them. "Now, we don't need any busybodies in here, do we?" She places a hand on Pearl's shoulder, facing her toward the door. "Why don't you two go downstairs and watch a video."

Pearl elbows past Kaylee, and the two fly down the stairs. A video. A rare treat in our home; we don't have cable or internet— just an ancient VHS player and a box of old tapes in cracked cases.

Momma follows them out of the room, saying nothing as she shuts the door behind her. Rachel smooths the single white pillow on the bed and picks a non-existent piece of lint from her blouse.

"I'm sorry. I didn't mean to take your room. Your mom…insisted. I wanted to wait until you were home. I thought I would be sharing with you; that would have been fun," she smiles with a tilt of her head.

"Really? I ask. I can't be mad at her.

"Really. I always wanted a sister," Rachel says. "I'm sorry how this happened. You can come in here whenever. It won't be for long, either. I'll be going to Bethel soon."

"Thanks," I sigh. How could I *not* give up my room for Rachel? She deserves it. She's giving up everything to serve Jehovah: her family and marriage (for now). She's going to Bethel, Truth headquarters. The place where our Prophesies come from. She'll be one of the volunteers that work for Jehovah. I could never make it to Bethel, not with my secret.

Plopping down on the edge of the bed, I keep my books close to my chest while Rachel rambles on about her day out in Field Service, preaching to the Worldly about Jehovah. I'm not listening. My thoughts are on the cabinet at the back of the closet and what I had hidden there. The cabinet was the perfect spot to hide my sketchbooks, the ones with the art Jehovah disapproves of. The ones filled with faces of the Worldly and the projects from Mr. Balentine's art class.

I know it's wrong. Jehovah has no place for an artist in Paradise or now. I can't seem to stop myself from drawing. My fingers tingle, and I'm not sure if it's from where I'd touched Gabe or because I needed to draw something.

In second grade, I won first prize in the school Art Show. Afterward, I brought my painting and blue-ribbon home and held it up to Momma, my face beaming with pride. She forced a smile, her lips pulled back tight, as she admired the watercolor in an off-hand way. She said I had talent, but I had to be careful, or art would become the most important thing to me and take me away from Jehovah. Everything the world said was good, always did, she said, clicking her tongue.

She'd said I should use my talent to draw bible figures, especially those Jehovah used as examples for us, like Job, Lot's Wife, Wise King Solomon, Dinah, and Samson.

With a mix of fear and sadness, I'd thrown the painting with its rows of sunflowers, their yellow faces pointing to the sun, and the small blue butterfly in the foreground. But now, I have a secret. A secret that's bigger than the painting from second grade. Does Jehovah hate me now?

"Sara, what do you think?" Rachel asks. She holds a dress, still on its hanger, out in front of her over her t-shirt and pants. Momma would never let me wear a t-shirt, but somehow, on Rachel, it's modest.

"What?"

"What do you think? For Meeting tomorrow?" She smiles, tilting her head. "Is this modest enough? Or is it too revealing?"

I eye the dress of pale pink fabric and white flowers. A zipper runs up the side, the collar rounded up at the base of the neck, and the full skirt falls below the knees.

"It's perfect," I say, wishing my Meeting clothes weren't hand-me-downs from Cheri Wilson, a girl six inches taller than me and whose favorite color is purple.

She puts her hand on my shoulder, and I flinch. Her eyes soften. "It may not feel like it now, but Jehovah will reward you for your loyalty to Him and your sacrifices. He's rewarded me many times already. Look at all He's done for me in such a short time. And I get you as a little sister as a bonus."

Yes, but you don't know about the closet, I think to myself.

"I have to take my Mom's car back." Rachel jangles a set of keys out in front of her. "Want to come along?"

"I can't. I have to help Momma," I sigh, wishing I could call Neena and tell her about Rachel instead. With the only phone in our house in the kitchen, that won't happen. Without a cell phone or a computer, my first chance to talk to her is at Meeting tomorrow. If I can wait that long.

I wander across the hall into Pearl and Kaylee's room, now my room, with its walls covered in pink and white candy-striped wallpaper left over from a little girl who lived here before. I toss my school books onto the cluttered dresser, pushing aside the row of worn stuffed animals, hair ribbons, and a shoebox of broken crayons. A pink, worn-out bean bag chair is wedged in the corner between the dresser and a small bookcase.

The only empty space in the room is a narrow section of floor. There is no place for a bed. There is no place for me.

Holding my sketchbook, I check for a place to keep it safe from the prying eyes of Kaylee and Pearl. I shove it underneath Kaylee's mattress. Not exactly a great place. I'll find a better place later.

I close the door behind me, glancing across to my room—correction—Rachel's room, with its pale blue walls and the wide window overlooking the street.

My room was the only place I had to myself. Where I could be alone to read a book, dream, or draw anything I wanted—the place where I could watch out my window and see the stars at night. Or see the back of Gabe's house. Where had that thought come from? I push it down to the bottom of my stomach, which begins to boil again.

Rachel deserves it more than I do.

Would it be so bad if I stayed in the art contest? If I didn't tell Mr. Ballentine to take me out of it? What if I won?

I swallow the burn in my throat. Pausing at the top of the stairs, I ask Jehovah again, for what seems like the thousandth time today, to forgive me, to keep Satan from me. I promise I'll do better. Satan keeps putting thoughts in my head, making me question things. If I were stronger in the Truth, the thoughts and questions would disappear.

Chapter 3

Downstairs, Momma flips open the ironing board in one quick movement. Behind her in a lopsided basket is a pile of Brad's black slacks, white dress shirts, and Kaylee and Pearl's dresses full of frills and ribbons, all waiting to be pressed. We must dress our best and be groomed when we go to Meetings to show Jehovah how much we love and respect Him. In return, He will continue to reward us.

As Pearl thumbs through the box of used VHS tapes, the cardboard sleeves worn and faded, another gift from one of the older Sisters, Rachel, with her perfect hair and teeth, glides down the stairs. Her skirt flows around her as if she walks on air. The light from the window behind illuminates the ends of her hair. She sparkles. I glance down at my drab gray and brown school clothes, feeling the full impact of our differences.

"Sister Michaels, I have to take my mom's car back. You can still pick me up, right?" Rachel slips her cell phone into her pocket. Sun shines through the window on the landing behind her, bathing her in light.

Momma picks up one of Kaylee's pink dresses and snaps it in the air before smoothing it flat on the ironing board. "Of course, Sister Rachel. We'll see you at 5:45 on the dot."

"I'll be ready," Rachel flashes a smile at me, tucks her curls of red hair behind her ears, and shuts the door softly behind her.

When I hear the car drive away, I say to Momma, "Rachel said she wouldn't mind sharing my room with me."

"Rachel needs her own space. She's getting ready for Bethel," Momma says, refusing to meet my eyes.

"Why didn't you wait for me to get home? Let me pack up my stuff?" I dare ask.

The iron spits and hisses, sending a halo of steam around Momma's face. "Do you have something to hide?"

"No," I say quickly, wondering if she'd found my secret.

If she had, though, I'd be sitting at the kitchen table with the Truth That Leads to Eternal Life book under my nose, or worse, a meeting of encouragement with one of the Elders.

"Instead of complaining and asking so many questions, you should be grateful. My mother died when I was five, and my father went before I was born. I never had anyone to help me. I had to do it all myself," Momma says.

I sink low into the sofa. My mouth clamps shut, hoping she won't go into her story again about living with her Great Aunt who smelled like dust and moldy potatoes and was never happy. Momma left that place as soon as possible and went to live in the world. Blah...blah...blah. Her life finally changed for the better when she found the Truth. I've heard it countless times and am in no mood to hear it again. It has nothing to do with me.

"Sara, work on pleasing Jehovah, doing all he requires, and he will reward you for your sacrifice," Momma says.

Jehovah tells us we must give Him our time; time in study, time in service, staying separate from the World, modest clothing, and attending all the Kingdom Hall meetings. But did He mean for me to give up my room to Rachel? I hadn't done that. It wasn't my choice. It just sort of happened.

"But giving up my room? Is that what he requires?" I ask out loud and regret it immediately. I shouldn't think such things, let alone say them.

Momma stares at me, a bead of sweat over her brow, her mouth in a straight line. "Sara, I am surprised at you. You know we are living in the Last Days. Time is precious. Rachel is here until she fulfills the requirements to get to Bethel." She snaps one of Brad's white shirts into the air. Dust motes float around.

"I was only asking," I say. It's true what Momma says about Bethel and the Last Days. Jehovah can come at any second; we all need to be ready. Rachel will be gone to Bethel soon, and I'll have my room back unless Armageddon comes first.

"I don't have time for any of your games and questions. You're old enough to know better. I have all this ironing, then dinner to make. There's family Bible Study tonight, and I have to get Rachel in a little bit," Momma says.

"I'll make dinner, Momma," I say, pulling to a stand. Kaylee and Pearl remain glued to the TV.

"I'll get Rachel. I've got to get something from Brother Peters. I'll get her on the way back," Brad says over my shoulder, making me jump. I hadn't heard his car pull into the driveway or the garage door rumble open.

"Daddy, daddy," Kaylee cries and runs to wrap herself around his knees.

Momma pushes her hair out of her eyes with the back of her hand. "Would you? I don't want to take you from study time. If you need to prepare or anything."

"I'm all prepared." He turns to me, shaking his head. "What about you? You should be making dinner instead of whining about your room?"

"I was just going," I say. I should have already been helping, not whining.

The pantry door squeaks as I open it. Under the flickering light, I stare at the rows of canned beans, sweetened milk, and pasta sauces, our stockpile for end-times, right before this System of Things is over. Pulling down a dusty box of macaroni and a can of tuna, I try not to think of my secret or where I'll be sleeping tonight.

As Kaylee places the last fork on the table and I fill the milk glasses, Brad returns from picking up Rachel. He drops his keys in the bowl by the door. His hair is messed up, and there's a red mark on one of his cheeks.

"Dinner ready? I'm starved," Brad rubs his belly, his shirt untucked.

Rachel, a few steps behind, darts in, her face pale. She hurries up the stairs without saying anything. I move to go after her, but Brad puts his arm out to stop me.

"Leave her," he says, sending a ripple of fear through me. The hairs on the back of my neck raise; something isn't right.

"Rachel's upset," I say, looking to Momma for help.

"I'm sure her family tried to stop her from leaving. Those without the Truth don't understand," Momma says as she places the steaming dish of macaroni and cheese in the middle of the table. "You did a fine job on this, Sara."

"Rachel is sad," Kaylee frowns.

"She'll be fine," Brad says. He pulls his chair out and motions for Kaylee and Pearl to follow.

"She should be happy to be here. Rachel's family doesn't have the Truth like we do." Pearl flops down in a chair next to Kaylee.

Momma eyes the fading mark on Brad's face. "What happened?" She asks, touching her cheek.

"Nothing," he says, his voice irritated as if Momma had done something wrong. "Let's eat."

"You can check on her after dinner if she doesn't come down. Give her some alone time," Momma says to me softly.

"Okay," I say, my gaze fixed on the stairs as I take my seat across from Brad. The red mark on his face has faded. Is that the outline of fingers? Had someone slapped him? Rachel's mom, maybe. The Worldly hates it when someone they love comes to Jehovah and His Truth. I'd read in our books and in the videos we watched. And here it is coming true in my own home.

We eat dinner in silence, nothing but the clang of our silverware. Even Kaylee is quiet for once. I push my food around with my fork from one side of the plate to the other. I'm not hungry.

"Can I be excused? I want to go see if Rachel wants anything," I say.

Momma folds her napkin, places it beside her plate, and glances at Brad. He nods, and I push away.

"Bring her down for Family Study time," Momma calls.

"Reading Jehovah's words will encourage her," Brad adds.

Upstairs, I tap on Rachel's door. "Rachel, it's me. Sara. Can I come in?" I ask. She doesn't answer, so I tap louder. "Rachel? You okay?"

"I'm fine," she says through the closed door.

"You missed dinner. It's almost Family Study time," I say, trying to sound happy and excited. Silence. "Rachel?"

The door opens slowly. She peers out, her eyes red and puffy like she'd been crying. "You by yourself?" she asks. I nod, and she pulls me in, shutting the door behind me. She's changed her clothes. She wears a loose sweatshirt and baggy sweatpants.

"I'm sorry about your family," I say. I peek out the window at the streetlights flickering on the back of Gabe's house. My cheeks warm. My mind should not be on a Worldly boy, not now, not ever. I glance at the pictures of her family lining the dresser. "It's got to be tough leaving them." I shift on my feet, not sure what to say to her.

Dabbing at her nose with a tissue, she plops down in the middle of her bed. "I'm fine. All my studies to know the Truth and make me a Sister are paying off." She pulls the sleeves of her sweatshirt down over her wrists, covering her hands. "Besides, I have you."

"Did they say evil things about you and Jehovah?" I ask.

"No, nothing like that," she shakes her head. "Can we not talk about it?"

I swallow, my throat dry, wondering what could be so bad that she couldn't tell me. We are Sisters in the Truth. Neena and I tell each other everything. Rachel said I was like a sister to her;

she should tell me anything. That's what sisters do. I stand there, my arms hanging at my sides, feeling useless.

I recall the words I learned to say when I was Kaylee's age. "Rely on Jehovah. Stay loyal to the Truth, and He will take care of everything," I recite. The words will make Rachel feel better.

Momma calls from downstairs.

"We need to go." Missing dinner is one thing, but missing Family Study, which Jehovah requires, is never good.

Rachel pulls herself up in slow motion. "Sure," she says weakly. She smooths her sweatshirt and sucks in a deep breath.

We usually have Family Study in the family room off the kitchen, each of us taking a seat on the orange sofa or one of the chairs that wobble. Tonight, we're in the living room, the room reserved for when the Sisters or an Elder come over.

The sofa is faded and worn around the edges, like everything else in our home. Momma keeps it covered with a pale green sheet tucked in tight around the corners. The stains in the carpet, from someone else before we moved in, are hidden under rugs and a carefully placed chair. The only seat left is a hard-backed chair next to Brad or the pile of pillows on the floor. I take the pillows, knowing Momma will be upset if I sit in the chair, leaving Rachel the floor.

Rachel hesitates before she takes the seat next to Brad, and I know whatever happened with her family was bad, really bad. They must have tried to stop her, and Brad stepped in. Satan is working hard to keep Rachel from serving Jehovah and the Truth. I say a silent prayer to Jehovah, thanking him for bringing Rachel to our house and forgiving me for my thoughts about my room and Gabe too.

"Well, glad you two could make it," he reaches over and squeezes Rachel's arm. She moves her hands to her lap, gently pulling her arm away. "If you're ready, I will start reading." He holds up the Truth book. "Tonight's chapter, The True Church. Girls, open your books to page forty-five."

I could recite this chapter, and all the chapters in the Truth Book, nearly by heart. But I know it's important to go over and over the prophecies, keeping them on our mind continually, giving Satan no room to slip into our hearts and pull us away from Jehovah.

Brad pauses and pats down his coarse hair, flattened into place with gel. Satisfied we're all paying attention; he starts to read. *"If we want to live eternally in God's New System, Paradise on Earth, we must acknowledge the true church. Won't it be a wonderful time when the wicked organizations and people on earth who cheat and oppress are gone?"* He stops and looks up at us, his dark eyes scanning the room. "Who can tell me who the wicked organizations are?"

Pearl's hand flies up. Brad nods at her, and she says, "The wicked organizations are all the churches everywhere in the world. Everyone who isn't in the Truth." She sits back, a wide grin on her face.

"Correct. And when will Jehovah destroy these wicked organizations? Who can answer? Rachel?" His eyes lock onto hers.

She flinches, and her jaw tightens. "During Armageddon," she says quietly.

"Very good," Brad nods.

We continue reading paragraph after paragraph. Brad's voice is low and clear, harsh at times if we don't answer fast enough. Finally, at nine o'clock, we are done. Momma carries a sleeping Kaylee to bed.

Rachel hurries ahead, shutting her door before I can tell her goodnight.

Chapter 4

Sun streams through the pink lace curtains. Dots of light dance on the bright pink walls, and I am wide awake. Air hisses from the almost flat air mattress. I roll to my back, my shoulders and neck aching from the hard floor beneath.

I pull the blanket up, covering my eyes, light seeping in through the edges. I wish for my bedroom with its pale gray-blue walls covered with my art, my books. Most of all, I want my bed, lumps and all. I wish I could stay in that bed until noon, for once. But it's Saturday, and Saturday is Meeting day—two hours of sitting in the hard-backed folding chairs at the windowless Kingdom Hall. Two hours of singing songs and one of the Elders instructing us from the Truth book. He'll ask the Congregation questions, and we must all be prepared to answer. My stomach clinches, and a spot of ache forms in my chest. I need to draw.

As I reach for my sketchbook, still hidden under Kaylee's mattress, she whispers, "Sara, you awake?"

"Go back to sleep. It's too early to get up," I say softly. My hand falls to my side as the ache in my chest grows larger. There will be no drawing today.

"I can't sleep anymore," she peers down at me, wiping the sleep from her eyes. "Your bed is flat."

"I know."

"You want to come up here with me?" She pulls her covers back, and I climb in.

We lay there, snuggled close, her cold feet pressed up against me, listening to the sounds of the house waking up. As Momma makes breakfast, there is a slam of cabinets and drawers in the kitchen. The pipes clank and ping as Brad gets in the shower. At the smell of bacon, Kaylee and Pearl both hurry downstairs.

I linger in Kaylee's bed, waiting for the hum of the water from Rachel's shower to stop. When it finally does, and I get my chance, there is no hot water. Rachel used it all.

By the time I get downstairs for breakfast, Brad is pushing a forkful of pancakes around on his plate, soaking up what is left of his syrup. He swallows it down with the last of his coffee. Rachel slides over on the bench, making room for me. Her curls of red hair are pulled back into a tight bun, and her face scrubbed so that her cheeks are pink.

"Wonderful breakfast again, Nancy," Brad stands, tossing his napkin on the table, his eyes on Rachel. Under the table, she grabs my hand; hers is like ice.

Momma beams. My gaze goes from one to the other. Brad never compliments Momma on breakfast. It must be a show for Rachel.

After breakfast, I help Momma with the dishes while Brad goes back to his office to pray and study Jehovah's word. There is so much to learn and prepare for when you're the Spiritual Head of a family. And Brad is on his way to becoming an Elder, which will change life for all of us.

As an Elder's wife, Momma will be admired by the other Sisters, elevated and important. Her time will be devoted to ministering to the other Sisters and traveling to other Congregations in our District at Brad's side. She will be able to hire someone to clean the house and send out Brad's clothes to get pressed. And me, I'll have new clothes, not things handed down from older girls in the Congregation, like Cheri Wilson. I wonder if my secret, hidden in the closet upstairs, has kept Jehovah from letting Brad be an Elder. He might have been one sooner if it wasn't for me. My stomach twists in knots.

"Time to go. Everyone in the car," Brad yells and flicks off the TV. Pearl whines. Brad's eyes darken. "Car. Now," he hisses.

I grab my bible with its silver cover from the kitchen table. I run my thumb over the letters embossed in the bottom corner that read *Sara Stephens*. The bible I'd earned last summer after working every day going door-to-door and doing street corner preaching. Momma had given it to me as a reward for my work serving Jehovah.

Ushing Kaylee and Pearl outside, Rachel is on my heels. Brad opens the sliding door of the van. It catches partway. He tugs it, muttering under his breath until it jerks open with a screeching metal-on-metal sound. His eyes cut to mine as he wipes his hands on the front of his pants, the pair Momma had spent so much time on getting the crease sharp and down the middle. With pale doughy fingers, he adjusts the red and black pens in the pocket of his shirt.

"That's a pretty dress you're wearing today," Brad says, his eyes running up and down Rachel. A line of red creeps up the back of her neck.

That was weird.

I slide into the back with Rachel, and Momma finally appears. Tugging her skirt into place and pulling the silver clip from her hair, she shuts the door behind her, catching her purse. Brad shakes his head.

"I'm so sorry," Momma says, out of breath.

His fingers tighten on the steering wheel, his knuckles white. If Rachel weren't here, he'd yell at Momma for making us late. Only bad Witnesses are late. They are too lazy to serve Jehovah properly. Being late will make it harder to be an Elder. Then

Momma would apologize and ask Jehovah to make her a better wife.

We pass Val's house, and I wonder what going away to camp with her would be like, and Neena too. Something inside me wishes I could go. Last year, in eighth grade, I heard about an art camp in Santa Cruz. It was for two weeks and meant sleeping over. I knew what Momma would say about camp; it could never happen, so I never asked. There was no point. The acid bubbles up in my stomach. I push it down, along with the wishes of all the things I want to do. All the things Satan puts in my head to take me from Jehovah.

The Kingdom Hall, a square windowless brick building, is set back from the busy road like a nondescript office building. There is no cross, no stained-glass windows, no dome top, or steeple— all things the Worldly do in their places of worship to call attention to themselves. I smile and lift my chin—our building is free of the Worldly ideals. It makes Jehovah proud, and I am proud to be one of his children. Brad hums as he pulls the van into a spot near the front by the neatly groomed bushes and pots of white flowers the Sisters planted.

Rachel and I follow Momma, who holds tight to Kaylee and Pearl. As we near the entrance, Cheri Wilson, my mentor and clothing donor, calls me. I want to find Neena. I need to talk to Neena.

"Ugh, Cheri. She's so bossy," I lean and whisper to Rachel, who giggles.

"I'll distract her," Rachel says, and she walks up to Cheri and starts talking while I slip away.

I weave through the Brothers and Sisters, who chatter in clumps near the entrance, passing the room where the shunned must sit, so we don't talk to them. I scan for Neena but don't see her tall silhouette in bright colors like tangerine, orange, or fuchsia she usually wears. Momma says the bright colors are improper because they draw attention to one's self and distract from Jehovah. I think they're pretty. Momma doesn't know everything.

"Hey," Cheri says, planting herself in front of me. Over her shoulder, I see Rachel shrug and mouth, *sorry.*

Today Cheri, with her bushy eyebrows and dry, cracked lips, wears a tomato-red dress with narrow ruffles trimming the neck and sleeves. Momma doesn't mind this bright color because Cheri is an Elder's daughter; she can do no wrong. And next year, when she grows tired of it, it'll be mine. Red is not my color. It washes me out and makes my skin look splotchy. When Brad is an Elder, it won't matter. I will have clothes of my own.

"Why did you ignore me?" She asks.

"I wasn't. I mean, I'm not." I try to step away.

"Do you remember we have our mentor study this week? You ready?" She asks. I strain to look around her. "You lookin' for Neena?" she asks.

"No, I mean yes," I say.

"She's not here. And good news," she points to a row of index cards on the bulletin board behind her. "You've got a Talk next month."

"I do?" I squint up at the card pinned to the board, with my name and topic assigned by the Elders. My partner is Neena, this is good. But still, I hate public speaking. Already my throat is dry, and my hands are sweaty.

"You excited?" Cheri asks.

"I guess, maybe," I stutter. Can she tell I'm scared?

"It's only a little talk. Don't be scared.

"I'm not." I lie. But it's not just a little Talk. It's two long minutes of me talking and teaching about Jehovah up on the stage in front of all the Brothers and Sisters. Everyone's eyes will be on me.

"I can help you with it," Cheri offers, her voice humming in my head.

I reread the card as I fight down my panic. I know this is important; a Talk helps us know what to do when we're in different situations with the Worldly. I won't be facing the

Congregation since Sisters can't directly educate or inspire Brothers. Neena will be with me. I'll be okay, maybe.

"I'll work on it with Neena. She's good at writing Talks," I say as I hurry away. I maneuver around Sister Winchester with her droopy eyes like a basset hound to the bathroom. I'm not in the mood for her yeasty breath or the handful of stale butterscotch candy she seems to think I like.

Shutting the door behind me, I lean up against the coolness of its wood. The air is thick with the scent of lavender air freshener and bleach used to clean the toilet. My stomach boils up into my chest, burning my throat. I fumble in my purse for the silver roll of antacids, finding them faster without my sketchbook in the way.

Cheri's right. It's a Talk. Easy. I've got to do it to prove myself to Jehovah. Show Him I am loyal and faithful. It's the only way he'll love me and save me. I'd done my hours, study time, and gone to all the Meetings. But the two things I hate the most, giving a Talk and answering at Meetings, are what keep me from being fully loved by Him.

Well. That and my art.

I chew two more antacids.

If I show signs of disobedience to Jehovah, Brad will not become an Elder. Momma will be stuck. There's no way around the Talk. I've got to do it.

With my hand resting on the knob, I take a deep breath and count down from three, open the door, and head toward the front of the Kingdom Hall to sit with my family and Rachel. As I hurry to my seat, I pass Neena sitting in the back row, the place for late Witnesses, with her mom, Sister Nichols, and little brother, James.

Mom scowls at me as I move down the narrow row of seats to sit, just as Brother Wilson, Cheri's dad, wearing his usual Saturday Meeting chocolate brown suit, steps up to the dark wood podium. His gray socks peek out from beneath his shiny slacks. Soft music crackles from the speakers fastened to the ceiling around the edge of the room. He clears his throat and stares down his long nose at the Congregation and taps the microphone. Those left standing in the Kingdom Hall move to their seats.

I sideways glance at Momma. She sits straight like she has a board against her back, her face lit up and fixed on Brother Wilson as he reads from the Truth book, the same chapter we studied last night. Wiping his brow, he pauses and surveys the Congregation. I don't have to look around to know that all faces, even the little kids like Kaylee, are turned toward him. Everyone pays attention during Meetings; it makes Jehovah happy. I will do better. I can do better. And I'm sorry for the thoughts which Satan keeps putting in my head. I should be stronger.

Brother Wilson asks the question printed in fine print at the bottom of the page he'd read. Momma elbows me, her eyes focused on Brother Wilson, her mouth pushed into a forced smile. It's time for me to raise my hand and answer. If only my voice didn't sound like I talked through my nose. I keep my eyes fixed on my book and the sections I'd underlined while I draw the wings of a butterfly in the margin.

"Pay attention," Momma hisses into my ear as she pinches the skin under my arm, and I yelp.

"It appears as if Sister Sara knows the answer," Brother Wilson nods down at me.

Brother Peters, a new Ministerial Servant with duties like holding microphones and setting up chairs, thrusts the microphone under my chin. There's a static sound in my head and a high-pitched buzz that grows louder. I open my mouth, but no words come.

"Sister Sara, do you know the answer?" Brother Wilson taps his fingers, his eyes flick to the clock on the back wall and then at me again. Brother Peters wriggles the microphone under my chin, urging me to speak.

Momma holds her Truth book under my nose, tapping the underlined sentence with the tip of a red fingernail. The words blur. Someone behind me coughs. Pearl giggles.

I hear myself squeak out the answer as if someone else were talking, using my mouth.

"Correct, Sister." Brother Wilson's lips go up in a Cheshire grin, and I know Jehovah loves me even more.

"Good job," Rachel leans over and whispers. My stomach stops churning, and I feel myself breathe again.

We sing our final song two hours later and say our final Amen. I hurry to the doors leading outside. Neena waits for me on the bottom step, her little brother, James running around one of the planters with Kaylee.

"I have so much to tell you. You'll never guess," I say, low enough for only Neena to hear.

"Is it about Rachel? I already know. Everyone knows she's living with your family now," Neena says.

"I wish I had a phone." I sigh.

"Me too. More important, Cheri called me this afternoon and asked me to be her Field Service partner tomorrow. I told her I couldn't. I'd already been assigned. You and me, right?" Neena asks.

"Did you set it up with Brother Reed? Is he okay with it? Remember the last time we got assigned together. They said we didn't focus enough on the people at the door."

"I already asked him. I told him we're in high school now, and we'd both matured in Jehovah. I also said I had some new scriptures I wanted to teach you to use," she says. "Any chance your mom and stepfather are going to let you have a phone anytime soon? I thought the deal was ninth grade you could get one."

"They changed their minds. Now it's next year. You know how my mom is. A cellphone is the gateway to me leaving Jehovah," I mimic Momma's voice.

Momma keeps a tight watch on me. Her and Brad's rules are strict. Stricter than most of Jehovah's followers. It's like she's I'm going to mess up with Jehovah. I swallow, wondering what she'd do if she found my secret hidden under the eaves.

Neena sighs. "I know she thinks my mom is a terrible Witness because I have a cell phone, and my mom can't attend all the meetings."

I want to say no, but she's right. Momma says things all the time about Sister Walker, Neena's mom, not applying Jehovah's word in her life.

"Your mom isn't a bad Witness. She's trying," I say, and Neena smiles weakly.

Sister Walker calls to Neena from her car. "Mom has a shift. Call me later if you can."

"I'll try," I say.

As I slide into the back seat of the van next to Rachel, I feel a pull of my dress and hear the tear of fabric. I wince. I'd ruined the only dress that's a color I like and isn't two sizes too big on me.

Tugging free, I slide in next to Rachel and bite back the tears.

"We can fix it," she says, holding the hem of my dress. She pokes a finger through the small grease-stained hole. "You won't even notice it when I'm done with it."

I press my forehead to the window. I can never be like Rachel. She's giving up everything for Jehovah. She answers questions at a meeting, her voice not quivering like mine. Her clothes stay neat. She's a living example of what suffering for Jehovah means by giving up her family and serving Him fully. I could never be like Rachel, ever. I can't even give up my art.

We come to a stop. I push the small window open and breathe in some fresh air as a car pulls up next to us, music blasting. Brad grumbles and tells me to shut my window. Pearl covers her ears and urges Kaylee to do the same.

I peer down at the red car. One of Gabe's older brothers is driving. He taps out the beat on the steering wheel. In the back is Gabe, staring down at his phone.

Momma says something about the music and how wonderful it is that Jehovah protects us from such things, and what kind of parents allow their children to listen to music like that. Almost as if he knows what Momma is saying, Gabe lifts his head. He spots me, and his lips curve into a smile, and I want to look away but can't. Instead, I smile too. As the car jerks away, he waves. I wave back.

Why had I waved? Jehovah hates me now.

Chapter 5

Sitting on the lumpy bean bag chair, the smell of the plastic burning my nose, Kaylee flits and spins around the room, showing me her new dress. Pearl leans over her bed rail and growls at Kaylee for her to stop.

"I'm just happy, Pearl. Quit trying to make me be grumpy," Kaylee says. She spins until she gets so dizzy and falls to her bed.

"Whatever," Pearl says.

If only I had my own room, I sigh, laying my head back and closing my eyes, my neck and shoulders sore from laying on the air mattress last night. I have nowhere to go for a minute of silence or to draw. We're leaving soon for Ministry Work at the Kingdom Hall, where Momma cleans the bathroom, and I wipe fingerprints off the glass. Pearl, old enough to work now, has a job of vacuuming. Kaylee will run up and down the empty rows of chairs. Brad and the other Brothers will work outside on the grass and bushes. When he becomes an Elder, we won't have to do this anymore. Neena won't be there, but Cheri will.

I wish I could stay home. I wish Ministry Work were a choice because if it were, I'd choose to go to the tiny art shop near the Library or the Museum of Art instead. As I think the words, my heart feels heavy. I've done it again. I can't go an hour without letting Satan's thoughts get into my head. Ministry Work is important. It's how I show Jehovah I am dedicated to Him.

"Come on, time to go," I sigh, gathering myself up from the beanbag. The girls race past me as we head downstairs. I stop for a moment outside of Rachel's closed door, raising my hand to knock just as Momma whisper-yells my name from the bottom of the stairs.

"I'm coming, Momma," I say, as I take each step one at a time, my heart still feeling heavy.

"I want you to stay home today," she says softly, and I hold back a smile. Jehovah had rewarded me.

"Why?" I ask.

"Rachel needs some encouragement. She's having a hard time with her family and the changes," Momma says as she adjusts the clips in her hair. "I can't stay. How would that appear to the rest of the congregation if I don't show up for Ministry Work."

"Okay, Momma," I say. I can't help but wonder if this is a test from Jehovah.

When the van is far away down the street, I race to the phone and call Neena. I have plenty of time to encourage Rachel. What's one call? It rings and rings, but she doesn't answer. Without a cell, I can't text her.

I race up the stairs to get my sketchpad from its hiding place. I move to go downstairs in case Neena calls back, when something falls from my sketchpad, the camp flier Val gave me yesterday.

Picking it up by the corner, so I don't catch any of Satan's lies, the shiny images glare back at me. One group is of girls about my age, standing arm and arm, jumping off a wooden dock into a lake with sparkling blue water. Another of faces lit up by a campfire. All fake. It's an organization ruled by Satan, who loves tricking the Worldly into believing they will be saved just because they believe in God or something. It's what we learned about in the Truth book last night. Jehovah has put this reminder here for me. I look up to the ceiling and ask for forgiveness for sinning again and again.

I'm about to tear the paper of lies into tiny pieces when I hear sounds of crying from Rachel's room. Momma was right; Rachel needs encouragement. Heavy with guilt for not going in sooner, I stick the pamphlet into my sketchbook and hide it back under Kaylee's mattress.

Padding across the hall, I tap on Rachel's door. "Rachel, it's me, Sara," I say.

The crying stops, and there's a rustle of papers. The door opens enough for her to see it's me.

"You by yourself?" she peers over my shoulder.

"Everyone is gone. Ministry Work," I say, and she nods knowingly.

Rachel pulls the door open all the way and motions me in. Behind her, papers are scattered across the unmade bed. A scrapbook lies open on the floor.

"Are you okay?" I venture.

She moves slowly and says nothing as she sits cross-legged on the floor. She pats the spot next to her, urging me to sit. I scan the page of pictures in the scrapbook: Rachel sitting between her parents on the beach, the sunlight dipping into the horizon behind them. Another of her and her brother, Paul, with a goofy grin and guitar in his lap. There's another of the four of them at a restaurant and another at a track meet, Rachel, holding a trophy.

I'd met her parents and Paul at a Jehovah's Paradise Picnic. Rachel had been excited to bring them. Mr. and Mrs. Cummings smiled and made small talk as if they were trying to support Rachel. Paul sat uncomfortably with the Witness boys while the girls clustered nearby. None of them fit in. None of them tried.

"You miss them a lot, don't you? It seems like you were close." I notice the poster of Paradise, with its bright colors of yellow, green, and pink that I'd made in fifth-grade art class, still taped to the back of her door.

"We were. But when I became a Bible Student, they told me Jehovah and the Truth are a lie, and I'm in a cult," she searches through the papers on the bed, grabs a handful, and holds them out for me to see. "I got my Bethel forms, I have to fill them out, and then the Elders have to approve them."

"Isn't that...a good thing?" I ask. Why would that make her cry?

"There's a lot of work to get approved. Not any Brother or Sister can go to Bethel. I have to be worthy of doing Jehovah's work." She drops the papers, and they flutter to the floor. "I'm not sure I am."

"You're kidding. You've done so much so fast," I say, trying to sound encouraging like Momma told me to do.

"Maybe," she shrugs and twists her hands in her lap. It can't be her fault that her family doesn't love Jehovah.

"Rachel, yesterday, I had bad thoughts about you. Negative things," I say, biting my thumbnail.

"Why?" Her brow shoots up.

"I was mad at you for taking my room. I'm sorry. You deserve it. You need it. I'm glad you're here," I say.

She wraps an arm around my shoulder and squeezes. "Thank you, Sara, that means a lot."

"I'm sorry about your family too. If only they'd come to Jehovah and the Truth, then you could be a family again," I say, and the words feel empty somehow. I gather her Bethel papers and put them in order. "Maybe you should put your family pictures away," I suggest.

"You're probably right. Thanks for that," she closes the scrapbook.

Thinking of what the Truth books teach us about encouragement, I decide the best thing to do for Rachel right now is to pray for her. "Do you want me to pray to Jehovah? Will that make you feel better?"

She shifts uncomfortably and nods.

I bow my head and begin to pray, knowing my words will comfort her. "Jehovah, please have Rachel's family leave her alone so she may follow you. Provide her the courage to stand up for you and do what you've commanded. Forgive Rachel where she has fallen short of doing your will."

I say Amen, and she says nothing. Her bottom lip quivers like she's holding back the tears. My prayer hadn't worked. She doesn't feel better.

"Rachel, are you sure you're okay? You can tell me anything. You said you always wanted a sister," I say, knowing I don't tell Kaylee and Pearl everything because they'd blab it to Momma. I shrink back. Does Rachel think that of me?

Pulling her knees to her chest, she says, "You are like my sister. But there are some things I can't tell you." She looks away.

"Do you think I'll tell someone else, like Neena or maybe the Elders? Because I won't," I say. "Whatever you tell me is between you and me, no one else."

"No, it's not that," her voice shakes. Still, she won't look at me.

A wave of fear spreads across my chest. Jehovah says secrets are never good. One secret leads to another, and soon the lies spread like a web.

"Secrets aren't good," I say.

"Sometimes they are," she snaps, and I jump.

"I'm sorry," I say, my stomach rolling. "I thought I could help you. I guess I'm not good at being a sister to you," I stand and start to go, my cheeks burning. I messed this up.

"Sara, wait," Rachel says and steps between me and the door. Her eyes shine with tears. "It's nothing you've done. It's me. I'm sorry. Please stay."

Feeling awkward, I sit on the edge of the bed, twisting my hands in my lap while she paces back and forth. I try not to look out the window, where I know I'll see Gabe's house.

"I want to tell you. I do, but..." her voice shakes.

"But what?" I ask. What is stopping her from telling me? Is she doubting Jehovah, and she can't bear to say it aloud? Maybe she doesn't want to go to Bethel after all. Or worse, she has a Worldly boyfriend.

"I can't tell you. He said he'd hurt Kaylee and Pearl if I did," Rachel says. Her eyes widen, and she clamps her hand over her mouth, shaking her head.

"Who will hurt Kaylee and Pearl? I don't understand. Rachel, tell me, what's wrong?" I beg. The room is eerily silent, and everything slows down, even the beating of my heart.

Rachel sinks to the bed, her arms wrapped around her chest. "If I tell you, you have to promise you won't say anything to anyone," she says, sadness wringing her eyes.

"I promise," I say, the back of my neck tingles.

She lowers her gaze to the ground, her face pale. "Yesterday, when Brad came to get me. On the way home. In the car. He did something."

My heart races like the thoughts in my head. What could Brad have done? He drives too fast and too close to other cars. Sometimes he yells out the window.

"Something?" I ask.

She bites her lip and rocks back and forth like the words hurt. "He tried to…he…I can't say it's too awful. You're going to hate me; Jehovah already does." She buries her face in her hands.

Confused, I say, "Rachel, Jehovah could never hate you. You've devoted your life to Him. You're in Good Standing, and you're going to Bethel. I've been in the Truth almost my whole life, and I'm barely able to answer at Meetings."

"I've not done enough. I'm going to die in Armageddon," she says.

"No," I say. If Rachel dies in Armageddon, I have no chance. "Rachel, what happened?"

"Brother Michaels, your step-father..." she stumbles over the words. "He touched me," she blurts out.

Time stands still. Her words hang in the air, waiting for me to respond.

"What do you mean? He touched you?" I tug at my blouse, pulling it tight.

She shakes her head, her eyes darting down to her sacred place. The place so sacred I cannot say its name. The place saved for our husbands when we marry—the place I am not allowed to touch.

"Your sacred place?" I whisper.

Dots of red blossom on her cheeks, and I know I am not wrong. The walls press in on me, darkness creeping in around the edges.

"In the car on our way home. Then last night...he came in here," she stops and buries her face in her hands as tears roll down her red cheeks.

My stomach bubbles up into my throat. I cover my mouth. It can't be true. Brad is the Spiritual Leader of our family. Rachael is lying. She must be. But why would Rachel make up this awful lie? Could it be she wants a way out so that she can go home to her family? The Truth book warns of tricks like this. Sisters who are unhappy accuse a Brother of something awful, shifting blame, the Elders call it.

"Rachel, is this true? You're not making it up, are you?" I ask.

Rachel's head flies up. She looks at me as if I'd slapped her. "I knew you wouldn't believe me. I shouldn't have told you anything."

Her words sting. I stand to leave; my knees wobble, and I reach for the edge of the dresser as the room spins. She can't be right. She can't. I don't want to have this conversation. I want to get out of here. But what if she is telling the truth? Now what? The last few days, Brad has paid extra attention to her. He'd touched her arm and commented on her dress. It gave me a weird feeling. Like, it wasn't right.

Then there are the other little things, the things I thought he was doing because he was trying to be kind to her. If Rachel is telling the truth, then Brad is a...I stop, my head a jumbled mess of thoughts—my stomach on fire.

"I didn't mean to call you a liar. What you're saying is a lot to take in," I say.

She wipes her eyes with the back of her hand. "You do? You believe me then?"

"Yes," I say softly. "But Rachel, you know what you need to do. You have to go to the Elders." As the words leave my mouth, I know it's not possible. She cannot, not without another witness. She'll have to face the Elders with Brad and tell them of his Wrong Doing. It's what Jehovah requires to keep the congregation clean and pure. Brad may never become an Elder. Rachel may never get to Bethel.

She shrinks away from me, becoming smaller. "No, I can't. Brad said he would hurt the girls if I told anyone. I told you because I trust you not to tell."

I swallow, my mouth dry. "Rachel, it's the only way. Go to the Elders. Rely on Jehovah. He promises when we do, He'll take care of us." Did I sound convincing? Will she go? I'd heard the Elders say it thousands of times when someone does wrong to you, rely on Jehovah. He will take care of it when the time is right. Don't shame Jehovah's name or his people by going to the police.

She shakes her head, her tears sliding down her cheeks. "I can't do that. The Elders will believe I'm reporting a Wrong Doing. There needs to be two witnesses to report any Wrong Doing. There were no witnesses, only me. I need to get to Bethel. I've worked hard. I can't go to the Elders now." Her voice drops.

"I'll say I saw it too. I'll be a witness," I say.

She shakes her head and shrinks even smaller. "No, Sara, that would be lying, and then Jehovah would never help me. And still, I would need another witness."

I know she's right. The rules are clearly laid out. My hands are damp with cold sweat, and my stomach burns. I wish I hadn't pushed her to tell me this secret. Now it's my secret too. And two secrets are going to be hard to keep.

"I promise I won't tell," I say.

Chapter 6

I can't sleep. There are too many places my mind wants to go, but I won't let it. I can't lay here anymore, listening to the questions in my head, asking Jehovah for answers when He seems so far away. There is something I can do to help Rachel. It's so simple. I reach under Kaylee's mattress for my sketchbook, wincing when she whimpers. Holding my breath, I tug it out gently. I gather my pillow and blanket, grab Kaylee's pink and purple flashlight from the dresser, and sneak into the hallway, shutting the door softly behind me.

I arrange myself in the hallway outside Rachel's door, careful not to make noise and wake her. Sitting here, outside her door, is the only thing I can do to help her while I wait on Jehovah. I'm still following the rules. I'm relying on Jehovah to take care of Brad – but Jehovah can't mean for me to do nothing? Can he? I start to draw in the dim circle of light from the flashlight, dragging my pencil across the smooth paper. My thoughts begin to melt away. Nothing matters right now except for the image flowing onto the page.

The pencil jumps, leaving a streak, when I hear what sounds like someone moving around in the darkness downstairs. Everyone should be asleep. I flick off the flashlight and listen in the darkness. A sliver of light from the seashell nightlight at the bottom of the stairs shines on the landing.

There are no sounds except for the hum of Pearl's fan clipped to the rail of her bed and the tick-tock of the clock in the kitchen. I let my breath out. It was only my imagination.

I go back to drawing, slow this time, my marks jagged and rough, not smooth like before. My pencil stills. I hear it again. A soft footfall on the steps below, as if someone were trying to be quiet. A long shadow moves up the wall. Before I can move, think, or do anything, he's there at the turn in the stairs. Brad.

He flinches when he sees me. Our eyes lock. I stare back. My skin simmers with heat, and my stomach rolls as I try to figure out what's going on. This is wrong, all wrong. Why is Brad coming up the stairs at night in the dark? He's not checking on Kaylee and Pearl. He's never done that before.

As quietly as he'd climbed the stairs, Brad backs away, his shadow shrinking as he disappears around the corner and back into the darkness.

Cold sweeps over me. Everything is wrong. My sketchbook falls to the floor with a thud. Unmoving, I sit there, staring at the empty landing. What just happened?

Rachel *is* telling the truth. I didn't want to believe her. I wanted it all to be a lie. But it's true. There's a monster in our house.

I rub the callous on my thumb, from where I hold my pencils too tight. Rachel is in trouble, she needs me, but I'd promised not to tell. What about Kaylee and Pearl? He will hurt them too. Why had I promised Rachel to keep her secret?

The Elders tell us to rely on Jehovah in all things. That's what I'd told Rachel, but had I been doing that? I lift my face toward the ceiling and pray silently to Jehovah. *Please forgive me for putting my art before you. Forgive me for my sinful thoughts about the Worldly boy Gabe. Jehovah, forgive me where I fall short, for my lies and mistakes. Help me to rely on you. Amen.*

I pick up my sketchbook, tears in my eyes. I have to get rid of this book and the rest of my secrets. Jehovah will not listen to my prayers if I cannot obey him fully. No more art. No more mistakes. Rely on Him, do not shame Him. The rules were simple.

At 6 a.m., when the muffled sound of Rachel's alarm buzzes, I drag myself back to the deflated mattress and lie there, my stomach a jumble of knots. When Kaylee and Pearl get up, I stay there, curled on my side, my eyes closed, pretending to sleep. When I have the room to myself, I somehow get up. With my eyes like sandpaper and a dull throb at the back of my head, I carefully choose my clothes for Field Service. Jehovah is watching and keeping track of my mistakes. Last night hadn't been a mistake. I know what I saw. I need His help. I can't mess up anymore.

I have a few choices: a floral print, which reminds me of a prairie girl, a purple short-sleeved sweater, and an olive-green blouse with bright pink stripes, all from the Wilson sisters. I decide on a yellow blouse with small white flowers and a navy-blue skirt from Thrift Towne. Even though they are slightly faded and worn around the hems and sleeves, they are modest, in my size and colors of my choice. I brush my hair flat and clip it back with a hairpin the same color as my hair.

I hurry to breakfast. Kaylee and Pearl are already done and seated in front of the TV, watching a grainy VHS tape. Rachel sits at the table, cradling a cup of coffee. She smiles up at me weakly and moves over to make room. Momma, focused on a large pot on the stove, glances over and nods approval at my choice of clothes. I slide in next to Rachel when Brad comes in. He scowls at me with a look of disapproval.

"Your top is too tight. I can see your bra straps. Very immodest," Brad snaps. Rachel flinches.

Feeling the heat rise on my cheeks, I drop my head. Rachel squeezes my hand under the table, and I squeeze back.

Momma leans over the table, placing a steaming plate of pancakes in front of Brad.

"Do what your stepfather says. You can't go out and represent Jehovah looking like that; what will the World think of us?" Momma says, and my mind whirls. A moment ago, she thought I was okay.

"I think she looks pretty," Kaylee calls out.

"Regardless of what Kaylee thinks, change now," Brad barks.

In my borrowed pink room, I choose the olive green dress, letting my "revealing" top fall to the floor. The olive top droops on my shoulders, and the sleeves hang below my wrists. Every bit of me is hidden under the folds of fabric.

At the Reeds' house, where we have our Pre-Field Service meeting, Neena waits on the path leading to the front door. Today she wears my favorite, a tangerine sundress, her brown shoulders covered with a light-yellow sweater. Shifting on her feet, she twists a curl of hair around one long finger.

"Those colors she wears. So bright. She calls so much attention to herself," Momma mutters. "It's such a shame her mother is putting her children's lives at risk by missing Meetings. Armageddon is so close; you'd think she'd show a little more concern." She clicks her tongue and glances at Brad. "I guess that's what happens when you don't have a man to guide your family spiritually."

Rachel shifts uncomfortably next to me. I pull an antacid from my pocket and slip it into my mouth, letting it dissolve on my tongue like a mint.

"She should rely on the system instead of working full-time. Then she could spend her time tending to the spiritual needs of her family. Or better, find a husband to do that job," Brad says as he shifts the car in reverse and slides the van in between two parked cars.

"Can you ask Brother Reed to partner us today?" Rachel leans over and whispers in my ear.

"I already promised Neena," I whisper back. Her shoulders slump. Suddenly I feel selfish. What if she's paired with Brad? "I can change. She'll understand."

Rachel hugs her bag to her chest. "No, don't. You go with Neena. You already promised."

"Sit close to Sister Winchester or Sister Reed; you'll get one of them as a partner. That always works."

Once out of the van, I hurry over to Neena, Rachel on my heels.

"Hey," Neena says to me, and then to Rachel, "Your dress is pretty."

"Thanks, so is yours," Rachel says, peering over her shoulder at the Wilson sisters as they walk past us. Brother Peters, hunched over the steering wheel of his tan truck, drives by, his head going from side to side as he tries to find a parking spot. He sees Rachel and quickly shifts his glance away.

"He's trying to become an Elder. I heard his last Congregation had no place for him. That's why he moved here," Neena says.

"You know a lot about him," I say.

"I was paired with Sister Winchester last Sunday. She talks a lot," Neena says.

"How can he become an Elder? He's not married. He needs a wife," I say.

"I think he has someone in mind," Neena gently elbows Rachel.

Rachel's eyes go wide, and she shakes her head. "Not me. I'm going to Bethel." But what if she can't go to Bethel? What if what happened with Brad mars her character, and she isn't accepted? I push the thoughts down until they press on the back of my head. Rely on Jehovah, rely on Jehovah.

"We better hurry if you want to sit next to Sister Winchester," I say to Rachel, and Neena's brow arches high. "She doesn't want to get stuck with Cheri," I say, trying not to give away the real reason – that she doesn't want to be paired with Brad.

"I never want to be paired with Cheri or any of the Wilson sisters," Neena rolls her eyes.

We make our way through the Reed's mint green living room. Folding chairs, in two neat rows, face a low brown chair with gold feet and trim, which looks like a throne—Brother Reed's chair. Neena and I weave around, past Cheri and her sisters, to our usual spot—two chairs where the branches of a giant potted palm dip low, hiding us.

Sister Winchester, in her handmade gray bumpy sweater, and Sister Reed sit side by side, squished into the old sofa. Rachel twists her hands and backs away as Brother Peters hurries in, taking the seat at the end. The only place for Rachel to sit is next to Brad unless she can squeeze in between Sister Reed and Winchester. As I move to let Rachel have my seat, she leans down and says something to Sister Winchester, who grabs her purse and bible and scoots down the sofa giving Rachel room. Everyone loves Rachel. I sit back, knowing that Brother Reed will pair them up. My plan worked.

"That'll be us someday," Neena says.

"Us?" I ask, confused.

"Two old married Sisters, remember?" She asks.

"Uhm, sure," I say.

We'd planned our weddings since we were little girls. A double wedding. We'd each marry an Elder. Our dresses would be the same, long trains, sleeves of lace, bouquets bursting with flowers and snowy white veils drifting like clouds down the length of our backs.

"Are you okay? You seem a little distracted."

"I'm fine," I smile too big. I can't give away anything. This is between me, Jehovah, and Rachel.

"If you say so. What's up with Rachel?" Neena leans in and whispers.

My heart drops. "What do you mean?"

"Are you blind? Look at her hair," she says, and I do. I hadn't noticed before, but her part is crooked, and her curls frizzed as if she hadn't bothered to brush it. The makeup she'd smeared on under her eyes doesn't hide the dark circles.

"It must be because she's sharing a bathroom with three other girls," I say, hoping Neena drops the subject of Rachel.

Kaylee squirms next to Momma. Brad scowls and motions with a slight jerk of his head at Momma, who reaches out and slaps Kaylee on the leg with a sting. Tears well in Kaylee's eyes, and she sits back, her legs straight, the toes of her shoes touching. I rub my leg, remembering when that was me.

Brother Reed clears his throat and adjusts the cuffs on his shirt. The room goes quiet as all eyes fall on him. He asks Brother Peters to open in prayer.

Brad's mouth narrows into a straight line, his lips pressed tight. Momma can't hide her frown. Brother Peters prayed last week; it should be Brad's time to pray. If Brad is not acknowledged as a leader, he will never become an Elder. Brother Peters is single and new to our Congregation. Single men can't become Elders. What is going on?

Brother Reed opens the little green book, the Field Service Guide. He speaks with his familiar gentleness and kindness like we are small children, and he wants us to understand. Behind his glasses, his blue eyes twinkle.

Then I get an idea. Brother Reed. He can help. He has always been like a grandfather to me. He's the one who encouraged me to draw more pictures of Paradise instead of focusing on drawing the end of this System of Things. He framed one of the pictures I'd given to him and Sister Reed and hung it up over their kitchen table. When we first moved here, and Kaylee was still a baby, he and Sister Reed would take me out in service and go for ice cream afterward. He said I was like their granddaughter, who lived on the other side of the country. Brother Reed can Counsel Rachel on what she should do and how to rely on Jehovah without messing up her chance of getting to Bethel.

But I'd promised Rachel I wouldn't tell. She has to go on her own, which she won't. I wipe the cold sweat from the palms of my hands and slip another antacid into my mouth.

After a short prayer from Brother Wilson, we're paired up. Sisters Winchester and Reed are paired. Momma is paired with Pearl. Rachel shrinks down next to me as Brother Reed decides on a partner for Brad. Please, Jehovah, not Brad, I pray silently.

"Brother Michaels, you go with Brother Wilson," he says, and Rachel makes a muffled sound in the back of her throat. "Sister

Rachel and Sister Cheri, you may go together. And Sister Sara and Sister Neena, you may go together."

I let out my breath. Jehovah is watching.

After the pairing up, we're given street assignments and divided into cars. Neena and I end up in Brother Reed's car with him and Brother Peters.

"You were right," Rachel says as I pass. And I nod with a smile knowing that Jehovah is taking care of everything, just like He promised.

Chapter 7

Neena and I sit in the backseat of Brother Reed's car. Up front, Brother Reed and Brother Peters talk about the scriptures they plan to use for the day while Neena and I are quiet. We should always listen to what the Brothers have to teach us. We take the expressway past a blur of strip malls and low apartment buildings. Brother Reed makes a left turn, and we pass the Koffee Stop, where Val goes with Bailey and Zoe every day before school and the McDonalds' where Gabe works. Why had I thought of Gabe again? What is wrong with me? I clutch my service bag, full of magazines and booklets we are ready to give out for donations, to my chest, my hand cold and damp with sweat. We're going toward my neighborhood.

Everyone needs to hear the Truth to live in Paradise, but I can't face people from school like Bailey, Zoe, or worse, Gabe. Not today. Val would get it, but I don't want to see her either, not after she told me I'm miserable.

We pass Harvard Avenue, the street Gabe lives on, then mine, and I relax, letting my service bag fall to my feet. We keep going, away from my neighborhood, when Brother Reed pulls to a stop. Craning his neck, he reads the faded and bent signpost on the far corner. He smacks the steering wheel with the flat of his hand and laughs. "Went too far. I was caught up in Brother Peters' story."

He steers the car in a wide-sweeping U-turn and then makes a left onto Harvard Ave. My stomach twists. I slip another antacid into my mouth without Neena seeing it.

Brother Peters squints to read the house numbers. I slide down in the seat, a faint hum at the back of my head, as we drift past Gabe's house with the red geraniums in boxes under each window. Abandoned bikes lie on their sides across the lawn. A messy row of shoes sits outside the front door. Why am I thinking about him so much? He's a boy, a Worldly boy.

We go another block and park under the shade of a row of straggly maple trees with bright green buds. Standing on the sidewalk, I shift from foot to foot as Brother Reed and Brother Peters peer over the tiny paper map deciding which way to go. My eyes dart down the street toward Gabe's house. Neena follows my gaze.

"You're being weird again," she leans in and whispers.

Before I can answer, Brother Reed says, "Well, Sisters, we're going to go this way." He points away from Gabe's house, and I exhale. "You take the west side of the street. We'll take the east and meet you at the end of the block."

Neena and I walk away, our backs to the Brothers, and I pray silently to Jehovah, telling him I'm sorry for the thoughts I'm having. And that I'm sorry for letting Satan get in the way of Field Service.

With a rolled-up Watchtower magazine in hand, Neena says, "I'll take the first door."

Our first house has a bright red door, its paint thick and shiny. Plastic Easter eggs balance in a large pink bowl on a table nestled between two chairs. I nudge Neena and roll my eyes; she nods in disapproval. Easter another Pagan holiday the World celebrates.

Neena steps up to the door and taps gently with the back of her knuckles. Her taps so soft no one inside can hear them. Sometimes, Neena and I don't feel like talking to the Worldly; they don't care about Jehovah or Armageddon. They'd prefer to die than live in Paradise. Like Rachel's family, she'd told them all about the Truth and Jehovah; instead, they said she was in a cult.

"No one's home." I hand her one of my neatly folded pamphlets, reserved for Not at Homes. While she slides it under the doormat, leaving a corner sticking out, I fill the house number in on our Door-to-Door record sheet and write "NH" (Not Home) and "LM" (Left Material) in the small space provided. We always have to leave something; it's what Jehovah requires. The more houses we go to and the more pamphlets we leave or people we talk to, the more Jehovah will love us. His loving us is the only way we'll get to Paradise.

We walk side by side in silence to the next house. Only I'm not silent on the inside. I'm thinking about Rachel, her secret, which is now mine. Rely on Jehovah, I repeat to myself. He won't let me down. He will take care of everything. We pass the Brothers, who talk to a lady across the street, a baby squirming in her arms, and a small child, wearing Easter Bunny ears, clings to her legs.

"You always get quiet when something is wrong, or you can't draw. What's going on?" Neena asks.

"Nothing," I say, hoping she didn't notice the catch in my voice. My sketchbook has never been a secret from her.

I sigh. "I've been drawing, see," I open my bag showing her the edge of my sketchpad.

"You might as well tell me; I'm going to keep bothering you until you do," she says.

"I can't tell you. I made a promise," I say.

"A secret? That doesn't sound good." Neena pulls me to a stop.

Smoothing the front of my blouse, I glance across the street. Brother Reed and Peters are talking at the curb.

"I can't tell you, Neena. I promised," I say.

She looks worried now. "Did someone commit a Wrong Doing? Is this like a talk to the Elders kind of problem?"

Neena is my best friend. I can trust her, and she is closer to Jehovah than I am. I can ask her without giving away Rachel's secret.

"It is a Wrong Doing, but not to me. It's a Sister," I pause. I shouldn't say anything else. But this is Neena, and Rachel needs help. Brad needs to be stopped. "There were no witnesses. Isn't there anything she can do?" I know the answer; nothing can be done without getting into trouble with the Elders and Jehovah.

Neena's mouth tightens, her brows knit together—the serious Neena face. Had I made a mistake confiding in her?

"Wow, I see why you're so quiet. That's rough. There's no getting around the two-witness rule. But there is something that might help this Sister," she says.

"What?" I ask. Brother Reed eyes us from across the street, and I pull her to walk.

"She can get counsel from an Elder," she says. My heart beats fast. Why hadn't I thought of that?

"Really? Counsel? That's it. She can just go to the Elders and say she needs help?" I ask.

"Well, not exactly. She needs someone in Good Standing to go with her or ask the Elders to Counsel her. She can't exactly report anyone for a Wrong Doing. She can talk about a problem she's having. Jehovah put the Elders in place and given them the ability to guide us, especially when we're having trouble dealing with the guidelines He gave us," Neena says.

"That's true. When you say Good Standing, you mean like Rachel level?" I ask, coming to a stop.

"No, more like your mom or Sister Reed level." Neena brushes her hair back off her shoulder.

My feet drag heavy, like my heart. Rachel will have to tell Momma or another Sister why she needs counsel. Rachel will never do that, and Brad will hurt the girls if she does. If only I'd been better at Jehovah's requirements. I haven't put in enough Service time. I haven't told enough people about Paradise on Earth and the Truth. I could answer more at meetings. I have a whole school of Worldly, and I've never witnessed to them about Jehovah. If I just did more, I could help, but it will take time, and I don't have time. Rachel doesn't have time. What if I go to Momma for her?

"Sara, maybe it's not as bad as you're making out to be. We must rely on Jehovah to do what's best for us. He promises he'll take care of every situation. He probably already is," Neena says.

He probably is, I think, biting my nail. Last night, if I hadn't gone to the hallway, Brad would have gone back into Rachel's room. Maybe Jehovah is using me to help Rachel. That can be it. But there has to be more. I can't be with her 24/7.

A car pulls up and trails slowly next to us. I pull close to Neena.

"You're not going to say hi?" A familiar voice says through the open passenger side window.

Heat prickles up my cheeks, and my palms become damp. I turn to find Gabe, his hair flattened on one side from sleep, his broad smile showing off his straight white teeth and a dimple in his left cheek. And a net of soccer balls in his lap.

His brother, Phil, who looks the same, except his hair curls around his face, leans around from the driver's seat and nods with his chin.

"Hi," I say in a too-loud high-pitched voice. I cringe.

"What are you doing here?" Gabe asks.

I try to speak, but nothing comes out. My stomach is ready to lurch out of my throat. Neena pokes me in the side. A million things run through my mind, none of which have anything to do with Jehovah. Suddenly I'm aware of the too-big olive-green blouse that hangs on me like a trash bag.

"Oh, wait," he taps his forehead. "You're doing your church thing. How do you get up so early on a Saturday? I have soccer practice, and I can barely drag myself out of bed."

"Because we have the Truth," I manage to squeak out.

His mouth opens as if he wants to say something, but he doesn't.

Neena fidgets next to me. Watching from across the street, Brother Reed begins to walk toward us, Brother Peters, with his sharp nose, close behind.

"I have to go. I'll see you around," I stutter and take a step away.

"Ya, I'm late for soccer. See you," Gabe says, and the car pulls away.

"Who's that boy? He's Worldly. You shouldn't talk to him," Neena scolds, and I shrink down, watching the back of the car as it heads down the street.

"It's Gabe. I've known him since fourth grade," I say, glancing back at the Brothers, who've already moved on to another house.

"Be careful. Remember how Satan likes to trick us." She sounds like Momma, and my heart sinks a little. It's just Gabe. What's the big deal? The spot on my hand where we'd touched at school burns again.

"This door is mine," I say.

The house is different than those on the rest of the block. The lawn is overgrown and brown on the street, where the others are deep green and crisscrossed with the gardener's mower lines. Plastic bags and greasy pizza boxes overflow from the trashcans along the side of the house. Between hanging baskets of dead flowers on the front porch, rusted metal butterflies dangling from a wind chime ting in the gentle breeze.

"Nice, this one has a doorbell. The old kind." She smiles from ear to ear as she presses her finger to the button. Inside there's a muted buzz. A large orange cat wanders to the window. Pushing the curtains aside, it stares at us, blinks slowly, and then licks one of its front paws.

We wait the appointed amount of time, my service bag of books and magazines digging into my shoulder. I shift on my feet, about to leave, when the door creaks open. A little boy in a pair of too-small Superman pajamas peers at us. He rubs the sleep from his eyes with a yawn.

"Hey," I say down to him. "Didn't your mother tell you not to open the door to strangers?"

"She's dead. Besides, you're not a stranger. I seen you before." He points a finger at me, his face a mask of sadness.

"You're Andy. From Kaylee's class?" I ask, and he nods.

Andy, the little boy whose mother died in January. Kaylee had told us all about it. And Momma had something about her not knowing Jehovah. If she had, she'd be in Paradise with us. I was the same age when my dad died, Momma said the same thing to me.

The butterflies hanging from the wind chime dance and let out a gentle song.

"Come on, give him the Watchtower, and let's go," Neena whispers.

I check over my shoulder; the Brothers are farther down the street, their backs to us.

"Where's your dad?" I ask. The cat jumps from the sill and weaves in and out of the boy's legs.

"He's sleeping," the boy sniffs. "I want my mom."

When I found out my dad was never coming home, I felt as if my insides had been emptied. I was hollow with an ache that nothing could take away. I longed to feel his whiskers scratch my face and smell the spicy scent of his aftershave. Momma didn't comfort me. All she said was my Daddy was rotting in the cold ground with worms because he didn't have the Truth. Jehovah didn't care about him. That's what I should say to Andy. But I can't.

"Andy, your mom is okay." Behind me, Neena sucks in a loud breath. I've gone too far.

The boy wipes his nose with his sleeve and shakes his head. "She's dead."

Neena tugs at the back of my blouse, pulling me to come away. I can't leave him, not like this. More than anything, when my daddy died, I needed someone to listen to me, to care. To tell me he wasn't just dead and lying in a hole in the ground. "When I was the same age as you, my daddy died. And you know what?"

He shakes his head. The wind tosses the chimes behind me.

"He went to heaven, a beautiful place up past the clouds. He watches me all the time." I focus my eyes on him as if we share a secret. Something tickles in the back of my head—a distant memory of being hugged tightly by my daddy and his laugh from deep in his belly. "Your mom is there too, and she's watching you. She wants you not to be sad; it makes her sad. Can you do that?" My voice catches in my throat; I'm not sure why I'm telling him this.

His bottom lip quivers. Tears stream down his grubby cheeks. "Really?" he asks.

The cat weaves through the space between us, its tail curved up in what looks like a question mark.

"Yes. Can you do something else for me?" I ask. He nods with a sniff. "Next time someone comes to the door, go get a grown-up to answer it." I reach into my bag and find a sticker sheet I'd meant to give to Kaylee. Taking it in both hands, he looks up at me with big eyes. Neena taps me on the shoulder and curls her finger for me to follow her. The Brothers wait at the end of the driveway. Had they heard me?

What I'd told this boy was a lie; his mother is dead. There's no place called heaven. Without the Truth, she won't wake up in Paradise. She's in the ground with worms. A chill sweeps over me as Jehovah pulls away from me. There's more room now for Satan to slip into my heart for what I'd said to Andy.

Andy scoops up the cat and shuts the door. We wait until we hear the lock click before leaving the porch.

"Why did you say that? That was all wrong," Neena says, voice tinged with anger and disappointment.

"I'm not sure," I shrug. But I do. I wanted him to be happy for a little bit.

I fill out the Field Service slip writing down the house number and scribbling down that I gave him a Watchtower. I write CB (call-back) in thick letters. I am the Sister promising to return to the house and teach them about the Truth, starting with a free Bible Study. The house will be mine; no one will visit again — except me. And I won't be going back.

"Why did you tell that little boy that lie? There's no heaven, and his Mom is in the ground. I think it's you who needs to get counsel from the Elders," Neena says. Her words sting.

Neena is right. I hid the Truth from this boy. I'm not going to be able to help Rachel. And Jehovah is not going to save me during Armageddon. I'm going to be one of those people standing behind the Witnesses as fire reigns down from the sky and the earth cracks wide open. Everyone not in the Truth dies.

Chapter 8

After Field Service, Brother Reed drops Neena and me off at the Kingdom Hall. Rachel is already there, standing alone in the shadows of the porch.

"I'm sorry," I say to Neena.

She tilts her head to the side and eyes me like she's thinking hard. "I guess we all have times we slip up. But Sara, that was big. You better ask Jehovah for forgiveness."

"But are we okay?" I point from me to her.

"Ya, we're okay. You said you were sorry. Let's go and stand by Rachel. She looks like she could use some uplifting or some encouragement."

As we start toward Rachel, Brad and Momma pull up in the van. Brad climbs out and goes to where the rest of the Brothers stand, sharing their Field Service stories and handing in the slips we'd filled out. They shake hands, patting each other on the back. Momma waves me over.

Momma leans out the open window and looks around the parking lot, "Neena, I don't see your mom. Need a ride?"

"Thank you, Sister Michaels. She's around the corner." Neena holds up her cell phone. "She just texted."

"Okay, that's good," Momma frowns. But the frown isn't because Neena's mom is coming; it's because of the cell phone.

"Can you come over later?" Neena asks, loud enough for Momma to hear. Even though I'm old enough to decide for myself, I don't dare say yes.

"Sara is going on Call Backs with me," Momma says as Rachel slides open the back door. "We're going to take Rachel and Brad home first."

I peer into the back. "Where are the girls?"

"At the Wilson's," Momma says.

Rachel and I exchange glances.

"Can Rachel come with us?" I ask, my stomach twisting. I'm getting used to the feeling now.

Momma frowns. "Three is too many; you know that. We go in pairs."

"But..." I start to say as Rachel climbs in, the color draining from her face. I say a quick prayer to Jehovah. Rachel can't be alone with Brad. As I say amen, Sister Winchester hurries over.

"Oh, Sister Michaels, I'm glad I caught you. I'd love to take Rachel with me this afternoon. She is so zealous for Jehovah. I'll have her home for dinner," she gushes.

"You don't have to ask me," Momma says. "Rachel can do as she pleases."

"Well?" Sister Winchester eyes Rachel. "You up for an afternoon with an old Sister?"

Rachel tucks a frizzy curl behind her ear. "I am." She squeezes my hand as she passes by, and I smile weakly.

That was close, I think. That can't happen again. My stomach burns up into my throat. Rachel has to talk to the Elders soon, but first, I have to tell Momma.

"Can Sara come over after Call Backs?" Neena asks, jarring me back to reality.

"We'll see," Momma says, which means no.

Neena's mom pulls into the parking lot and parks at the far end. She's on her phone. Momma scowls.

"Call me later," Neena says, then leans over and whispers. "If your mom will let you. I know she hates me because of my phone and clothes."

A pang of sadness, mixed with anger, hits my chest. Momma makes too many choices in my life.

"I'm sorry," I say to Neena as she hurries away.

Brad comes toward the van. Like last night in the dark, his eyes lock in on mine, I'd been too afraid to move then, and I'm still afraid, but Jehovah will make this right. Rely on Him. I say over and over in my head.

Momma and I ride in silence. I stare out the side window, watching the world as we pass it by, trying to work up the courage to tell her. Rachel will forgive me. This is the only way.

"Sara, you seem out of sorts today. What's going on?" Momma asks.

"I'm tired, that's all. The air mattress has a hole in it," I say. I face forward, trying to act normally. As normal as I can with my world falling apart.

"I'll have to see about getting a new one. Sara, I am proud of you," Momma says. "Giving your room up for Rachel shows how you are maturing in Jehovah's will. He will reward you for that."

I squint out the front windshield. If Momma only knew. I'm not maturing in the Truth. What I just told Andy was a lie. My art is hidden away. Then there's the contest and my lustful thoughts about Gabe. I rub my temples, trying to make it all stop.

"When I was your age, my Great Aunt gave me a place to live. But it came with stipulations. I had to clean and cook," Momma goes on. I stop listening. She's trying to make me feel better by telling me how terrible her life was until she found Jehovah. I'd heard it a million times. Finally, she stops, and I have the chance to say what I've been holding in—the words building up in my head.

"Momma..." I say as my courage slips away, draining out through my fingertips. What if Brad hurts Kaylee and Pearl? Is this how Rachel felt when she tried to tell me.

"Well, what is it?" Momma asks.

"Do you think I'll ever be good enough like Rachel to get to Bethel?" I ask, but those aren't the right words. I shift, so she can't see the tears I'm trying to hold in.

"Is that what's been bothering you? Going to Bethel is between you and Jehovah," Momma says. "It is up to you to do all the things Jehovah requires. If you can't, then it's for certain you will never make it to Bethel."

I'm sure I'll never make it to Bethel; I can't do anything right for Jehovah. I will end up getting married to someone like Brother Peters when I'm eighteen.

Our conversation over, Momma flicks the knob on the radio and sings along to an Elton John song.

At 3:00, we're done with our Call-Backs. My hair is limp and won't stay in its band, my face oily, and my feet hurt from the old shoes. We'd gone to 10 homes, and not one person was home. It was as if they knew we were coming and left on purpose. We pressed Watchtowers into their door frames with hand-scrawled notes about how we missed them and would revisit them next Saturday at the same time.

Our last stop is at Ralph's Grocery. "You get the ice cream," Momma points to the frozen food section, and I am grateful to be on my own. I walk down the aisle, lit by the freezers, examining all the frozen dinners and gluten-free options for breakfast foods until I get to the ice cream. I open the freezer door, and the cold air swirls around me as I examine all the flavors: Chocolate Chip, Rocky Road, and Strawberry Cheesecake, wishing for once I could choose one of those. It's always Neapolitan in the big plastic tub because it is the cheapest and what Brad wants.

A woman behind me says, "Excuse me," as she reaches around with a long tan arm. A gold bracelet filled with butterfly charms jingles as she grabs a tub of ice cream. I recognize her profile, Sister Torrez. She's not Sister Torrez anymore; she's been Disfellowshipped. Shunned. I shouldn't be near her. I can't talk to her. Jehovah requires we avoid people like her who threaten the Truth's purity with their sin. I could be Reproved by the Elders, my privileges as a Sister taken away just by talking to her. I could be shunned too.

As I pivot to leave, she says, "Sara, is that you? You've gotten so tall since the last time I saw you." She holds her arms open to hug me, and I step back stiffly, making sure she feels the cold from me.

"Uhm, hi," I mumble. I need to get away from here, fast.

"This is Isabelle," she says, and Isabelle giggles up at me. She has the same brown curls as Mrs. Torrez.

I blink and look past her toward the end of the aisle for Momma.

"I understand you can't talk to me. But I can talk to you, right?" Mrs. Torrez tilts her head and twists the bracelet on her wrist.

I nod, my lips glued shut, my voice caught somewhere in my throat. I'd already said too much. It's not for me to decide if I can talk to her or not. No one gets Disfellowshipped unless they've committed an unforgivable sin, like cheating on a spouse, smoking, or talking badly about the Truth. Until the Torrez's say, they are sorry and ask for forgiveness from the Congregation, they cannot begin the process of getting reinstated into the Truth. Until then, we must shun them.

"You can call me Rory," she says. In the shopping cart, Isabelle kicks her feet and giggles.

The last time I'd seen Rory, she was still Sister Torrez. She was pregnant, about ready to pop. Two weeks later, she and her husband, Brother Torrez, were Disfellowshipped. They never came back to meetings. I never got to say goodbye. What could she do that was so wrong that Jehovah no longer wanted her as part of the Truth? Why didn't she want to come back? Jehovah always let you come back if you were sorry, and you followed what the Elders told you to do to get reinstated back into the Truth.

I can talk to Isabelle. She's a baby and didn't do anything wrong; she isn't Disfellowshipped.

I glance over my shoulder. Momma is nowhere in sight. "Hi, Isabelle." I hide behind my hands, and she laughs.

Rory unbuckles the straps around Isabelle, picks her up, and holds her close, nuzzling her neck and kissing her forehead.

"Sara, you know, I didn't do anything bad. I'm sure that's what you've been told. I had a blood transfusion. If I hadn't had that, I wouldn't be here, and neither would Isabelle." She twists to face me, tears in her eyes.

A blood transfusion. One of the worse sins. She chose to get the life blood of another person in her body instead of relying on Jehovah to heal her.

When Rory was pregnant, she was sick all the time. Brother Torrez would bring a pillow to each meeting, grab a chair, and prop her feet up on it. Her swollen hands lay in her lap, dark circles ringed her eyes, and her skin had a yellow tinge. Momma and the other Sisters whispered about Sister Torrez and her inability to attend meetings and how her Field Service hours dwindled to nothing.

I wrap my arms around my chest. What if Rory had relied on Jehovah and the Elders? What if she had listened to the Governors who gave us the words straight from Jehovah? Would there be a baby Isabelle? Would Rory still be here? If she'd remained loyal, she'd be in Paradise. But not now. Now she will die in Armageddon with the rest of the World.

I should go.

"I sure wish you could babysit for me. I could use a good sitter," Rory says.

I couldn't in a million years babysit for someone who'd turned their back on Jehovah. My eyes widen, and I hurry down the aisle, forgetting the ice cream, and run right into Momma. She grabs my elbow and spins me around.

"Were you talking to that horrible Apostate woman?" Momma growls at me, her hot breath on my ear.

"No! We were both getting ice cream at the same time, and I got trapped. I tried to get away. Look, I didn't even get the ice cream." I hold up my hands as proof. Momma lets out a gust of air through her nose and storms off to the checkout.

I place our items on the sticky belt as Momma makes small talk with a lady in front of us. I glance sideways, two aisles over at Rory. Isabelle squeals, and I realize the sacrifice Rory made. Rory's parents will never talk to her again. They'll never meet Isabelle, hold her in their arms, spoil her, love her.

I swallow the lump in my throat, wondering if my mother would ever do the same for me – or if she'd let me die.

Chapter 9

By the time Momma and I get home, Brad has left for Brother Fellowship at the Kingdom Hall. As I reach into the van to grab the groceries, Sister Winchester drops Rachel off.

"Are you okay? That was close. You could have been alone with Brad," I say all in one breath as Rachel bends to scoop up a bag.

"I am okay; Jehovah saved me with sister Winchester," Rachel says. "You are such a good little sister Sara. Please, don't worry so much," she says. She's working too hard to convince me nothing is wrong. But she can't hide the red in her eyes or the shake of her voice.

"You can get counsel. Go to Momma. She can help," I say. Rachel has to listen. This is the only way.

Her face pales, the same color as the white flowers on her dress. "Sara, I can't do that. Have you been talking?"

"No. I haven't, I promise," I shake my head. "But you can get Counsel," I plead, my stomach twisting in knots. "The Elders want to help you."

She bends and gets another bag. "I can't risk losing my chance at Bethel. I'm leaving it in Jehovah's hands. I am relying on Him like we are told. I will not shame Him. He will take care of everything," She smiles down at me before hurrying into the house, leaving me alone.

Relying on Jehovah is a good thing. It's not shaming Him, and it's definitely not a sin. Getting Counsel is not shaming Him. Going to the police would be shaming Him. Going to the Elders to report a Wrong Doing without two witnesses is a sin. All I want to do is help Rachel. Momma is the only way. I wish Rachel would let me help her. A wave of nausea sweeps over me. What if Brad tires of Rachel and moves on to me, or worse, Kaylee or Pearl?

Momma decides to order takeout from the Peking Palace. Dinner arrives, and Rachel places the boxes around the table while I get the plates. I'm not hungry. My throat tight, I push a snow pea around on my plate, shoving the rice from one side to the other.

Momma wipes her hands on a napkin, crumples it, and leaves it beside her empty plate. "Since it's only the three of us, let's read from the Daily Scripture book and then watch a movie."

Rachel says nothing as she presses her fingers to her forehead and rubs. Her face is still pale from before, and dark circles ring her eyes. She's not okay like she pretends to be.

"Sara? You want to pick the movie?" Momma asks.

"Sure," I say. I'm not in the mood to watch a movie or read Jehovah's words, though I should be. I pick through the box of old VHS tapes and find one of Momma's favorites, an old musical.

Momma picks up the stack of fortune cookies and tosses them into the trash. "I told them I didn't want these things. Fortunes. It's a gateway for Satan." She stares down at the trashcan, her hands on her hips.

"Sister Michaels, I don't feel so good. Do you mind if I skip the movie? I'll stay for the reading, of course," Rachel says.

"I wondered if you weren't feeling good. You should go to bed and get some rest. Sara and I will read it." Momma puts her arm around Rachel's shoulder.

"No, I'll stay. It's important," Rachel says. She moves to sit. Momma waves her away toward the stairs.

"Dear, your dedication and zeal are something to be admired. You should get some rest. The last few days have been stressful for you." Momma scans the shelf for the Daily Scripture book.

"Thank you, Sister Michaels," Rachel says. "Sara, we'll do something fun tomorrow, I promise."

"Okay," I say. I watch as she walks up the stairs, her shoulders hunched, taking each step like it hurts to move. This is not right.

Momma scans the shelf sagging with the weight of the books. Finding the right one, she plucks it out with one finger. She sits back down, her hands pressing flat the smooth cover of the book. I sit on the bench across from her, my head heavy.

"I guess I'll read," she smiles at me as if she told a joke. As the spiritual guide of our family, Brad is the one who reads, always.

Momma clears her throat and starts to read. I barely listen. I've heard the words many times before. I've memorized the words that Jehovah wants me to say and believe.

"This world has nothing good to offer you. Those who have gained the most of what it has to offer are among the most unhappy, selfish and burdened people of all. Note how the Bible appraises this world: "Everything in the world—the desire of the flesh and the desire of the eyes and the showy display of one's means of life—does not originate with Jehovah, but originates with the world. Furthermore, the world is passing away and so is its desire, but he that does the will of Jehovah remains forever."

The words hit me like a slap in the face. I haven't focused fully Jehovah, I've focused on the things of the world– Gabe, the boy Andy, my art. No wonder I feel so mixed up.

Momma stops and looks up at me. "Sara, what is Jehovah telling us here?"

"I should focus more on Jehovah than my Worldly desires. If we don't, then when He destroys the world during Armageddon, we will die with the rest of the people who didn't follow the Truth." As the words come from my mouth, a voice taps at the back of my head. Val and Andy, does Jehovah mean to destroy them? They aren't evil. And what about Isabel? She is too young to understand the Truth. Is Jehovah going to kill her too? I quickly shut the voice down. It's wrong to judge Jehovah's ways.

Rachel has given up everything for Jehovah. She has no Worldly desires. Jehovah will take care of her, He promises. She needs help. And there is only one way.

My eyes flick to the clock. Brad will be home soon. The girls are gone. Rachel is in her room. Now is the time. I don't care if Rachel is angry with me; this is for her spiritual good. I may never get this chance again. I suck in a deep breath and work up the courage.

"Momma, earlier when you were driving, when we were talking, and I said nothing was wrong?" I venture.

"Yes." She nods and slips the ribbon back into place, closing the book gently.

"I didn't tell you the truth. Something is bothering me, but it's about Rachel," I say, lowering my voice.

Momma wrinkles her brow. "You're not gossiping, are you?"

"No, Momma," I say, feeling my courage slip away.

"I hope she's not regretting leaving her Worldly home. This System of Things is ending soon; it would make Satan so happy to have her run back to them and away from the Truth." Momma says all in one breath.

"It's nothing like that," I say, my voice quivering. "It's Brad. He touched her. He touched her...Sacred Place," my voice fades to a whisper.

The corner of her mouth twitches as she stares at me silently, her face hard and eyes dark.

"He said if she told anyone, he would hurt Kaylee and Pearl," I say, and still, she says nothing. "Momma, did you hear me? Brad..."

She puts her hand up to stop me. A vein pulses on her forehead as she pushes away from the table and glares down at me. "Why did you tell me this? What do you expect me to do?"

"Go to the Elders, get Counsel for Rachel," I say.

Moving away, Momma's hands flutter around her neck as she paces across the kitchen. "How can you suggest that? I can't do that. I'm not a witness to what happened. There needs to be two witnesses to take any wrongdoing to the Elders. I'm not even sure anything happened. Rachel is young; she's probably lying because she wants to go home. She moves to the sink, flicks the water on, and squirts in a stream of blue soap–too much soap.

"Momma, how can you say that? It's Rachel. She gave up everything. Why would she lie?" My voice shakes, and the familiar burn returns to my stomach, moving up into my chest.

Momma faces me, her arms crossed over her chest. "This is all Satan's doing. He's trying to stop Brad from becoming an Elder.

We cannot break the laws. You know the scripture, *'Rely on him, and He will act on your behalf.'* And do I need to remind you again, there must be two witnesses – TWO."

My chest feels like someone is squeezing my heart. "But Momma, all I'm asking is for Counsel for Rachel, not to report a Wrong Doing. She needs spiritual guidance while she waits for Jehovah's will to be done. Did you see her tonight?"

Momma shakes her head, her face red. "Sara, I am surprised at you. Have you forgotten what Jehovah requires of us as His true believers? You know the rules of the Truth. There's nothing for me to do." Momma falls into the chair, her legs no longer able to hold her. She buries her face in her hands, and her shoulders shake. I move to comfort her when I hear the rumble of the garage door opening.

Momma sits up and tucks her hair behind her ear. "No more of this. Not another word. You are to rely on Jehovah. He will take care of this. We cannot shame His name." She shoves the book back onto the shelf.

Brad comes in with his gray bible tucked under his arm and a plate of leftovers in the other. "Lot of food tonight. The Sisters went all out."

"That's wonderful," Momma says, trying to sound happy, but her voice comes out high and strained. Robotically she takes the plate and places it in the fridge.

Brad's eyes darken. He looks from her to me and back again. I shiver. He knows I told.

"I'm going to bed," he announces. "Bushed."

"Good night," Momma says, her back turned to him. She rinses a cup in the sink and places it in the drainer. "We'll watch the movie another time."

"Yes, Momma," I say.

I trudge up the stairs. I've failed again.

I sleep in the hallway in the dark space between Rachel's door and mine. I don't care if I don't sleep. Rachel is more important than anything right now. The house is eerily quiet. My eyes become heavy, and I wish I'd brought my sketchbook. But then, I promised Jehovah I was done with that. Then I hear it, just like before, the sounds of feet padding across the kitchen floor, the flicker of the nightlight as someone walks past. And then Brad is there, at the landing, looking back at me.

Something rages deep inside me. "Go away," I hiss, surprised at my own voice.

He moves forward like he's going to push me aside. Instead, he steps back and walks away, muttering something I can't understand.

I realize in that second, as my heart pounds in my chest and my breath catches in my throat—it's all up to me. Rachel shared her secret with me for a reason. She knew I'd help her.

I pull my blanket up to my chin and lay back against the wall. I have one chance and one choice: Brother Reed. He will listen to me. He's like my Grandfather. He will Counsel Rachel. He will tell her what to do. Going to him won't shame on Jehovah's name, and private Counsel will be good for Rachel.

A shade of doom slides down, and my thoughts go dark. Am I doing the right thing? Jehovah's laws are in place for his true believers for a reason. If I fail, I will never live in Paradise on Earth. I won't survive Armageddon.

Chapter 10

At breakfast, Kaylee, home from her sleepover, giggles, and thrusts a paper under my nose.

"Look what I drew over at the Wilson's last night," she says.

Yawning, I turn the page.

"You got it upside down," Kaylee turns the paper around and smooths it on the table.

On the paper, she'd made five oblong shapes. Each shape has a lopsided head. People maybe? They stand in the grass made of bright yellow and dark green lines. In the background, a squiggly rainbow spreads across the paper.

"Is this us in Paradise?" I ask.

"Yes! See Momma, Daddy, me, Pearl, and you." She presses her finger to each person as she says the name.

"What are these?" I ask, touching the dark shapes lying flat on the grass, flowers growing out of them.

"Those are the Worldly. They're dead. They didn't live through Armageddon," Kaylee says, and my heart prickles with sadness. I recall the pictures I'd drawn when I was her age: sunflowers, houses with wide windows and a straggly line of smoke from a crooked chimney, and people with smiles. Not death.

"It's a terrible picture. Your people don't have any faces," Pearl says over my shoulder.

"It's not!" Kaylee pouts. She takes the picture back and holds it close to her chest.

"I think it's good," Rachel says, sitting across from me. Instead of one of her usual Field Service dresses, she wears pants and a blouse. Her makeup doesn't hide the red and puffy eyes. She doesn't attempt a smile.

How can I tell her I told Momma, and Momma won't help? I swallow the lump that's growing in my throat. She doesn't need to know; it will only make things worse for her.

Momma places a plate of steaming scrambled eggs and sausage in front of us. In a swift movement, she picks up Brad's plate from his empty spot and scrapes the remains of his half-eaten egg and crusts of toast into the trash as if she were trying to hide him from Rachel and me.

"Where are you going?" I ask Rachel.

"Job interview," she says, and I wonder why she hadn't told me until now. But then, I am keeping secrets from her, too.

Brad walks in with his hair slicked back, a sharp crease down each leg of his black slacks. Momma's best ironing. Rachel puts her head down like she's interested in the yellow glob of eggs on her plate. She doesn't see him fix his gaze on me. Anger flashes across his face, and heat rises on my cheeks. Momma is busy with Kaylee, and Pearl doesn't see it either.

"Have a fruitful day," he says to Momma. "And you girls behave." He pats Kaylee and Pearl on the head as he heads to the garage, and I want to scream.

Holding her coffee between her hands, Momma slides in across from Rachel. "How will you work and do your full-time Field Service?"

How can Momma act as if nothing happened? Doesn't she care? The lump in my throat grows larger, pushing on my chest.

"Most places, when they find out you're a Jehovah's Witness, pile the hours on, make it hard for you to serve Jehovah. The World hates the Truth," Momma says.

Rachel pierces a piece of sausage with her fork. "I don't need an interview; it's a formality. I'm going to work at Brother Wilson's insurance office. It's 15 hours a week. My parents cut off my cell phone. And I need to save for Bethel."

"You could apply for assistance. A lot of young Witnesses do that. Then you can focus all your time on Jehovah," Momma says. Her voice sounds hopeful like she can't wait for Jehovah to destroy everything around us.

"That will take too long. I need to get out..." Rachel stops, pink rising on her cheeks. I look to Momma, who looks away. "I'm close to Bethel," Rachel finishes.

"We'll help you any way we can. Right, Sara?" Momma says, her eyes locking in on mine, her mouth in a tight line.

"Sure," I say, knowing Momma isn't helping Rachel in any way she can.

"What corner did you get assigned?" Rachel asks.

I raise my brows.

"For street preaching this morning. It's today, right?"

Today is my day to do my service work downtown, and I'd forgotten. Brother Reed set it up last week. There's a chance I can talk to Brother Reed alone.

"I have to meet everyone by the Main Library," I say.

"Street corner preaching, that's how Rachel became my bible student. Remember that Rachel, what was it two or three years ago when we met?" Momma asks.

"It was two," Rachel says. "I was sixteen."

"Sara, you can ride the bus with Rachel, then I won't have to drive you," Momma says, and Rachel agrees. "Your own service cart. What a wonderful reward. It's just as the Elders and Governor Body say, do everything Jehovah requires, and He will reward you."

Her words are a reminder to keep my mouth shut, to not bring shame on Jehovah's name.

The phone rings, jarring the silence we'd fallen into. Kaylee jumps from her spot in front of the TV, lurching for the phone before anyone else can answer it. Momma crosses her arms over her chest and frowns.

"It's for Sara," Kaylee says.

Why did Neena have to call now?

"It's a stranger," Kaylee says, and I wonder who it could be.

"Hello," I say, aware of the roomful of eyes on me and wishing again for a cell phone. Maybe I need a part-time job like Rachel.

Momma would never allow that.

"Sarah, it's me, Rory."

"Um," I say, a little too loud.

Momma's eyes lock in on me. She mouths, "Who is it?"

Before I can say anything, Rory says in a rush, "I'm hoping you can help me out. I know because I'm disfellowshipped, you're scared of me. But I'm desperate. Miguel is out of town, and daycare is closed for the Easter holiday. Can you babysit Friday afternoon? I have a shift. I can't get out of it." In the background, Isabelle laughs.

I wipe the sweat from my palm on my skirt.

I look from Momma to Rachel, who stare at me like I have something growing out of my head. I picture Rory's swollen belly and the blood transfusion she needed to save her life. I hear Isabelle laugh again, and the knot in my throat threatens to burst.

"Sara, I really need your help. Everyone is on Spring Break. I can't find anyone to cover my shift. It would help me out. You don't have to talk to me. It will be a good deed, and I'll pay you.

I'll leave cash on the table. It's for Isabelle, not me," she pleads. There's a pull in my chest like someone tugs a string. She's right. I don't have to talk to her. Isabelle is a baby. Maybe...maybe this is what I'm supposed to do? Maybe Jehovah is giving me an opportunity to teach Isabelle the Truth? I can use the money to help Rachel. It's one step closer to a cell phone or clothes of my own. I've never had a chance to make real money before – all my babysitting for Sisters is done for free.

"Let me check," I say, holding the phone to my chest. "Momma, can I babysit Friday afternoon? It's for one of Sister Walker's bible students," I ask. In my head I ask Jehovah to forgive me for the lie. I am doing something good with it.

Momma taps her finger on her mug. "Aren't you already babysitting for Sister Winchester's grandkids?"

"That's tomorrow," I say.

"A bible student of Sister Walker's?" Momma asks, and I nod. "You'll have to find a way over and back. And, of course, you'll be home for family study at 7:00."

"I can take the bus. It's not far," I say.

"Fine then," Momma says.

"Okay," I say into the phone.

"See you at two. I promise no talking," Rory says and hangs up.

I hope I've done the right thing.

Rachel and I wait for the bus at the stop in front of the Koffee Stop. I look for Val and her friends, but then remember she's at camp. Rachel stands with her arms wrapped around her waist like she's cold even though it's warm out. She keeps her eyes fixed down the street, like doing that will make the bus come faster. She's quiet, but I need to tell her what I did, even if she hates me. I'm going to make it right. She'll feel better.

"Rachel," I venture. "I have to tell you something."

Fear flashes across her face. "You told, didn't you? I knew it."

"What? Wait? I did, but it's not what you think," I say.

She drops her arms to her sides. "How could you? I asked you not to. Jehovah is taking care of this." She flops down onto the bench. "I thought I could trust you."

I suck in my breath. "You can. You're in bad shape. You need Counsel. The Elders...they'll help you...they'll know what to do," I blubber. Tears begin to fall. "I tried to get Momma to help me, but she said no."

She looks up at me, her bottom lip shaking. "She said no?"

I nod, wiping the tear from my eye.

"I'm sorry, Rachel. I thought this was what Jehovah wanted. I thought after I saw Brad in the hallway two nights in a row, and then yesterday after Field Service, that Counsel is the only answer," I say.

"What do you mean you saw Brad in the hallway?" She asks. The cars behind me whir by, covering the sound of my heart pounding in my ears.

"I slept outside your room. He came up the stairs in the middle of the night," I say to the ground.

Rachel looks at me, her face full of sadness.

"Sara, I'm...I don't..." tears fall down her cheeks. Behind me, the bus squeaks to a stop, and the doors open with a swish.

She stands slow, her knees shaking, her face paler than before. She climbs the stairs. I follow her as she moves to sit in the back, plopping down next to her so our shoulders touch.

"I'm sorry, Rachel," I whisper.

"It's okay, Sara," she says, her voice ragged and tired. "I shouldn't have put all this on you. That was wrong."

"It wasn't wrong. You should have told me. But maybe you should get help," I whisper, and then our conversation is over. She sits her face like marble. When the bus pulls up to her stop, Rachel says nothing and hurries away.

As the bus bumps along, my hands itch to move, so I pull out a pen and begin to draw on the back page of my bible, the only thing I have to draw on, my sketchbook hidden away at home. By the time I reach my stop, the page is covered. A face, eyes filled with sadness, almost hopeless, stares back at me – mine.

I've written a string of words around the edge, over and over: *Rely on Jehovah*.

Brother Reed, Sister Winchester, and Cheri, in her favorite tomato-red blouse, wait for me at the corner of 18th and R by the library. Brother Reed checks his watch, then looks up at me with a frown.

"You're late," Cheri announces.

Sister Winchester wears her normal thick gray sweater, the same color as her hair. She pats Cheri on the arm. "Now, now, that's not very Sisterly of you, is it? We should pray to Jehovah to strengthen her instead of pointing out her mistake."

I shift uncomfortably.

"Cheri, why don't you take our cart to our corner while I help the Sisters with theirs," Brother Reed points down the block.

With a frown, Cheri grabs the cart. She hurries down the street, the wheels of the cart squeaking and bumping along the pavement as she drags it behind her.

Brother Reed helps Sister Winchester set up our cart, opening it and locking it into place, and arranging the Truth literature, making sure we have enough to hand out.

He rubs his hands together, clears his throat, and looks down the street. "I'm going to be on the other corner with Cheri. If you two need anything or anyone starts harassing you, fold up the cart and come over to us. Anything else?" He asks.

"Thank you so much Brother Reed," Sister Winchester says. She pulls out a butterscotch candy and twists off the plastic wrapper. "You two have a fruitful morning."

As Brother Reed walks away, I feel panic rising. I reach into my pocket for the familiar foil tube of antacid, break off two and chew them slowly. This might be my only chance to get him alone.

Rachel's face, full of fear when she told me, flashes before me. And Momma's face, full of anger.

Rely on Jehovah. Do not shame His name.

Jehovah put me here, now, with Brother Reed. Exactly when I need to talk to him alone.

I have to do it.

"Be right back," I say over my shoulder to Sister Winchester and hurry away before she can stop me. "Brother Reed," I call when I near him. He faces me, and I pause again, fear creeping up over what I'm about to say.

"Yes, Sister Sara, did you forget something?" He smiles down at me, the sun catching the edge of his glasses.

"N-no. It's something else," I say.

His smile fades as he peers over my shoulder over to Sister Winchester. "You shouldn't leave your partner alone unless it's important."

"It is. It's very important."

He pushes his glasses up and waits while I stare at him mutely. A million thoughts run through my mind. Am I doing the right thing? Am I relying on Jehovah? Why had I told Rory I'd babysit?

"Well, what is so important you left your post?" He says as he tugs his cuffs down over his wrist.

"I need Counsel," I blurt out, but it's not me; it's Rachel.

His eyebrows knit together. "Of course, anytime you need Counsel from the Elders, you have it. Why didn't you call about this?"

"There's no privacy at home." My heart beats like it's about to explode out of my chest. "And I want you to give me Counsel, not anyone else." I twist my hands behind my back, not looking away from him.

He lets his breath out with a heavy sigh. He rests his hand on my shoulder. "How about this afternoon, after we're done here? I have some time to spare."

"Okay," I say. Have I done the right thing? Am I disappointing Jehovah?

Chapter 11

When I asked Brother Reed for Counsel, I thought I'd feel better, but I don't. My face is hot, my hands cold with sweat, and I am a jumble of knots. I force myself to smile at the Worldly people passing by, remembering what Val said about not being miserable. It seems like weeks ago, but it's only been days.

I lift my chin, step closer to the plastic card filled with Truth literature, and try to make eye contact with each person who passes. Some look at me knowingly, like they feel sorry for me. Most shake their heads, frowning in disgust. All walk away. No one asks for a free home bible study so they can learn the Truth. No one seems to care the world is ending soon, and they will die.

"You okay, dear? You seem far away," Sister Winchester says, interrupting my thoughts.

"I'm fine. I guess I just expected, out here, it would be easier to teach the Worldly about the Truth," I say.

"This is your first time out here, isn't it?"

"Yes," I say.

"Sara, the Worldly don't believe they need Jehovah. If only they understood that this System is ending soon. But they are blind. It's our job to keep Jehovah's commandments close. We need to preach to the Worldly as Noah did when he built the ark.

We must courageously obey Jehovah and remain loyal. When we do, Jehovah will reward us with life in Paradise," she reminds.

I'd heard the words thousands of times before. Today they seem foreign, and I do nothing to soothe the uneasiness building inside. If anything, I feel worse. I am not courageous. I am not loyal.

My gaze darts down to the end of the block. I can see the red blob, Cheri, and Brother Reed in his dark blue suit, their backs to us.

My bladder is on fire, and I desperately need something to drink. "Is it okay if I go get us something to drink? There's a place around the corner." I thumb over my shoulder.

She sits back on the edge of the cement planter and wipes her brow. "I would love one my dear. I'm parched." She rifles in her purse for some money.

"My treat," I say and hurry away before she can press her wadded-up bills into my hand.

I head for the coffee shop I'd seen when I'd gotten off the bus. It's ahead, not far. As I near the front door, I spot a girl about my age sitting at a table alone. She has a sketchpad like mine, laid open, and wears earbuds. She sips a tall pink drink with a swirl of whipped cream on the top, eyes something in the distance, stops, and then her pencil dances across the paper. I wish it were me sitting there. There is so much to draw, the people waiting for the bus, the lost young couple bent over a phone looking for directions, and the library across the street with its pillars and gargoyles.

Quick as the thought comes, I swallow it down and hurry inside.

Everyone must be thirsty because there is a line to the door. I duck in and slide to the bathroom in the back. By the time I get our drinks and walk back to Sister Winchester, she's already folded up the cart so it's the size of a small-wheeled suitcase. "You were gone so long I was about to come to find you."

"Sorry," I say, handing her an iced coffee. "Long line." I take a slurp of my frosty drink and look away from her. The lunchtime crowd has drifted back to work, the sidewalk empty. "Why'd you close up? We still have twenty minutes," I say. My time report will be short today, and that's not good. I need to do more than is required. I'll have to make up the twenty minutes somewhere else.

"A homeless person kept asking me for money. When I told him I didn't have any, he asked for a free home bible study." She clicks her tongue and shakes her head. "He doesn't even have a home. So, I shut down the shop."

"I guess he doesn't deserve to know about Jehovah," I mumble into my straw.

"What, dear?" She cups her ear.

"Nothing," I say up to her.

Pulling the cart behind her, we walk to where Brother Reed and Cheri wait.

"Oh, Sisters, you finished for the day?" Brother Reed asks, not looking at me.

"Yes, Brother Reed, the need is not very great down here today, and my back is aching," Sister Winchester rubs the small of her back. "I will make up my time with some Call Backs or letter writing."

"You ready for Wednesday?" Cheri asks as we climb into the back of Brother Reed's car.

"Wednesday?" I echo.

Her eyes bulge out in question. "Don't you remember? I'm coming over to mentor you. Our bible study," she says, stretching the words out like I don't understand.

"I forgot," I say.

Her brows knit together in one fuzzy line. "Forgot? How can you forget? You don't want Satan slipping into your heart and taking over, do you?"

A spark of fear burns in my chest. I shake my head, feeling the heat on my cheeks. "No. With Rachel moving in and all the extra Field Service hours I've been doing, I just forgot. I'm sorry. Do you mind, can we start next week?"

She sits back, her lips pinched tight. "Is that a good idea?"

"What if we do two chapters instead of one?" I suggest.

"And next Field Service, we'll partner," Cheri adds. My stomach knots again. What if Rachel needs me?

"Fine," I say, anything to get out of this week.

"It's so good seeing you two youngsters leaning on each other and following Jehovah. A true friendship will last forever," Sister Winchester says, leaning around to face us. Cheri grins from ear to ear, revealing her yellow teeth.

In the back of Brother Reed's car, I am trapped with Cheri, who babbles about her experiences out in Ministry Work. She says something about Rachel and Bethel, and my ears perk up. But then she switches subjects back to herself, and I quit listening and try to figure out what I will say to Brother Reed.

Instead of taking me to the Kingdom Hall for Counsel, Brother Reed takes me to his house. "This will be much more comfortable and private," he says as he leads me to his office at the back of the house.

Sister Reed follows with a plate of cookies and frosty glasses of lemonade. "It's so good to see you, Sara. We miss you around here." She places the snack down on the table and kisses the top of my head. "We need some new artwork."

"I will make you something," I say. If she knew about my sketchbook and the art I'd hidden away, she might not be so nice to me right now.

"Wonderful!" She claps her hands together. "I'll be in the kitchen should you need me."

Brother Reed places his worn bible on the table between us and waits until he hears the click of the door behind him before he starts.

"Let's pray first," he says. I bow my head and fold my sweaty hands in my lap while he prays.

He pushes his glasses up his slender nose. "Why do you wish to seek Counsel, Sister Sara?"

My words freeze somewhere between my head and mouth. I try to keep my hands still by grabbing hold of my bible. It's just Counsel; why am I so nervous? Brother Reed will tell me what to do and pray to Jehovah. He'll give me scriptures to read to encourage Rachel.

"It's okay. We're imperfect creatures. As followers of the Truth, we all need to receive counsel occasionally. And, as a reminder, whatever you tell me will stay with me and not be repeated to anyone else," he says, his voice kind and gentle, urging me to speak.

"Anything?" I ask.

"Anything. I will give you sound biblical counsel, which you will take and enact upon." He straightens the bible between us.

I cannot waste an Elders' time any longer. Focusing on the tree outside the window and not on his face, I tell him what Rachel promised me to keep secret. I tell him about Brad in the hallway in the middle of the night and, the red mark on his face, how Rachel was upset about messing up her chance for Bethel. His hands remain still, and his face gives away nothing, a perfect poker face, if he played poker.

"That's quite a story," he says when I finish. He takes a sip of his lemonade.

"It's not a story," I say.

He taps his bible, then flips it open. "Sara, Counsel is for adjusting *your* behavior with scriptural guidance. It sounds like you're reporting someone for Wrong Doing."

"No, that's not what...I couldn't. It's Counsel. And...it's Rachel who needs the Counsel, but she wouldn't come, and I thought," fumbling over my words, my tongue seeming to grow as I talk. Why couldn't I find the right words? Why doesn't he believe me? I push back, wanting to leave, but Brother Reed brought me here, and Rachel needs me.

Brother Reed sips his lemonade again and opens his bible, turning each page with a crisp snap. "I'm surprised by this behavior. I feel you've purposely misled me. You're a baptized

Sister, so you are aware of Jehovah's requirements. No Brother or Sister can be reported for Wrong Doing unless there are **two** witnesses to back it up. What if Rachel is making this up? Perhaps she has a crush on Brad? You know that happens with girls and young women; they develop feelings for the older men who help them out of sticky situations."

The churning returns to my stomach. "Rachel wouldn't lie. She said for me to rely on Jehovah. He will take care of it."

"We don't know why Brad was going upstairs. And Rachel is right. You need to rely on Jehovah. His rules and commandments are in place for a purpose," he spits. Why is he getting angry with me? Shouldn't he be mad at Brad?

I shake my head. "You have to help. I saw Brad outside of her room at night. He's going to keep hurting her. Now he's going to hurt Kaylee and Pearl because I told." Hot tears pour from my eyes. I've messed everything up.

"You made a mistake. There's no proof. It truly is in Jehovah's hands." He pushes his chair back and hands me a tissue. "I'm taking you home. I don't want to hear any more about this. There will be no bringing shame to Jehovah's name."

I stand, my fists at my sides. "How can you not help? You're an Elder?"

Anger flashes across his face. "Enough. You are a Sister and not a very obedient one. You should never talk to an Elder in that way." He runs his hand through his hair and shakes his head. "You need to go home and start working on your obedience and getting right with Jehovah. You understand what that means don't you?"

I say nothing.

"Do you?" He asks again.

"Yes, it means I'll die in Armageddon. I won't live in Paradise on Earth." My voice trembles.

"Exactly," he says. I follow him out, my head down.

"Leaving so soon?" Sister Reed calls from the kitchen. "Sara, don't forget, I need a new painting."

I mumble an almost silent goodbye.

I've messed up again, badly this time. I hope it's not too late to make it right with Jehovah. What am I going to tell Rachel?

Chapter 12

Brother Reed drops me at home. I am glad to be out of his car. A dull achiness has seeped into my skin, making me feel empty.

Kaylee and Pearl fight over what looks like a new box of crayons. Momma is in the kitchen. I sit silently at the table, wishing for my sketchbook.

The phone rings, and Momma picks it up before I can. I wish it to be Neena.

"Oh, Brother Reed, thank you so much for assigning Sara to do downtown work this morning. It's such a privilege," Momma gushes. Her tenses, and she turns away quickly, so I can't see her face. My stomach clenches with dread.

She says nothing now, her head bobbing up and down as Brother Reed does all the talking.

"I understand," Momma says and hangs up. The air in the room is still as the rooster on the clock crows. She takes a deep breath, smooths down the front of her dress, and calls me over with a wave.

"Yes, Momma," I say, the feeling of dread settling in.

Momma's face is as hard as stone as she pulls me into the dark living room, the blinds pulled closed, and the furniture covered in white sheets – a room frozen in time, fake.

"What have you done?" Momma asks.

"Nothing," I say. But I had.

"One more time. What did you do?" She hisses through her clenched jaw.

"I did what Jehovah..." I start to say. Momma moves fast, so fast I don't have time to move away from the flat of her hand. She slaps me hard, my head snaps back, and my teeth rattle. My cheek burns and I raise my hand to cover the spot, biting back the tears.

"That was Brother Reed. After I forbade you to, you went behind my back and sought Counsel from an Elder. Do you realize how that makes *me* look? Like I can't control my own daughter? You accused the Spiritual Leader of this family of Wrong Doing without having any witnesses, as Jehovah requires. I am a Sister in Good Standing. That's hard to gain. I can't get that back so easily," her hands flutter around her neck. "Now the Elders want to meet Brad and me at the Kingdom Hall about you. They'll probably call Rachel in, too," she pauses, biting her lip. "I'm sure you've ruined Brad's chance to become an Elder. And Rachel will probably be delayed in going to Bethel now."

"I was trying to help Rachel. It was for Counsel," I say softly, keeping my head down and my hand to my cheek. If Brad doesn't become an Elder, all the work Momma has been doing is for nothing. And Rachel, she'll be stuck here.

"I told you to rely on Jehovah. You're so *stubborn* and willful; you've always been that way. Jehovah isn't going to save you. You're going to die in Armageddon. What if you'd gone to the police? You would have brought Shame on Jehovah," she shakes her head as she whisks her purse and keys up from the table. "Watch your sisters. And make dinner. This is probably going to take a while."

Rachel comes home as I pour the spaghetti box into the boiling water. I hide my face from her, hiding the red mark from Momma's slap.

"I got the job," Rachel says. "Where is everyone?"

Water spills over the edge of the pan, sizzling on the burner. I flick the knob off.

"Momma went," I stop, catching myself from telling Rachel exactly where Momma is. My heart constricts. She'll know soon enough. "She's out. Kaylee and Pearl are upstairs playing Kingdom Hall in their room." I grab the milk and butter from the fridge, forgetting about my face.

"What happened to you?" Rachel asks, her eyes wide.

"It's nothing," I say quickly, letting my hair fall over my face in a curtain.

"It doesn't look like nothing. Someone slapped you."

I shake my head.

"I can *see* it. Sit, tell me." She jerks her chin toward the kitchen table, and I follow. Sliding in across from her, I tuck my hair behind my ears. There's no point in hiding the mark any longer.

"What happened," Rachel asks, the concern on her face matching her voice. It nearly undoes me.

"Momma did it," I say, my voice flat, a wave of nausea rippling through me.

"Why? No one deserves to be hit. No one," she says.

"She...I did something. I...I told Brother Reed about Brad. But it wasn't to report a Wrong Doing. It was for me and you to... to get Counsel. I only wanted to help. It wasn't supposed to be like this," I say quietly.

Rachel sits unmoving. I make my hands still, laying them flat on the table.

"I know."

I look up at her, searching her face. "How?"

"Brother Reed called me," Rachel says, her voice flat.

"I didn't mean to get you in trouble. I was trying to do what Jehovah wanted me to do. I thought — I thought it would be private," I pause and wipe a tear from the corner of my eye. "I thought Brother Reed would listen to me and help. I thought I was close enough to Jehovah that it would work out. You hate me, don't you?" I ask.

"No, Sara, I don't. I shouldn't have burdened you with this problem. I can see you were trying to do the right thing," She reaches across the table and grabs my ice-cold hands. "You are close to Jehovah. Don't doubt that. What happened with Brother Michaels was my fault. I led him on. Probably my immodest clothes. Or maybe it was my thoughts about missing my family and doubting Bethel. I left room for Satan to slip into my heart."

I jerk my hands back. "What? No, none of this is your fault." But I recall the words of our Truth book, the two small paragraphs about women who are abused, beaten, or raped – they'd done something to cause it. But Rachel? What could she have done? It makes no sense.

"Before I moved in, I had a few doubts about Jehovah and the Truth. I wasn't sure about Bethel. Those doubts pushed me away from Jehovah and allowed Satan into my life. And that's when..." she stops and wipes tears from the corners of her eyes with her fingertips. "It doesn't matter what happened. All that matters is I understand what I did wrong and will get the biblical correction I need to get back on track."

I stare at her.

"I'm meeting with the Elders tomorrow for my Counsel," she says, as if it were nothing. "For now, I have to read *Organized to do Jehovah's Will* and go through the Bethel materials again.

They're going to guide me back spiritually. In a way, you've done a good thing, Sara. You're helping me with my faith."

This is happening the wrong way. It feels like *she* is being punished.

"I don't understand. What about Brad?" I ask.

"That is between the Elders and Jehovah. My focus will be on proving to the Elders and Governors that I am spiritually sound and ready for Bethel." She stands, her hands flat on the table. "Promise me you're done with all this. I'm relying on Jehovah like I should. He will take care of everything. He already is."

Is this what Jehovah wants when He commands us to rely on him? Study more of the Truth? Do nothing?

"I promise," I say, then hurry to the bathroom, where I throw up.

Chapter 13

Momma sits on the sofa, her eyes closed and her body limp, like she's melted into the cushions. I'd been gone all day, morning Fields Service with Cheri like I'd promised and babysitting Sister Winchester's grandchildren. All I want to do now is sit upstairs in the pink room that is not mine and draw in my sketchbook. Except I'd promised Jehovah no more drawing. No more art. It was done with that.

Not wanting to wake Momma, I pad toward the stairs, grabbing a banana from the big bowl of fruit as I pass.

"Finally, you're home," Momma says, making me jump.

"Sister Winchester and her daughter dropped me off. Remember, after Field Service, I went to babysit," I say, snapping the banana open.

"Yes, I forgot," Momma rubs her temples like it hurts to hear my voice. Sucking in air between her teeth, she gathers her limbs, pulling to a stand, her navy-blue dress wrinkled and creased. "Put your things away and get ready."

A cold shiver runs up my spine. "Ready for what?"

"You've got a meeting with the Elders," she says.

My stomach flutters, but not in a good way. "Now? Why?"

Momma stares at me, her eyes blank. She doesn't need to say it. I know I am the one the Elders chose to discipline.

"This is between you and them. I tried to tell you, but you're too defiant," Momma's voice is cold and flat. She bends and picks up toys scattered across the floor, tossing them into a basket.

Something pulls at my chest, taking my breath with it.

"I did what I thought Jehovah was telling me to do," I say, hiding the shaking in my voice.

She exhales through her teeth as she stands with her hands on her hips, like she's being kept from something important. "Be thankful that you didn't ruin your stepfather's chances of being an Elder or in Rachel getting to Bethel."

We stand there in silence for what seems like forever, the ticking of the rooster clock over the kitchen sink louder until it bangs in between my ears like a drum. A lawnmower starts up somewhere outside. I wish more than anything to talk to Neena. She'll listen to me. She'll understand. Won't she?

Momma pulls into a spot hidden behind the dumpster at the back of the Kingdom Hall. Here, Momma's faded blue van won't be seen from the street. This time of day, a lone car in the parking lot and the Elder's cars would spark a chain of rumors with the Sisters. They'd spread it around fast that our family is having troubles. Or worse, someone is being disciplined, and Momma's Good Standing status will slip even farther down.

She flips the tiny mirror on the visor down and peers at herself. She tucks a strand of hair that escaped its clip behind her ear and wipes a speck of mascara from the corner of her eye. Snapping the visor shut, she lets out her breath. "Well, we're here. What are you waiting for?"

"Nothing," I mumble, unclipping my seat belt and sliding out.

The gravel crunches under my feet as I follow behind her. I keep my head up, positive I've done nothing wrong and this is all a mistake. Surely, they will listen to me and make things right. Does it matter that no one saw what Brad did except Rachel? Across the street, at City Park, there's a *ting*, the sound of an aluminum bat as it hits a ball, followed by the roar of a crowd. I wonder if Gabe is playing in the game, his family in the bleachers. Or if he is in Santa Cruz. I wish I were there too, sitting on the bleachers, the sun hitting my face.

Why had I thought about Gabe, a Worldly boy? Why had that popped into my head right now? I push it all to the back of my brain, and suddenly, I'm alone. Empty, as if I were floating above myself, looking down.

Like a guard waiting for his prisoner, Brother Wilson stands outside the dented steel backdoor of the Kingdom Hall. His black pants held up over his round belly with a pair of suspenders, a sliver of white sock showing at his ankle. Another layer of dread builds inside me, and I can't seem to will it away.

Ushering us, he leans down and whispers to Momma, his droopy eyes never leaving my face. Momma nods and shuffles to a bench along the far wall. Smoothing her skirt, she sits, her hunched shoulders now straight, pressed against the wall. With a sniff, she tugs her dog-eared book, *Draw Close to Jehovah*, out of her purse. I pass her, begging her with my eyes to come in with me. She opens the book and pulls it close to her nose, her face hidden. She's sending me to the wolves on my own.

Brother Wilson motions me to the Elder's Room. The ominous, mysterious Elder's Room, where couples receive permission to court with the intention of marriage. The room where single women receive spiritual guidance because they have no husband to guide them. The place where a family, like Rory's, where a blood transfusion saved her life but got her Disfellowshipped.

What's going to happen to me? I beg Jehovah, in silence, to come near to me. Still, I feel alone. Where has he gone? Why has he left me?

A high-pitched hum starts at the back of my head as I stumble into the dark, windowless room, Brother Wilson on my heels. A single fluorescent tube flickers like an ominous warning, casting a dull yellow glow on the dark paneled walls.

Brother Reed arranges three chairs around a small wooden table at the center of the room.

"Good afternoon, Sara. I'm glad you could make it," he pats a chair for me to sit on.

Brother Wilson squeezes into a chair reserved for him, his stomach pressing up against the edge of the table. "Brother Reed, please lead us in prayer before we begin," he says, lacing his fingers like plump sausages.

Brother Reed clears his throat and begins to pray. His voice is gentle, crisp, and clear. His prayer, an endless string of words such as doubt, shortcomings, wrongdoing, shame, disgrace, and rebuke, hit me like sharp points of arrows. It's clear why I am here. I mutter an almost silent amen and raise my head to meet their gazes, to see a mix of scorn and disappointment.

Brother Reed flicks the corner of his Bible with his thumb. "Sister Sara, normally, we would have all the Elders here. But as I feel you are like one of my grandchildren, I'm keeping this between us. You've made some accusations of Wrong Doing against your stepfather, Brother Michaels."

"It wasn't an accusation. I told Momma and Brother Reed what happened with Rachel. I sought Counsel to help Rachel," I pause, bending my head and folding my hands in my lap, the way I'd been taught to show submission to a Brother.

Shaking his head, Brother Wilson shifts in his seat. Leaning forward, he lifts one corner of his mouth into a smile. "This is why we have the two-witness rule, Sara. You can't go around accusing

Brothers of Wrong Doing. That's how rumors are spread and names defiled."

I look from Brother Wilson's soft doughy face to the sharp nose of Brother Reed, who shakes his head slowly and says, "It's harmful when these stories are started."

"It's not a story. Rachel told me," I say. Shivering with cold, I wrap my arms around my chest. The hum in my head grows louder. I wish I could erase this moment, or paint over it like it was a bad drawing.

Brother Wilson flips through the tissue-like pages of his Bible, nodding quickly when he finds the passage. He turns it toward me and slides it across the table. "Let us examine what the scripture has to say. I'm sure you're already familiar with the words of Deuteronomy 19:15, but I'd like to hear you read them aloud."

The light flickers overhead as I read aloud, keeping my voice steady, "*No single witness should rise up against a man respecting any error or any sin, in the case of any sin that he may commit. At the mouth of two witnesses or at the mouth of three witnesses, the matter should stand good.*"

"Sara, we've been through this. You understand that there needs to be two witnesses, or in some cases three, as the scriptures say when a brother commits a sin against another." Brother Reed stretches his fingers, tapping them on the table's edge.

"So, when Brad did this awful thing to Rachel, if there were two witnesses, you would listen?" I ask, almost pleading, not understanding why it's me here in the chair when all I'd done was try to help Rachel.

The two exchange glances. The tips of Brother Reed's ears redden a vein pulses on his forehead.

Ignoring my question, Brother Wilson flips through his Bible. He says, "Bringing false accusations against someone is disgraceful in Jehovah's eyes. What if you'd reported this to the police? You would have brought shame on Jehovah's name."

"I would never shame Jehovah," I say. The coil in my stomach winds tighter and tighter.

Brother Reed runs his finger around his collar, the edges yellowed with age. "We have spoken to everyone concerned. Brother Michaels acknowledged his actions might have been misinterpreted by Rachel. And Rachel, too, was open to our wisdom and insight. She has come to understand the source of the problem and is working to make it right."

The chair groans as Brother Wilson leans back. "Sara, we are imperfect, and this is something we must leave in Jehovah's hands. He gave his Governing Body insight, and in turn, they've placed specific laws in place. It's not up to any of us to question. This is what you agreed to when you became a baptized member."

"We called you here to talk about you. To give you a chance to apologize and make things right with Jehovah," Brother Wilson says.

The light flickers on and off again. The coil in my stomach springs open. I pull myself to a stand, knocking my chair to the ground behind me.

"I haven't done anything wrong, and neither has Rachel!" I say it loud enough for Momma to hear.

The room goes silent, except for the hum in my head. Both look at me, their faces blank as if they were puppets without feelings.

"Well, I wouldn't have believed it if I hadn't seen it myself. You are defiant, like your mother says. Why is that, Sara?" Brother Reed asks, using his grandfatherly voice again.

I want to run, not sit here listening to these empty words. But something makes me stay. It's not the familiar fear of displeasing Jehovah and dying in Armageddon. It's worse. It's the horror of knowing Brad can continue to hurt others, and Rachel blames herself. And what could I do? I am powerless. I right my chair and sit back down, my body covered in a cold sweat.

Brother Wilson sniffs and pulls out a manilla folder filled with loose pages. From the other side of the table, I can clearly see my name written in neat square letters across the top of the page. Below my name is a series of columns with dates and numbers.

My Field Service time record, my time being mentored, how many Talks I'd given, and how often I participated in Meetings by raising my hand and answering questions.

Brother Wilson runs his finger down the page. "It does appear since your last Weekly Time Report you've put in a sizable number of Field Service hours, which is great. But you're not doing too great at participation during the Meetings, you've done only one Talk in the last six months, and you canceled your mentoring?" He slides the notebook to Brother Reed.

"I didn't cancel. We agreed to delay for a week," I say.

"You will have to do better than this. You're failing to serve Jehovah fully. And instead of showing remorse, you're defiant," Brother Wilson says.

"What about your art? Are you letting that get in the way of you and Jehovah?" Brother Reed asks like he read my mind.

Numb and suddenly mute, I shake my head slow.

Brother Reed clicks his pen. "Well, you are forcing us to discipline you with Reproof."

Reproof. I suck in my breath. That's one step away from Disfellowshipping. "Reproof? Why?" I fight the urge to scream.

"Because you're going against what we..." Brother Wilson pauses and clears his throat. "What we, under the guidance of the Governing Body and Jehovah, have commanded us to do to keep the Congregation clean. I'm sure you've already felt Jehovah slipping away from you. He does that when you break the rules. But that's why we have discipline. And, since this is your first time being disciplined, Jehovah is giving you a chance to change. Then He'll come back to you when you've made your heart ready."

The words wash over me. I feel nothing, not the coil in my stomach, the pressing on my temples, not even the numbness. They exchange glances again as Brother Reed flips to a new page.

"Sara," Brother Reed says, his pen hovering above the blank page. "Reproof is more than keeping Jehovah's Congregation clean. It's a way of drawing you closer to him."

"Jehovah will forgive you if you ask. We'll assign you a course of spiritual discipline designed to give you a glimpse of what it would be like to be away from Jehovah," Brother Wilson pauses and waits for me to answer. "If you fail with your reproof, if you don't humble yourself, ask for forgiveness, and follow all the steps we give you, we will have no choice but to Disfellowship you."

Disfellowship. The word echoes in my head. Shunned. My family won't be allowed to talk to me. Neena will change too. She'll ignore me and act like I'm non-existent. I will be invisible to everyone. I would have to leave home. Where would I go? I have no other family. No aunts or uncles. I would be out in the World, far from Jehovah. Can they really do that to me?

I shiver, thinking of Rory and others who'd been Disfellowshipped. We never talk of those people again; they are dead to us. I'd talked to her. Fear flashes through me.

"Are you sorry for what you've done, Sara? You want to live in Paradise on Earth, don't you?" Brother Reed asks.

The walls close in around me. My chest tightens, so it's hard to breathe. I want to live in Paradise, but I'm not sorry for helping Rachel. What Brad did is wrong. He lied. But I'm trapped in their world of Jehovah's rules. If I don't say I'm sorry, I'll be Disfellowshipped. I won't have anywhere else to go. Reproof, I can do it. It's a punishment, not shunning. It's short-term. But no one can know.

I hear myself say the words, but I don't believe them. "I was wrong. I hope Jehovah can forgive me for where I've fallen short. Please tell me how to make this better."

They pass me a yellow sheet of paper and asked me to sign at the bottom. Something inside me feels dirty and unclean, like I've done something wrong. But I haven't. It wasn't me; it was Brad.

Right?

Chapter 14

Biting back the tears, I race toward the double doors leading out to the front. All I want to do is scream, cry–breathe. Momma, who is standing like she is afraid to move, calls my name, cutting through the silence of the small lobby. I stop, my hands clenched at my sides and slowly face her, erasing the anger from my face.

"I was going to walk home. I need some time with Jehovah," I say, my voice not sounding like my own.

Momma smiles with fake pleasantness. "That's not a good idea. You need to come home."

Brother Reed and Wilson exiting from their Elder's room, come and stand beside her, the three of them making a half-circle. Brother Wilson tugs at the knot on his tie. All eyes on me as I push down the anger threatening to bubble up out of me.

"I need some quiet alone time with Jehovah. There's no way at home," I say, my voice soft, almost pleading with her.

Momma shifts on her feet and glances around uncomfortably.

"My opinion, as a spiritual leader, is it would be wise to let her do this Sister Michaels. It would be good for her to have this time to contemplate and consider her actions. And ask Jehovah to draw near to her again," Brother Reed says, handing Momma a book, the one they'd assigned my mentor, Cheri, to read with me. "This is for Sara."

Momma looks at the book with its powder blue cover and gold lettering: *How to Remain in God's Love*. The book is meant for effective Counsel.

She nods and slides it into her purse. "Yes, Brother Reed is very discerning. He knows what's best. You come straight home, don't dawdle," she says like I'm twelve.

"Yes, Momma," I say, biting back tears. I can't let any of them see me cry. Not one drop.

I don't go straight home. Instead, I cross the street, heading toward the park. The baseball game is over. My legs shake as I climb the bleachers behind first base and sit on the highest bench, where I can view the field and the park beyond. I pull my knees up, wrapping my arms around them, and the tears flow.

I'd done everything I could to please Jehovah to make him love me, ensuring I would make it through Armageddon. I'd spent hours and hours studying the Watchtower books and going to all the Meetings, even when I was sick or didn't feel like it. Then, there was all the time in Field Service and Street Corner Preaching. I'd dressed modestly. I'd stayed away from the World, blending into the background at school.

What else can I do? Where had I fallen short and let Satan lead me?

Val, for one. I need to stop talking to her. I did it before, back in fifth grade, when I devoted myself entirely to Jehovah. Why had I let her back in?

The Art Contest—I can't be in that. I'll ask Mr. Balentine to take me out. And Gabe, no more thinking about him or talking to him. Don't even look at him. And then there are Andy and Rory. Both are huge mistakes. But there's one more thing, one more secret that only Jehovah knows. My secret under the eaves. Is that why Jehovah has been so far from me? Is that why this is happening? Because of my art? I suck in a deep breath between my teeth. Is that what Jehovah is asking of me?

Now that my name is written in the Elder's Book of Discipline, I need Him more than ever. I must follow the corrections they laid out for me. One mistake, one slip-up, and I'm disfellowshipped.

Being Reproofed is a mild discipline. It is just a taste of what it would be like to live without Jehovah. My privileges of answering at meetings and giving Talks with other Sisters are taken away, which I'm okay with. I'm assigned bathroom cleaning at the Kingdom Hall every Saturday and Wednesday. My Field Service, door-to-door hours are restricted to 10 hours a month, and then I must be paired with a Sister or Brother who are in Good Standing with Jehovah. No more door-to-door with Neena. What am I going to tell her next time she asks?

Brother Wilson reminded me to stay off the internet, away from social media, and avoid the World. Satan has found a weak place in me, and the only thing to drive him away is to stay close to Jehovah.

There's only one thing to do. And it's going to be hard. Very hard.

Chapter 15

After everyone is asleep, I'm awake with the bedroom door open, wide enough to hear Brad coming up the stairs. Now that his secret is out, he'd be stupid to try again. Every time I close my eyes, I see him laughing at me, the Elders pointing at me, and I feel the sting of Momma's slap. I feel dirty and ashamed. Like I've done something wrong.

I have. I've slipped far from Jehovah. Can I ever get back to the place I was?

I decide to take a shower. I turn on the water as hot as I can stand. The sharp spray stings my skin like thousands of needles as I scrub away the dirty feeling. I stay, crying and scrubbing my body, my hair, and every part of me until the water grows cold and I no longer have any tears.

The dirty feeling is still there.

Morning comes, sand scratches at my eyes, and they water from the light. I quickly dress, choosing something bright, not dark, like how I feel. When I get downstairs, Kaylee and Pearl are ready for Field Service. Momma eyes me in my spring dress, my hair loose. I look down. My dress is long and pale yellow, falling below my knees, the collar high on my neck. It can't be immodest. I can't be drawing attention to myself, I think.

"Girls wait for me in the car," she says with a little too much happiness.

I grab my sweater from the back of the chair and start to go when Momma stops me. She puts her finger to her lips and shakes her head, and we wait for Kaylee and Pearl as they skip away. Pearl glances back over her shoulder, her eyes resting on me with a sour look like she knows I'm Reproved.

"It seems you've forgotten your discipline from the Elders," Momma says when we're alone.

"I haven't," I say, slipping into my sweater. "I'm going to do Field Service."

Momma shakes her head. "Your hours are limited. You've done more than enough. I've spoken with Cheri, and she's coming to have her Mentor study with you. After she leaves, I expect you to keep reading the book Brother Reed gave you. I left it on the table."

I start to say something, then stop.

"And no drawing. Don't think I'm not aware of your silly sketchpad and doodling," she says, and my heart jackrabbits. Pearl. It had to be Pearl. My other secret is still safe in the back of the closet.

"I won't draw. I promise. I gave it up to serve Jehovah better," I say, my voice shaking. Could she tell?

"It's important you do all the things the Elders tell you. You want to get to Paradise, don't you?" She folds her arms over her chest.

"I do. Of course, I do," I say as the phone rings.

I reach for it, and Momma scowls. "I'm not done."

"This could be Cheri," I say and then answer the phone not giving Momma a chance to say anymore. She glares at me as if her insides were on fire.

"I am so glad it was you who answered. It's me, Rory," the voice says. Momma taps her watch.

"Uhm. Hi," I say. I shouldn't be talking to Rory.

"I'm reminding you about later. We're still on?" She asks. The blood drains from my head, and the room spins. I lean against the counter. I can't babysit, not now, not ever. I want to hang up, but Momma would only ask more questions.

"You there?" Rory asks.

"Yes," I say, giving away nothing.

"See you at two?" She asks.

"Uhmm," I am about to say no. My brain screams no, a million times NO. I can't let Rory down and Isabelle too. I might be the only person to show her about Jehovah and the Truth. Maybe this will be a way for Rory to return to the Truth, too, by my example. What she did; was it really any more wrong than what I did?

"I have to go. Who is it?" Momma slips into her jacket, the one that makes her look like she should be handing out packets of peanuts and tiny cups of ice on an airplane.

I swallow the knot in my throat and silently ask Jehovah to forgive me, then say, "It's Sister Walker's bible student reminding me about later. It's still okay, right? It'll be after Cheri leaves. I can take my study book with me. She is in great need." I lower my voice for full effect.

Momma sucks in a breath as she thinks. Pearl runs in from the garage, a purple stain bleeding down the front of her pink dress.

"Look what Kaylee did. She spilled her juice box on me," Pearl cries, fanning her dress.

"It was on accident," Kaylee cries behind her. "I didn't mean to."

Momma looks from me to them and waves for Pearl to go upstairs. "Yes, fine. But no pay. You're doing this for Jehovah."

"Of course," I say and wait until Momma is up the stairs. "I'll be there." I hang up before Rory can say anything. The less I talk to her, the better.

When the house is quiet, and I'm waiting for Cheri, I start up the stairs to Rachel's room. The sooner I get rid of my secret, the better. As I reach the top step, the doorbell blasts three shrill rings – Cheri. The secret will have to keep a little longer.

Chapter 16

Opening the front door, I find Cheri in her in a green and yellow polka-dotted dress, the sleeves puffed and edged with ruffles falling to her wrists. The neck buttoned closed with a single tiny pearl button that looks ready to pop off. My mouth fills with a sour taste. Next year, when she grows tired of the dress, it will hang in my closet. She plops down on the sofa in the room reserved for Elders or Sisters, her book in her hands before I can tell her *not this room*. Maybe Momma won't notice.

Cheri starts reading from the first page of "How to Remain in God's Love, *"It is not always easy for us to obey God. We live in a wicked world that is ruled by Satan. He tries to influence people to do what is bad. We also have to fight against our own imperfect thoughts and feelings, since they can lead us to disobey Jehovah..."*

This is going to be a long study. Cheri is going to drag this out. I glance at the clock and sigh.

I climb the steps to Rory's house, the front door opening before I can knock. With her finger to her lips, Rory steps out onto the landing in her bare feet. She's wearing a t-shirt with a grape jelly stain on the sleeve, and shorts. Short shorts. Shorts that if I could see the show part of her butt. Her legs are toned and tan like she goes to the gym. I look away from her immodesty.

"Isabelle is asleep on the couch," she whispers. "Come in."

I feel the rumble in my chest. I hesitate.

"Sara, it's okay. You're doing nothing wrong. I promise. I know how hard this is for you. You don't have to say a word or look at me. You'll feel loads better when Isabelle gets up." Her lips curve up in a smile, and her eyes sparkle. Except for her immodest clothes, she doesn't look scary or dangerous.

I follow her into the dark living room with my hands twisting behind my back. Isabelle sleeps on the overstuffed sofa, curled up under a blanket with blue butterflies. A pink pacifier wiggles in her mouth as she sucks it in her dream. With her finger to her lips, Rory jerks her head for me to follow.

In the silent kitchen, she slides two sheets of paper across the white marble countertop to me. Scanning them, I find directions for Isabelle and important phone numbers. Rory fills two tall glasses of iced tea from her fridge.

I want to tell her about Brad and Rachel, how I was disciplined - Reproved. Rory will understand. But then, will she call the police? That would bring shame to Jehovah's name. I'll be Disfellowshipped for sure — my family torn apart. When Armageddon comes, I won't survive. Jehovah won't save me because I'd shamed him.

"I understand how scared you are to be here. Truly I do. I promise I'm not trying to get you to leave the Truth. I knew you'd be good with Isabelle when I saw you at the store," she says, her voice kind and soothing – how I wish Momma talked to me. The unease begins to slip away as I slide onto one of the stools.

Without looking up at her, I ask, "Can I ask you something?"

"Sure, anything," she says.

"Why did you get the blood transfusion if you knew you'd get Disfellowshipped?" I ask, lifting my chin but still avoiding her eyes.

She leans back, folding her hands in her lap. "Because I was about to die."

"How could you break Jehovah's rule? Putting someone else's blood in your body – it's unclean," I say. I shouldn't be asking her this. This is wrong. I stand to go, but I can't leave Isabelle. I'd made a promise.

"That's true to some point, and I'm not going to talk about science and misconceptions with you because I promised I wouldn't persuade you to leave the Truth. What happened is I was sick when I was pregnant with Isabelle. No one at the Kingdom Hall came to help us; they only judged us for not attending Meetings or going out in Field Service. The Elders counseled Miguel and me several times. I tried hard to do everything Jehovah required but couldn't keep up."

She pauses and sips her tea, her red lipstick leaving a mark on the straw. "When Isabelle was born, I lost a lot of blood. And I needed a transfusion, or I would die. The Elders came to the hospital and strongly urged Miguel not to let me have one. I don't even know how they found out," she shakes her head. "Miguel and I refused. I wanted to live for Isabelle. I prayed and prayed, and I couldn't see how God wanted me to die when the fix was right there in front of me."

"Oh," I say. Momma wouldn't have taken the blood. If it were me, she would let me die.

Rory leans over, putting her hand on my arm, and I flinch. "Are you still afraid of me?"

I hesitate a moment. "Yes. You are Disfellowshipped. Me talking to you is displeasing to Jehovah."

"I understand. As I said, we don't have to talk. You're here for Isabelle. Okay?" she asks, and I nod. "You can use my laptop if you want until she wakes."

"Thanks," I say, but I'm not sure what I'll do. It feels wrong. She's being so nice. Not how Worldly people are supposed to be.

Isabelle makes a sound from the other room and then quiets. "I must get ready for work. Help yourself to some food," Rory whispers.

I make the okay sign, and she tip-toes to the back of the house. I fumble in the fridge, find a loaf of bread, sliced cheese, and lunch meat, and make myself a sandwich. I sit on one of the tall stools around the white stone countertop. The kitchen is so bright. Everything gleams in the sunlight, the exact opposite of our kitchen with the black stove, which isn't exactly level, the terra cotta tiled floor, and cabinets someone had painted a muddy brown long ago.

Brad said there is no point in painting or renovating since this System of Things is ending soon. When we get to Paradise, we'll have our pick of houses from all the people who died in Armageddon. A pinprick of discomfort grows in my chest.

I open the laptop and type in the password she'd written on the paper. I fumble around, careful not to read anything that comes up on the homepage. I log into my Facebook account. I'm not even sure why I have it. I can barely get on the internet. Neena's not on here. And the only friends I have are a few Sisters at Bethel and a Missionary Family that went to Brazil. I haven't been on it since the last time I'd been to the library alone, a month ago, and I only have one friend, Val. I squint, looking at the screen and the blinking friend notification. Rory touches my shoulder, and I jump.

"Sorry," she whispers and thumbs over her shoulder toward sleeping Isabelle. "You've got a good hour of silence."

"Okay," I mouth.

Rory reaches for the doorknob, her hand hovering before dropping to her side. She comes and kneels next to me, and I stiffen as she takes my clammy hand in hers.

I shouldn't fear her; she's not what everyone says. But still, I can't help it. Biting my lip, I look down at the silver rings on her fingers and the colorful knotted bracelets on her wrists, not meeting her gaze.

She smooths my hair down, tucks a strand behind my ear, and lifts my chin. "I promise you; you're going to be fine. Jehovah is not going to hate you for this."

She pats my hand again, and then she's gone.

I go back to the friend request and click on it. There is another below that, a lady with the same last name as mine, Stephens. Alyce Stephens.

I click on the profile. She's definitely a grandmother, her skin smooth across her cheeks, creased around her eyes and mouth as if she spent a lot of time laughing. Her gray hair falls around her in soft curls. She wears a flowy top in purples, reds and green. Around her neck are strings of beads in matching colors. There is a picture of her painting in a field of tall grass, another of her standing in front of Half Dome at Yosemite, and one at a volcano in Hawaii.

I decide she looks harmless. And we have the same last name. Could we be related? I know nothing about my dad's family. Momma never let me see them. They didn't have the Truth, so I was never allowed near them.

Isabelle cries from the other room. I accept the friend request and close the computer.

Chapter 17

At Meeting, I wait for my turn to put my Weekly Time Report into the narrow metal box, painted a shiny white. A tiny gold lock dangles from the lid, and I wonder why the Elders keep it locked. Not for me to worry about. Today is my new start. Jehovah will see I'm willing to do anything and everything he requires.

And then it's my turn. I look down at the dog-eared time report in my hand, and the voices of the Brothers and Sisters around me talking become a dull hum. At the bottom of the paper, written in heavy pencil, my total - twenty hours. I run my finger down the list: hours door-to-door, number of callbacks, number of bible studies, and how much Truth literature I handed out. Everything has a number next to it.

Last Saturday, when I did this, and all the Saturdays before, my heart swelled, and my head felt light – I'd done it all for Jehovah, and he would save me. Today, I don't deserve to be here. I will make it better. I'd already stopped drawing, my sketchbook no longer in my purse. Tomorrow at school, I'll be more invisible than before. All that's left is my secret, hidden from everyone except Jehovah.

I let the paper drop into the slot and wait for the feeling of accomplishment and pride in knowing I am doing all that Jehovah requires to wash over me. To feel as if I'm being wrapped in a warm hug. It doesn't happen. Instead, there is an emptiness in the deepest places inside, behind my ribs, at the pit of my stomach, all the way to the tips of my toes. I plaster a smile on my face and go.

I go to our usual seats, ignoring the people in the glassed-off room, where the Disfellowshipped people trying to get back into the Truth sit. This way, we don't have to be near them. A smile spreads across my face. Everyone I pass will see how happy I am in Jehovah. I look for Neena. I need a friend right now. All I see is Cheri and her sisters, with their shiny faces sitting in one row. Cheri peers over at me, her lips pulled tight, and points to her book in her lap – the book she'd read to me yesterday. I hurry past and take my seat between Momma and Rachel. Where is Neena? I need her. I need my friend.

Up on the stage, behind the pulpit, a narrow piece of wood stained the color of coffee hangs with a scripture. It's new. The old one had been up for a long time. The letters had faded, and the wood had yellowed. This one seems like it was placed there just for me.

"Your strength will be in keeping calm and showing trust."
Isaiah 30:15

Brother Reed leads the Meeting. The Congregation sings, and I join, singing so loud Jehovah will hear my devotion to him, and so will all the Brothers and Sisters. There will be no guessing where my heart is. When we're done, we bow our heads in prayer, asking Jehovah to forgive us where we fall short of his requirements.

I say amen, keep my head bowed and wait for the empty feeling to disappear. It doesn't. Jehovah is still far from me. I have a lot of work to do to get Him back.

With no pen to draw with, I have a hard time paying attention throughout the whole Meeting. Pearl raises her hand a few times and is called on to answer. The answers flow from her straight from the book. Momma nods her head in approval. It seems to go on for hours. Finally, we sing one last song and say a final amen. I stand next to Momma while she talks to a group of Sisters. Through the glass in the doors, I see Neena outside, cornered by Cheri. Neena and I had barely spoken all week, and right now, I could use my best friend. I pull away from Momma.

Neena looks up at me as I push through the doors.

"Cheri, Brother Peters has something for you. A new study book or something. He's looking all over for you," I say, Neena and Cheri looking confused.

"Book?" Cheri squints, looking through the glass panes on the door.

I shrug. "I'm telling you what he said."

Cheri's dress swirls around her ankles as she turns and hurries back inside to find Brother Peters.

"Why'd you do that?" Neena leans in and asks, her eyes following Cheri.

"What?" I raise my brows.

"Send her after Brother Peters," she covers her mouth, hiding a grin.

"You looked like you needed to be rescued."

Neena shifts back on her heels. "I did. Thanks. Where have you been all week? I thought we were going to do some stuff together. It's like you disappeared."

"Remember, no cell phone, no privacy," I frown. "I tried to call you, but you didn't answer."

"If only you had a cell phone. Won't your mom let you if you buy your own?" She twists a coil of hair around her finger.

"It's never going to happen," I say, and right now is not the time for me to push it. I have to get right with Jehovah.

"Can you spend the night tonight?" Neena asks.

"I'm sure I can, but you know how my mom and stepfather are," I roll my eyes. "I have to ask."

"She'll say yes," Neena says. I wish I could be so sure. Momma doesn't like Neena, and I'm being Reproved. If Momma only knew, Neena is a much better Witness than I am or will ever be.

I find Momma as she puts her time record into the white box. a look of accomplishment on her tired face.

"Can I spend the night at Neena's?" I ask.

She rubs her temples as if I'd given her a headache by asking her.

"I'll take my study book. I want to prepare for my next time with Cheri. Sister Walker will be home, and Charlie too, Neena's little brother," I say, and Momma's expression doesn't change. "You could use a break. The girls will be gone. Rachel is doing something with Sister Winchester. You won't have to worry about me."

I'd said the right words. "Yes. Fine. Go," Momma says, rubbing her temples again. "I expect to see you tomorrow out in Field Service."

"I will, Momma," I say, giving her a quick hug. She stiffens.

Neena fans $20.00 under my nose when I get to her house. "Mom ordered pizza, but we have to go pick it up."

"No problem," I say.

We walk the five blocks to Pietro's Pizza, the sun's warmth on our backs. Neena has her learner's permit, but we can't drive without an adult in the car, so we walk. The silence is awkward between us. We always had something to say. Now I feel like I'm a million miles away from her because of my secrets. I want to tell her about my Reproof and meeting Rory, everything. But I can't.

Even though she's my friend, the Reproof is between Jehovah and me -and the Elders.

"So, after that time with the boy at the door, when you told him about heaven instead of Paradise, I started to worry about you and your walk with Jehovah," Neena says.

"I'm fine. I was just having a bad day. I'm better." As I say it, I trip over a small crack in the cement. I don't fall, but my arms windmill, and I look silly in Cheri's old green dress; we both laugh until our eyes water. Maybe I can tell her some things. She is my best friend; she'll understand.

When we stop laughing, I ask, "Neena, do you ever think Jehovah won't save you during Armageddon?"

"Sometimes. We can never be 100% sure He will spare us. That's why I do everything the Elders and Governing Body say I should, to stay close to Jehovah. This System of Things is ending soon. I'm not risking life in Paradise."

She sounds just like Momma and all the other Sisters. If she's not 100% sure, will I ever be good enough?

"What if someone loyal to Jehovah messes up a little? Does Jehovah turn away from them?" I ask.

"Yes, of course, He does. That person needs to get right with Jehovah, read the Truth Book, maybe go to their spiritual leader for guidance, or the Elders for Counsel."

"That's what I thought. Thanks," I say, forcing myself to smile. The emptiness comes back in a giant wave, drowning me.

"Are we talking about you?" She asks.

"No, not me. Just a question, that's all," I say, unsure if I'm talking about me or someone else like Rachel, Rory, or even Brad. My stomach sours again.

"I have a surprise. Guess what?" She asks.

"What?"

"Next year, I'm going to New System School," she says. New System School, the school for students in the Truth. It costs money, and Momma and Brad don't have enough to send me.

I cringe and pull to a stop. "Wait. What? New System School? Why?"

"Because I can't stand the Worldly school anymore. New System will let me learn at home four days a week. I can help my Mom more and do more Field Service." She eyes me with a slight frown. "You seem like you're upset about this."

"I'm... happy for you," I say. "How are you getting there? It costs so much."

"My mom is making it work. She got money somehow and said it was important," Neena says.

"Well, you'll get to go to school with Cheri and the rest of the Wilsons," I say with a wicked smile.

A car drives by and slows. I peer over, expecting it to be Gabe, my heart racing. Instead, it's just an old person squinting into the sun. I deflate and touch the spot on my hand again, where we'd touched. It was days ago. Why am I thinking about Gabe when I promised Jehovah I wouldn't? I look up to the sky and silently beg for forgiveness.

"Something *is* going on with you," Neena says.

"No, nothing," I lie. My chest tightens as I shake my head. What should I say? I can't tell her about my Reproof. I can't tell her about Brad and Rachel. I can't tell her anything like I thought I could.

We get to Pietro's, and Neena pulls the door open. The smell of sauce and greasy meat hits my nose, and my mouth waters.

"You should ask your mom to enroll you in New System School next year. We could be together, and then you wouldn't have so many Worldly problems."

"Good idea," I say. But is it?

Chapter 18

The first morning back to school after spring break, the sky gray, full of dark clouds, matching my mood. I should be happy. Everything I've done and am about to do will bring me closer to Jehovah. Somehow though, I can't seem to shake the feeling of disappointment. The emptiness grows. I pass Rachel's room and want to knock, but her light is still off. I'll talk to her later. She's tired from the extra study work the Elders gave her.

I walk the few blocks to school alone while everyone else gets a ride or walks with someone else. Momma is too busy with the girls. Brad offered to give me a ride. I told him I'd rather walk. Fine, he'd said. He wanted to say more to me, but I pushed past him out into the cold. No way am I being trapped alone with Brad anywhere.

I tug at the too-tight neck of my itchy brown sweater.

At school, my mood gets darker. The lights in Mrs. Winters' first-period Algebra class flicker, and the heater isn't working. Without my sketchbook, I find it hard to pay attention. I draw butterflies on the back of a paper, like I am in a trance or something, until I drop my pencil, ashamed I couldn't keep my promise to Jehovah.

When the bell rings, I dash out of class. Since I'm in the back, nearest the door, it's easy.

"Sara, wait," Val calls when I reach the crowded hallway.

I pretend I don't hear and weave through the clumps of students, but she's persistent and soon is next to me.

"Sara," she says, out of breath. "I guess you didn't hear me."

"Oh, no, I didn't," I lie and slow my steps.

"I wanted to ask if you wanted to volunteer with me to help with the school dance?" Val asks, stopping in front of me.

"No. I can't do that," I snap.

Her brows shoot up. "It's not like you're coming to the dance. You're so creative. We could use your help. I mean your art and all," she looks at my empty hands, where my sketchbook usually is.

"I don't do my art anymore; it was taking away from Jehovah," I say proudly, pulling my shoulders back.

She looks at me, a look of confusion on her face. "God doesn't like art?"

"Jehovah requires more of me," I say. She'd never understand about Reproof and being one step away from being Disfellowshipped. Val is Worldly; she can't help me with anything, not Brad, Rachel, the Elders...nothing. She'll only make things worse. I should have stayed away from her in the first place.

"Sara, what happened? I thought we...you and me... I thought we were friends."

Before I can answer, telling her I can't be friends with her because she doesn't love Jehovah, Bailey is there. She loops her arm through Val's. "Hey, we're gonna be late for Algebra," she says, eyeballing me. Today her eyes are outlined in blue, matching the ends of her hair.

"Since when do you care about Algebra?" Val asks.

"Since there's a new boy in the class," Bailey bounces, her eyes sparkling.

Val looks like she wants to say more, but she doesn't. Instead, she walks away with Bailey, looking over her shoulder toward me, her eyes filled with sadness.

Loneliness, worse than before, sweeps over me, so deep and sudden. Tears sting my eyes. It doesn't matter, I tell myself. Val doesn't matter, the stupid dance doesn't matter, art doesn't matter, none of it will save me from Armageddon. I bend my head low and hurry to Mr. Balentine's class.

My stomach a jumble of knots, I stand at Mr. Balentine's desk, where he sits, his head down, reading something on his computer. My brown dress itches around my neck, and I resist the urge to scratch.

"Mr. B," I say softly.

He jumps and looks up. "Oh Sara, I didn't hear you. I trust you had a good spring break," he says.

"Yes," I say and stand there in awkward silence.

"Did you need something?" He asks.

I gather my breath and hug my books tighter, my knuckles white. "Yes. I want to withdraw from the art contest."

"Why would you want to do that?" He asks as he takes his glasses off and cleans them with a tissue.

"I just do," I say quickly, looking away. Behind me, I hear the rustle of other students entering.

"Well," Mr. Balentine smiles fully, so the lines around his mouth are deep. "It's a little late; you already won first prize."

Mr. Balentine slips his glasses back on and keeps talking, but I can't hear the words over the ringing in my ears. All I see are his lips moving. He presses buttons on his computer, and the printer hums as it spits out a piece of paper.

"Here, this is everything you need to know," he holds the paper out for me to take, but I'm frozen. "Sara," he pushes it at me.

"Uhm, yes, thanks," I say, taking it.

"Make sure you read over the papers. You're getting an award. And you'll move up to the next level, the State. You'll need to submit two additional works." He rubs his hands together as he stands. "This is so exciting."

"Exciting," I repeat flatly, inching back as if my feet were in thick mud. I fold the paper and put it in my English book without reading it. It doesn't matter what it says. I'm not going. Why didn't I tell him to take me out of the State contest? Jehovah is watching and listening to everything I do and think. I've got to get this under control.

The moment I walk into the house, Momma is there waiting for me, her hands behind her back. She beams from ear to ear as if she has a secret she can't wait to tell me.

"Such good news," she says, and I'm afraid to ask. "Look what came today. The newest book from the Governors." She pulls out what she's been holding behind her back, a bright green book the size of a paperback. The title, in fancy gold script, swirls and blurs as she holds it under my nose.

"Wonderful," I say, trying to sound interested when all I want to do is collapse into bed, pull the covers over my head, and hide from everything. I can't even do that. I have no bed, no room, no place of my own.

"It is wonderful!" She pulls the book back, opening it so the spine cracks and reads the title to me. *"Your Youth, Getting the Best out of It."*

"I have homework," I say, and start to go up the stairs.

"Homework can wait. This is for you," Momma presses the book into my hands. "Tonight, we're having private study time. You, me, and your step-father," she bounces on her toes.

"I don't want to study with him," I say before I can stop myself.

A purple vein pops out on Momma's forehead, and she falls back onto her heels. "You have no choice in this matter; it's part of your discipline. And a reward at the same time. Jehovah has given the Governors great insight in writing this book."

My stomach burns. I wish for an antacid. "Okay, Momma," I resign.

"Much better. Now, you read the first chapter, *Moving into Womanhood*, so you can be prepared," she says.

I run up the stairs, my stomach threatening to spill over, even though it's empty; I hadn't eaten lunch. Flopping to the floor, I unfold the paper Mr. Balentine gave me. On it, congratulations from the judges. I'd won First Place for Pen and Ink.

Holding the paper to my chest, I shut my eyes and see the image I'd drawn – a woman's face. I'd seen her at the park. Her white hair pulled into a loose bun at the back of her head. She sat alone, but smiled so deeply that lines and creases appeared around her eyes and mouth. She was the oldest woman I'd ever seen, her back hunched, and she used a cane to walk. She must have been in pain, but her eyes were full of happiness. I wasn't sure how she could be so happy when she didn't have the Truth. The drawing, too, Momma and the Elders would disapprove.

It doesn't matter anyway. The awards ceremony is Friday night. There is no way I can go. Skip Meeting night? Jehovah would hate me.

I fold the paper back up and tuck it into the back of my drawer along with the camp flier Val gave me. Why am I keeping them? They are dangerous.

But something inside me cannot bear to throw them away.

What is wrong with me?

Chapter 19

Tuesday after school, Rachel is at work, and Momma has gone somewhere with Pearl and Kaylee. Finally, I am alone. I reach for the phone, my hand hovering over it. I want to talk to Neena and tell her what happened at school. I want to tell her how hard I'm trying to get closer to Jehovah, about my Reproof — everything I've been keeping from her. I realize, with a pang of sadness, she won't understand. She can never know.

Now that I'm alone, I can finish what I started. The last thing, and then Jehovah, will be closer to me like He promised. I toss my books onto Kaylee's bed and grab my service bag. After dumping the contents onto the floor, I hurry into Rachel's room, my old room. Before going in, I pause at the top of the stairs and listen for the sounds below. There is nothing.

I twist the knob, feeling guilty as I enter, like invading someone's privacy. The room seems smaller now. I glance out the window for Momma's van or Rachel walking from the bus stop. There is no one. My gaze lingers a little too long on Gabe's house. I bite my lip, hard, and turn away.

I slide open the closet door, revealing Rachel's clothes, spaced evenly apart on pink velvet hangers. Dropping to my knees, I crawl to the back, pushing aside an overstuffed bag full of donated clothes from the Wilsons, tearing the plastic open. I shove a box aside, wondering why Momma had left them here and my belongings are in the garage. Stretching out, I search for the latch on the cupboard with my fingertips and flick it open.

The side of my face presses to the plastic bag. I reach into the darkness for the stack of sketchbooks and the small plastic pencil box from grade school, filled with my pencils, charcoal, and a few tubes of paint. This is the last of the things keeping me separated from Jehovah.

I move fast, not looking as I load it all into my service bag. When it's full and the cabinet empty, I put everything in the closet back into place. I consider grabbing the bag of the Wilson's hand-me-downs and tossing it into the garbage, but it's too big. I adjust it, so the tear is in the back and push it back into the closet. Backing out, I knock one of Rachel's dresses off the hanger. I wipe my hands on my sides before carefully placing the dress back on the hanger, making sure it's spaced apart like the others.

In the garage, I push back the trash can lid, releasing the smells of sour milk, coffee grounds, and the faint lemon scent of the trash bags. I stare down until everything blurs into a swirl of colors, and I gag from the smell.

I hold my service bag out over the bin, ready to dump the contents. I can't seem to let it go.

My stomach presses up into my chest. I look up to Jehovah. He's watching me, and Satan is too. Only one of them I want to please. Still, I can't seem to let go. My sketchbooks are part of me. Letting them go is like throwing away pieces of me, my thoughts, and emotions that I pour out through my pencil onto the paper – the sounds, scents, colors, and feelings. My heart races, keeping up with my thoughts.

Maybe if I promise Jehovah to draw and paint only what He approves of, I don't need to throw everything away? I'll throw out the books I'd filled with Worldly things, like the old lady on the bus who'd fallen asleep with her bundle of bags around her or the father and son who'd shared a piece of birthday cake at the diner. From now on, I'll only create pictures of Armageddon, Paradise, and characters from the Bible.

No more dreaming about being an artist. No more letting my art take over my life and becoming my religion like the Worldly. Surely Jehovah would be okay with that. I could be an artist at Bethel, creating the images in our books and videos. Someone has to do that. My heart begins to slow, and I breathe in deeply. It's right. It feels right.

I decide to keep one blank book and my pencil box of supplies. The rest I will toss. But first, I need to find a hiding place; the tiny cupboard in Rachel's room is no longer safe. The room I sleep in won't work either; Kaylee or nosy Pearl will surely find it.

I look around the garage and the cabinets lining the wall. I pull open door after door, looking for a place to stash my stuff, but each one is crammed full of paper towels, toilet paper, cleaning supplies, and more of Momma's End of Times stockpile. Overhead are plastic bins and the cardboard boxes Momma had written my name on, my stuff. The only way up there is the ladder, and it's too clumsy to get. Then, I see it: the wooden workbench in the corner. It was here when we moved in, and Brad hardly uses it. The only tools he owns are a hammer and a few screwdrivers set on a shelf above.

It's perfect. I smile as I tug open the drawer at the bottom. I push aside a mound of rags —and my hand freezes midair. My breath catches in my throat as I find myself staring down at a picture—a woman, naked. The only thing covering her is her long brown hair draped over half her face, curling down between her breasts, two perfectly round breasts—the curves of her hips, her sacred place, everything out there for everyone to see.

My entire body shakes as I push aside the magazine to find another underneath. I'm hit with images of oversized chests and rear ends and puffed-up lips. I clamp my eyes shut. Jehovah will punish me for seeing these things. I drop the magazine and throw-up into the trashcan.

This is wrong, all wrong. There is no one I can tell. Nothing I can do. I can't report this without getting into more trouble or, worse, being Disfellowshipped.

It's not fair. Nothing is fair. Why does Brad get to continue with his sins just because no one saw him beside Rachel? Where is Jehovah?

As the waves of anger wash over me, full of rage, I shake out the entire contents of my bag. My sketchbooks flutter like deformed butterflies, landing with a dull thud on top of my vomit. I grab Brad's stack of magazines, the terrible secret he kept hidden away in the bottom drawer. I drop them into the trash — Brad's secret goes with mine. I throw some of the rags on top and run in and get the kitchen trash, covering all of the secrets.

Slamming the lid shut, the anger starts to fade. Emptiness hits me like a brick wall, worse than before. I did everything Jehovah wanted of me. I devoted myself to Him. I gave up friends like Val. I stopped drawing. I'd thrown away my precious work. Everything I did was for Jehovah to save me. Getting rid of everything and focusing on Jehovah, He promised me something. He lied. He gave me nothing except empty promises and punishment.

Val was right. I am miserable. Why hadn't I seen any of this before? A hum starts in my head, pressing in on all sides. I have to get away from here.

I rush inside, scribble a note out for Momma, telling her I'm at the library, and stick it to the fridge with a magnet saying, "Loving Jehovah, Best Life Ever." Lie. Lie. Lie. All lies, I say out loud as I throw the magnet in the trash. I leave the note on the table. Instead, the edge tucked under the empty fruit bowl.

I grab my bike and pedal down the street, passing all the almond-colored houses and neatly mowed yards. I ride to the park, heading into the empty baseball field. I lean my bike against the stretched-out chain link fence behind the dugout, climb the bleachers nearly to the top, and sit. I should be learning to drive, not riding a dumb bike. I should have a phone to text Momma and not leave a note.

My knees to my chest, I watch across the field where a man snaps pieces of a kite together. He holds it up. In the center is a blue butterfly, bright against the white of the kite. A little boy I recognize as Andy, the one I'd talked to at the door, jumps around him--his father. Andy's father kneels in the grass, says something to Andy, and hands the kite over. Together they run. A little girl on the swings squeals on the playground behind them as she is pushed high into the air.

I remember when I was that age, it was Momma, me, and Daddy. There was no fear of Armageddon coming and Jehovah killing me because I didn't answer a question at a Meeting or go out in Field Service. There were birthday parties, Christmas lights, and candy on Halloween with Daddy. There were the days at the park when he pushed me on the swing as I begged to go higher. Then he was gone. Dead. That's when Momma found the Truth.

After he was gone, I would swing alone by myself, pumping my legs until I was high in the air, while Momma sat on the bench reading one of her Truth books or talking to other parents about Jehovah. I loved to jump when the swing was at its highest point, feeling like I was flying, just for a moment. Maybe if I flew high enough, I could reach the sky and heaven where Daddy was, even though Momma told me since Daddy didn't follow Jehovah and have the Truth, he was dead and cold in the ground.

I didn't believe her.

Once, I jumped from the swing, landing on the ground, the bark digging into my knees and palms. A blue butterfly lay crumpled on the ground in front of me. I decided to test Jehovah to see if he was a fake.

I checked to see if Momma was looking, she wasn't, so I buried the butterfly and pushed a stick bent into the shape of a cross, something Jehovah said was bad, into the ground, marking the grave. I prayed to God to take the butterfly to heaven, if there was a heaven. Or, leave it in the grave if there wasn't. After my amen, I carefully pushed back the little mound of dirt and found an empty grave. Did that mean Jehovah was a fake?

I thought it did, but that was so long ago. I'd heard Jehovah's lie for so many years, over and over and over, and I believed it. I had no choice. There was no room for anything else. And the lie sounded so beautiful, so right – life in Paradise forever. All I had to do was follow Jehovah and do everything he asked me to do without question.

Andy's shouts of excitement from across the field snap me out of my memory and the haze I'd fallen into. Jehovah and the Truth's lies are all so clear now, laying out in front of me one after the other. Why hadn't I seen them before?

The butterfly kite darts up and down high in the sky, almost touching the clouds. I remember other blue butterflies – I'd seen so many lately. It was following me. The emptiness in my chest radiates into warmth, spreading, as if someone had wrapped me in a warm blanket.

My life is suddenly split in two – the Truth and the World.

I wipe the tears from my face with the back of my hand. The Elders are wrong. Jehovah is not real. Brad is evil. He's a monster. All of them are liars. The Truth is a lie, and I am trapped inside it like a fly in a spider's web. If I try to leave, if I reveal the lies, I will be shunned. Where will I go? Who will protect Kaylee and Pearl? Who will stop Brad?

Chapter 20

There is a lightness in me, in all the empty places where Jehovah tried to fit his lies, where the real me has been buried. At the same time, a heaviness is pressing at the back of my head because of Jehovah's lies and broken promises. I'm stuck. I'm split in two – one person in both worlds, and neither world can mix with the other. One keeps me safe from the other until I can fix it all.

Momma frowns at me when I come into the kitchen.

"You should have waited until I got home to ask about going to the library," she says.

"I'm sorry, Momma," I put my head down like usual, swallowing down the anger that simmers. "I had homework. It couldn't wait. We don't have internet here. It makes it hard."

"I'm considering strongly putting you in New System School next year," Momma says.

I cringe. "It won't happen again. Next time I'll wait. I promise," I say. She eyes me, looking me up and down. She knows. She can tell. "I'll still need the internet for New System School, Momma. They do everything remote."

She pushes her lips together. "That's different," she says. "You get going on fixing dinner. I've got to iron your stepfather's slacks and shirt. We have Mid-Week Meeting tonight, or did you forget?"

"I didn't forget," I say. The phone rings, and Momma answers it before handing it to me.

"It's Neena. Keep it short. You have things to do," Momma snaps like I am a little kid, not fifteen.

"Yes, Momma," I say as I take the phone from her.

"Bad time? Your mom doesn't sound happy I called," Neena says.

"She's not, but I am. You saved me from a lecture," I say.

The next day, I woke early. Mr. B. asked me for two new art pieces for the State Art Show. I have nothing; everything thrown away. All I have is a pencil. Mr. B. didn't ask questions when I asked if I could come in early to work on the pieces. What could I tell him anyway? Oh, hey, Mr. B., if my family sees this, I'll be shunned. Oh, and I threw away all my stuff and found my stepfather's secret stash of porn.

I dress for school in my best Service clothes: a polka-dotted blouse and navy skirt, so I will no longer be the invisible girl in my gray and brown clothes. Fearful Momma will notice and wonder why I'm wearing my Service clothes, I throw on an oversized olive-green sweater, courtesy of Cheri, roll up the sleeves that fall over my wrists, and slip into a pair of flat brown loafers. I put a pair of white sneakers into my backpack. Perfect.

Before I go downstairs, I get my sketchbook out of its hiding place under Kaylee's mattress. I'm glad I hadn't tossed it away with the others. I tug out the camp flier and the art contest winning notice — reading them both again. I shake my head. How can these send me to Armageddon?

In the kitchen Momma is at the stove flipping french toast. I grab a slice from the plate next to her and go to leave when she stops me.

"Aren't you going to join us?" She points to the table with the spatula. "We're about to do our morning reading."

Shifting on my feet, I look at the clock. Kaylee tugs at my sweater, pulling me towards the table.

"You should stay and study the Daily Scripture with us. It's what Jehovah would want," Brad says, and I squirm free from Kaylee. I feel like a million worms are crawling on my skin.

"Momma, I can't be late again. I'll get detention on Saturday," I plead.

Brad pushes his fingertips together in front of him. "You'll need to do better, Sara, if you want to return to Jehovah's family. Being Reproved is nothing to take lightly. It's your life."

My plan to get to school early to draw ruined. I drop my pack to the floor, where it lands with a thud. I slide into the seat next to Kaylee. She snakes her arm around mine and grabs my hand. Brad begins to read the daily scripture. The buzz starts in my head again.

On the way to school, when I'm blocks from home, I take off the ugly sweater and wad it up in my pack and change my shoes. At school, I take my usual spot in first period. I pull at the hem of my polka-dotted blouse and wish I had jeans, t-shirts, anything but this.

Someone taps me on the shoulder, and I jump. Turning, I expect to see Mrs. Winters. Instead, I find Val. She holds something out for me. I take it in both hands. It's a brown leather journal with a butterfly stamped on the cover. How did she know?

I hold my breath as I unbuckle the tiny clasp keeping the sketchbook closed. Inside, written in purple ink, is a note:

"For my friend. I will always be here for you – no matter what. Val"

I look up at her, unsure of what to do. Why does she want to be my friend? I've been horrible to her. No one has ever bought me a gift before. Momma gave me a new bible, but it wasn't a gift; it came at the cost of my whole summer going door-to-door. The Wilsons always give me their old clothes. Is this what Worldly friends do?

"Thank you," I manage to say, stumbling over the words.

Val takes her seat in front of me without saying another word.

I read Val's words, over and over, until the letters start to smudge from my tears. I look around to see if anyone has noticed; no one has. All eyes are on Mrs. Winters—I'm still the invisible girl.

Maybe...I don't want to be so invisible anymore.

First period seems like it's a million hours long; finally, it ends, and I hurry to step in front of Val before she can leave.

Bailey leans around Val, eyeballing my new journal and then the polka-dotted blouse. "Like the retro look," she says to me.

"I'll meet you at Algebra," Val says over her shoulder to Bailey.

"What? We always walk..." she stops and looks at me again. I feel the heat rise on my cheeks. "Whatevs," Bailey says as she walks away, leaving Val and me alone.

We walk to the hallway. I stand to the side, feeling as if all eyes are on me.

"I'm sorry," Val says, and I'm confused.

"Wait, why are you sorry?" I ask. "I'm the one who was mean to you."

She shakes her head and thumbs the cross on her necklace. "I know your family is super religious and super strict. I mean, you not hanging out with me anymore because of Jehovah. Remember, that's what you told me."

"I'm sorry about that," I say, feeling like I'd done so much to push her away, but she is still here.

"It's okay, really. I shouldn't have pushed you with camp stuff. And then what I said before spring break about being miserable, that was mean of me," Val says. "I want to be your friend, if that's okay. Try again."

A group of Seniors walks by, and I go silent as one of them laughs too loud. I can't help but wonder if it's at me. Val had always tried to be my friend, since fourth grade when we moved here. I could never let her in because she's Worldly. But the Elders and Governors got it all wrong about the Worldly; she's asking for forgiveness for something *I* did. She is more of a friend than any of Jehovah's people have been.

"Sara?" Val asks. "Are we okay?"

"Yeah. Yeah, we're okay," I smile. "Thanks for this," I hold up the new sketchbook.

She shrugs, "I figured you could use it."

The bell rings for second period to start.

Val smiles. "See you at lunch." She walks backward away from me, stepping into her Algebra class as the bell rings. Lunch? I'd never eaten lunch with anyone at school before. I've always sat alone, as far away as I could, staying invisible, far away from the Worldly.

I stand in the quiet stillness of the empty hallway, rubbing my thumb over the butterfly stamped into the smooth leather cover of the sketchbook. Would Neena have been my friend if I were never in the Truth? Would she and I have sleepovers, text each other, and share our deepest secrets? She wouldn't. I would be a nobody, just another lost Worldly person. Dead to her.

Chapter 21

At dinner, I push the shriveled pale green peas, the kind from a can, around my plate with my fork while Kaylee and Pearl argue with each other. Brad snaps at them, making Rachel jump. Dark shadows ring her eyes, her face pale, almost gray, like she hasn't slept in days.

A rigid ball forms in my stomach, pushing on my chest, and my breath catches in my throat. Has Brad gotten to her again? He can't have. I make sure Rachel is never alone with him. I keep my door open. It's not enough. Momma seems not to notice anything as she babbles about her day in Field Service.

I'm sorry I failed you, I think. I vow to sleep in the hallway again.

Momma faces Kaylee and Pearl and says, in her sweet you-better-do-this- voice, "Your dad and I are having a special study time with Sara; you two upstairs." My mouth goes dry. I can't do this. I won't. I have no choice. I've got to fake it.

"I'll take them," Rachel says without looking up. I want to grab her hand and tell her it will be okay. I'm taking care of everything. She takes the girls by the hand and whispers down to them something about dolls. She walks as if her steps hurt, and my heart hurts seeing it.

"I'll get everything ready," Brad wrings his hands together.

"You can do the dishes when we're done," Momma says to me as if I was worried about when I'd do them.

I follow her into the living room, where Brad waits on the sofa, the sheet Momma uses to cover it folded on the chair. He pats the cushion beside him, where I am meant to sit. Momma follows, sitting on my other side so I am wedged between them both.

Brad opens the book, holding it between us so we can all see. I feel the heat from his legs where they touch mine. My nose burns from his too-sweet cologne mixed with his sour sweat. I inch closer to Momma, but there is no room, no escape.

"I need my book. It's upstairs," I push to get up.

"No, this is fine. I'm glad you already studied," Brad says, and Momma agrees. "I'll read the first paragraph. We'll take turns." He clears his throat and begins to read, his voice sharp as he snaps each T and pauses too long at each comma. Momma sits next to me, her hands folded in her lap, her eyes fixed on the page.

"Chapter 1 – Coming Into Womanhood," Brad starts, and I shrink, wishing I was anywhere but here. Brad squints and reads aloud the question at the bottom of the page, "During this time of bloom, what might cause a girl concern as to her own physical growth?" He looks at me, and I push myself back into the cushion, trying to make myself small.

"I don't know," I whisper. I shouldn't have to sit here between them, reading *this*.

"I thought you said you'd studied," Momma says. "You're fifteen, Sara, but you're acting like Kaylee."

They both stare at me, their faces expectant. I'm no good at this. I'm failing already. My mask goes on, the one that hides the real me. And I start to become invisible again.

"Maybe, she's growing too fast, like her chest is getting big," I say, the heat rising on my cheeks. My mask goes on, the one that hides the real me.

"Good, very good," Brad grins from ear to ear, his yellow teeth showing. "Now, you read." He stabs at the place I am to start.

I read, trying to hide the shake in my voice. "*Do not draw attention deliberately to those parts of your body that relate to motherhood by wearing short, snug-fitting skirts, low-cut blouses, or tight sweaters. That would have a stimulating effect on the opposite sex.*" Having reached the end of the paragraph, I stop, my throat dry. Brad juts his forehead to the book, and I keep reading, the words catching.

"Why might wearing tight clothing lead to unwanted problems for a young girl?" Brad asks when I finish.

"Uhm...I..." I stutter and stop. Rachel doesn't wear tight clothes or anything immodest. I look down at my brown sweater, loose everywhere but the neck where it squeezes my breath. I want to wear t-shirts and jeans, flannels or leggings. I want to yell that they have it all wrong. Brad did what he did because he is bad, not because of Rachel and her clothes. Jehovah is a liar.

"Again, you don't have the answer," Momma says with a sting. "Sara, this is disappointing. This is not new knowledge or insight. These are things you should know."

"The clothing a girl wears can give the wrong signal to the opposite sex. She should not be attracting inappropriate behavior. Her mind should be on marriage and what kind of husband she wants." I recite the words they want to hear, even though I don't believe them.

"Good, very good," Brad agrees, and then it's Momma's time to read.

"The physical changes of adolescence may bring emotional changes..." I tune out. Nothing about this feels good. Nothing about this feels right. It's wrong, and I have to make it stop. Rachel is broken. Pearl and Kaylee can't go through this.

Chapter 22

Momma is in the kitchen, her apron tied tight around her waist, as she helps Pearl with her braid. Rachel sits alone at the table. She looks worse today—her hair matted in the back, her hands shaking as she sips her coffee. I'm stiff from sleeping in the hallway again, my head fuzzy. How long can I keep this up? It's only been a few days.

"Hey," I say, taking the chair next to her.

"Hey," she says back, her voice quiet.

Why does she stay? She should go home and be with her family, who loves her. How can she still feel so confident in the Truth after what Brad and the Elders did to her? Momma pushes Pearl to sit and eat breakfast, pours her cereal, and adds the milk. She places it in front of Pearl, who scowls up at her.

"I hate that cereal." Pearl crosses her arms over her chest.

Momma taps the table with a spoon and tells her to eat. "Jehovah gave us that cereal. Now you will eat."

Rachel sighs and puts her coffee down like she wants to say something. But she doesn't. Momma dumps a pan of burnt eggs into the trash, tossing the pan into the sink, where it rests with a sizzle.

"Where is Kaylee?" Momma asks.

"She's upstairs, getting new tights," I say.

"Oh, she's going to make me late," Momma says. She begins to put the clean dishes away and drops a glass. It shatters, and tiny shards of glass skitter in all directions across the terra cotta floor. "Great, now this." Momma throws her hands up in the air. "Nobody move!" She orders as she grabs the broom and begins to sweep.

Brad comes in. His mouth turned into a scowl, his Daily Scripture book in his hand. Rachel squirms next to me and buttons the top button of her blouse, so that her collar is almost choking her. I pull closer to her.

"What's all this noise? I'm trying to have some quiet time in my office with Jehovah before I go to work," Brad says. What he's really doing in his office?

"Momma broke a glass, and now we're going to be late for school," Pearl says.

"It's been a rough morning," Momma says. "New Bible Student today, and nothing is going right."

"I'll take the girls," Brad says.

A little noise escapes the back of Rachel's throat, and Brad shifts his gaze to her. She puts her head down. Rachel has been reduced to a quivering mess. Anger burns inside my chest.

"I was planning on walking them. No need," I say, meeting Brad's gaze.

"Won't you be late?" His eyes bore into mine. I don't flinch.

"No, I'll be fine," I lie. I will be late and miss finishing my art project for the State contest again. But I don't care. Pearl and Kaylee, they need me. Rachel does too. I'll work on my project at lunch. Mr. B. will let me work on it during class. I've mapped out, with every detail, what I'm drawing.

Brad disappears back to his study, and Rachel looks at me with a weak smile.

"Go get your stuff, Kaylee," I say as I usher Pearl upstairs. She pouts and looks back at Momma.

"It's fine. Go. I'll pick you up after school," Momma says.

The phone rings. Momma is distracted. I answer it.

"Sara! Oh good. Babysit tomorrow after school?" Rory asks, her voice low. Fear flutters in my chest, warning me to be careful. Not fear of Rory, but Momma.

"I...I don't think," I stumble over the words. Rory can help me. Can't she? Momma moves close, tapping her watch. "Let me check with my mom first," I say. I cover the phone with my hand. "It's Sister Walker's Bible Student again. She needs me to babysit tomorrow after school. Can I?" I wrinkle my nose, pouring on the innocence.

Momma twists her lips like she's going to say no. And the fluttering in my head gets louder. I need this.

"I'll talk to her about coming to Meetings. I'll be home in time for our Family Study." I say the magic words, "Family Study" – that cinched it.

Momma waves her hand and says, "Yes, fine. But no pay. This is part of your…" she starts to say and stops.

I nod. "And I have to be home by 7:00," I tell Rory.

"I can do that," Rory says.

Rachel helps me clean up the kitchen after dinner that night. Momma takes the girls upstairs to give them baths. Brad is back in his office preparing for a Talk he was assigned at our next Meeting.

"Are you getting excited for Bethel soon?" I ask Rachel, trying to make conversation with her. She's barely said anything these last few days. If I could tell her I had a plan, I'd worked it out, and if she understood the Truth is a lie, things would be better for her. She'd go to the police, back to her family where she belonged. Not here in this mess, we call home.

"Yes," Rachel says. She doesn't sound excited. Her voice is dull and lifeless like she'd rather be anywhere but here. Her hands shake as she rinses the soap from Momma's favorite mug.

"Wouldn't it be nice if we had a dishwasher?" I ask, taking the mug from her and drying it.

"Ya," she says.

"Are you okay?" I ask, even though I can tell she's not.

"I'm fine. What makes you ask?" Her voice high pitched. She reaches for a plate, scrubbing it too hard.

"Because of everything that's happened," I say, softening my voice, hoping she doesn't make me say the words.

Rachel stops scrubbing. Licking her lips, she looks over her shoulder.

"It's okay. Momma's still upstairs with the girls. And he's in his study," I say, unable to say Brad's name out loud.

Rachel stares mutely out the window over the sink, still holding the plate. I gently take it from her fingers. I rinse it in hot water, the steam fogging up the window.

"Rachel, are you doubting Jehovah? The Truth?" I dare to whisper the words. It feels good to say them out loud.

The corner of her mouth twitches as tears well up in her eyes. She keeps her eyes fixed on a point outside the window. She mouths something. Yes? I'm not sure.

I move closer to her, so our shoulders touch and lower my voice even more. "Why are you staying here? Don't you want to go home, be with your Mom and Dad, your brother?"

"I can't go back to them," Rachel says. "I've made a big mess of things. I tried hard to do what the Elders said, and...I feel worse." Tears stream down her cheeks, and she buries her face in her hands.

I put my arm around her. "You can go back to your family. They love you," I say and stop as Momma comes in. She rushes over to Rachel. How much had she heard?

"Rachel, Sara? What's going on? Are you okay?" Momma puts her arm around Rachel's shoulder, nudging me aside.

"I'm fine, Sister Michaels." Rachel looks at me, her eyes telling me not to let Momma know the truth.

"What did you say to make her so upset?" Momma asks.

"Nothing. I promise. She misses her family. I was encouraging her, telling her Jehovah is caring for her," I say. Can she see the lie on my face?

"Rachel, you don't need to help with the dishes. Go watch TV or something. Just relax," Momma says to Rachel. "Sara, you finish the dishes." She picks her bible up from the table, thumbs through the books on the shelf above the phone, and slides her bible in. "You better be careful with your defiant attitude. You're in Reproof right now," she says.

"I'll try harder," I lie. But it's true I need to be careful.

She sits at the table and flips through her bible. "We're living in the end times. Armageddon can happen at any moment. You must be prepared spiritually. I'm sure you understand the importance of obedience. There are some wonderful passages for you to read about defiance," Momma says. "There's Lot's wife. Remember, she was turned into a pillar of salt. Then there is…"

she keeps talking, and I focus my thoughts on the drawing for the contest.

Tomorrow, I will finish it. It needs a few more details, some lines, and shading. And then a pop of color, blue eyes. Rachel has blue eyes.

Chapter 23

In Science class, Gabe is already in his seat, two rows in front of mine, swiveled around so he faces my direction. He glances at me when I slide into my chair and looks away quickly. He despises me. I cringe remembering the last thing I'd told him, "Because I have the Truth." I sounded like a snob, like I was better than everyone else when I wasn't. I'm not. I'm just like them.

Mr. Arguelles, with his rumpled pants and a flop of brown hair over his eyes, rushes in. Standing at the front of the classroom, he rubs his hands together and smiles at us like he has a big secret he can't wait to tell.

"Good afternoon. I'm glad you could all make it," Mr. Arguelles laughs and turns to write on the whiteboard behind him.

Pushing his hair back, he faces us. "This year's Science Fair is going to be different. We're going to experiment with something new." He laughs again, and the class groans at his awful joke. "First, you're all going to partner up."

Everyone bursts into conversation, claiming their partners—Bailey and Zoe group up. Val's not in this class. I remain in my seat like a lump, unsure of where to go, and who to ask. Everything spins, and my palms start to sweat.

"Quiet down," Mr. Arguelles waves his hands. "I should have said, *I'll* pair you up. I'm assigning pairs based on skill sets, aptitude, and who I believe will work well together."

"He's like a mad scientist," someone says in the back, and class erupts in laughter.

Mr. Arguelles puts his hands on his hips. "Very funny. Next, no internet or Google searching allowed," he says, and the class groans. "I know, I know. This is part of your experiment. You can get your research done at that place called 'the library' where you'll use reference books. You can interview experts. Now for the pairing up. Your project idea must be turned in today before the end of class."

Lifting a sheet of paper from his desk, Mr. Arguelles writes a list of names on the whiteboard. Why is he choosing our partners? Are we in sixth grade?

Chewing my thumbnail, I sink low in my seat. The sunlight shoots through the tall windows, and the overhead lights seem to brighten as if shining down on me. There is no hiding for me anymore. Being invisible had its advantages. Dropping my sweaty hands into my lap, I wait for my name to appear on the board.

Nate - Rose

Zoe - Bailey

Sara - Gabe

Red creeps up the back of Gabe's neck. Is he mad about it? I'll ask Mr. Arguelles to change partners.

"No changing partners. I thought hard about this list." Mr. Arguelles puts the cap back on the marker and sits at this desk. "Get into your pairs. Slide your chairs around. And if you need ideas, I have some sheets here."

No one listens to him. They slide chairs and desks around the room. Gabe waves me to the empty desk beside him, his face returning to its normal color. I sit, my knees shaking and a cold sweat on my palms. I hadn't been this close to him since the day our hands touched.

"Any ideas?" he asks.

He smells good, like the outdoors. Focus, I tell myself.

"Not really. Maybe we need one of those sheets," I say, my voice cracking. Does he notice?

"I have an idea," he says and writes on a clean sheet of notebook paper. He rotates the paper toward me, his hand brushing against mine. He jerks away. "What about that?"

I start to read it out loud, and he shushes me. "Don't give it away," he says, his finger to his lips.

I open my notebook and write the idea at the top of my page, Are Fingerprints Hereditary. "I like it," I say. "How do we start?"

"Library. I guess," he says. "Should we meet there?"

The pit of my stomach drops a little, like I imagine it would at the top of a roller coaster, warning me something exciting is about to happen.

"The only day I can go is Sunday afternoon," I say, leaving off the part about after Field Service. More important, I wonder what lie I'm going to tell Momma. All of them are piling up now. I hope I can keep them straight.

"Sure." He smiles, and I get to the top of the roller coaster again and drop. This ride is going to be exciting. Jehovah had messed so many things up.

Isabelle squeals my name when Rory opens the door. Running out, she wraps her arms around my legs and says, "Sarwah!"

I peel her off and pick her up to carry her inside. Her curls bounce with each step.

"She's been waiting for you at the window since she got up from her nap," Rory says.

I put Isabelle down, and she pulls me by the hand to the middle of the living room, where a tea party waits. A small pink table is set with plastic teacups and a teapot, all in white, peppered with tiny cornflower blue flowers. I sit cross-legged while Isabelle pours pretend tea.

Rory sits on the edge of the sofa, her hands clasped in her lap. "I have time; you're early. Tell me what's going on."

My eyes shoot to her. How does she know? My instinct is to deny it. I can't tell her about Brad. If she goes to the police...the Elders will realize it was me. I'll be Disfellowshipped for shaming Jehovah, and I'll lose everything. That's not part of my plan.

"Nothing is going on," I say, taking a sip of Isabelle's tea.

"Sara, something is going on. You're here a second time. You were so scared of me in the grocery store like you'd catch something from me," she says. "You've changed. I can see it."

A knot tightens in my chest. If she can see it, then maybe the others can too. She understands. She knows Jehovah is a lie. I bite my lip and look out the window toward the puffy white clouds floating by. Maybe she needs to be part of my plan?

I look back to her. "I was figuring out ..." *If everything I know is a lie.* Heat rises on my face, and my voice starts to shake. No. I can't say it. I can't risk it.

"It's okay. I know it's hard. It was hard for me," Rory says. "I'm here for you. Whatever you need. Okay?" she says.

"Okay," I say.

"When you're ready to tell me, I'm all ears," she says, pushing her bracelets up her wrists. "I've got to get ready. I'm meeting Miguel in a half-hour."

Isabelle gives me one of her plastic cookies. I take a pretend bite and rub my belly. A bolt of fear hits me. What would Neena do if she knew I was here, at a disfellowshipped Sister's house? What would she do if she knew I was Reproved? My eyes water. I know the answer. After reporting to an Elder, she would never talk to me again. The irony – I'm protecting Rachel, who Brad is hurting. Reporting him was wrong, and it got me disciplined. But Neena can report me for talking to a Disfellowshipped person, and I'd be punished and Neena rewarded. And Val, the Wordly person Jehovah said I should stay away from, she's standing by my side – no matter what.

Rory appears a few minutes later, her hair piled on her head. She wears a flowy dress that swirls around her ankles and perfume that smells faintly of flowers and oranges.

"Sara, I have something for you." she holds a small silver cell phone and charging cord for me.

I take them, holding them uncomfortably in my hand.

"It's a prepaid phone. Charge it up. I'll send you my number. I'm a text or call away if you ever need me."

I stare at her, again feeling awkward and unable to say thank you.

Her phone beeps. "My Uber is here." She rushes away, stopping to kiss Isabelle on the head. Isabelle waves from the window as they drive away, and then we go back to playing tea party.

After Isabelle's dinner, and bath, it's time for bed. I carry her to her room and sit in the rocking chair as she curls up in my lap. I look down at her round face, long eyelashes, and tiny mouth like a rosebud. Isabelle will never meet her grandparents, aunts, uncles, or cousins because Isabelle will never be part of the Truth. They will never acknowledge her.

I flick on the night light, and an array of butterflies light up across the ceiling, something Kaylee would live in. I shut the door softly behind me, a pang of sadness in my chest.

I find the laptop Rory said I could use last time and log in to Facebook. I scroll through my meager page feed, which is mostly ads, hesitating with the mouse over the number five next to the message icon. I click it.

I have five messages from Alyce Stephens, the woman whose friend request I accepted in a hurry the last time I was here. The messages start on that same day. I read through fast and then again. Nothing makes sense.

Hi Sara. My name is Alyce Sara Stephens. I may be your grandmother.

I live in Michigan with my daughter and grandchildren. I have a studio overlooking the lake.

My son's name was Richard Kenneth Stephens. He died 12 years ago today.

Please message me back.

Then there's nothing until last Wednesday.

I know you may be scared. If you don't want to message, I understand. But here's my phone number, just in case.

She can't be my grandmother. Momma would have told me. But my dad's name was Richard Kenneth Stephens, and he died when I was four– twelve years ago.

She could be my grandmother.

I scroll through her feed, and a familiar face stares back at me. A neatly trimmed beard, aviator glasses, and a military uniform. My dad. Tears well in my eyes as a million thoughts swirl in my head. I do what I do when I feel this way. I draw.

I grab a pen from the cup on the counter and rummage around, looking for a sheet of paper, the tray in the small printer empty. I finally find a pad in the junk drawer. I flip through the pad, find a blank page and glance up at the face smiling back at me on the computer screen. Hunching over the pad, with the blotchy ink of the black pen, and using the person on the screen as my model, I draw without stopping. When I'm done, staring back at me is a face, the face of my father. His eyes crinkled in laughter. The way I remember him most. Happy.

Putting the pen down, I rub my hand, sore from holding the pen so tight. I carefully tear the page from the notebook, fold it, and put it in my backpack. Something I'll have to hide when I get home. If Momma finds it, she'll tear it up.

Before closing the laptop, I return to Facebook and Alyce Stephens. She is my grandmother. I add her phone number to the cell phone Rory gave me. I create a contact using Cheri Wilson as the name, incase anyone finds the phone,. I don't send anything. Not yet. I'm not ready. What would I even say?

Rory drives me home, and my head is spinning. My secrets are growing. The phone, my grandmother, Rory, and Gabe. I've got to be careful. We near the Koffee Stop by my house and I ask Rory to let me out.

Rory looks at me, her eyes wide with alarm. "I can't let you out   here."

"It's okay. It's only around the corner and then two more blocks. I walk this all the time," I say.

"But it's late. It's dark," she says. "I will take you to the end of your street and wait until you get into your house."

There's no point in arguing with her; her mind is made up. Momma or Brad can't see her car in the dark if she's at the end of the street, so I agree. Besides, they'll be expecting me to be dropped off. As I move to get out, she grabs my arm gently.

"Sara... I'm here for you, I promise. No matter what it is. If you need me, text me. We can talk, or I'll come and get you. Whatever you need. No questions asked," she says.

My breath catches. She's not supposed to be this nice to me. "I promise," I say, and I feel bad about not telling her everything.

Halfway down the block, I look back in the darkness. Rory's car still at the corner, the lights off. She's watching and waiting. In a patch of dark between the streetlights, I slip into the muddy brown cardigan that itches and change back into the scuffed brown loafers I'd stowed in my

backpack. I take a few deep breaths and arrange my face back into the dutiful Witness, full of love for Jehovah, dead to the world around me. Miserable status.

Brad's car is missing from the driveway. The house is dark except for the light in Rachel's room and the light on the front porch, and I'm happy... just for a moment.

The moment fades as soon as I walk in the door. Momma flicks on the kitchen light, startling me so I step back. In one hand she holds the camp flier.

"Looks like we need to talk," she says.

Chapter 24

Momma glares at me as she holds up the Christian Camp flier from Val, the one I thought I'd hidden so well. I scan the room for the paper Mr. Balentine gave me about winning the art contest but didn't see it.

"Why were you in my stuff?" I ask, remembering not too long ago, she'd packed up my room and all my belongings as if my feelings didn't matter. The only thing that matters to her is Jehovah.

"This is exactly why you are being Reproved. Your *defiance.* Didn't we just talk about this?" She spits the words at me, so I feel the spray on my face.

"I'm not defiant," I say and tug at the collar of my dress where it pinches on my neck.

"Explain this, then," she snaps the flier in my face.

"It was from Val. I was going to throw it away. I guess it got mixed up in my school stuff when I was moving rooms," I say, holding my breath while she contemplates what I told her. I can almost see the wheels spinning in her head.

Her lips curve into a tight smile. "Well, let's not let that happen again." She straightens her arm, the paper dangling from her fingertips. "This is nothing but trash." She rips the camp flier into tiny pieces and throws it in the bin under the sink. "Imagine if the girls found that. It has a crucifix on it. You could have let Satan into their hearts with your lazy attitude and forgetfulness." She taps her foot, her arms crossed over her chest. What would she have done with Brad's porn? Nothing.

"Can I go?" I ask, putting my head down.

"Be careful, Sara, very careful. You're treading on thin ice. Maybe we need to have a study time, you and me," she says.

I stand; still, my head still down, the rooster clock over the sink ticking away, while I wait for her to decide.

"It's late, and we have Meeting tomorrow. You read two more chapters of the book the Elders gave you. I'll expect answers in the morning," she says.

"I will," I say.

I climb the stairs, my head heavy, and wish Momma would be happy, like Rory. Doesn't she want to be happy?

I hang my purse on the hook in the closet. I'll have to find a better place to hide the phone. Momma is looking through my things. If she finds my purse and what's in it, there's no telling what she'll do.

Late that night, when all is quiet, and I hear the click of the light go off downstairs, I slide into the hallway with my blankets. Brad won't get past me; Rachel will be safe. By the glow of the nightlight at the stairway landing, I find the answers in the book, highlighting them in bright pink highlighter. That should make Momma happy.

Sometime in the middle of the night or early morning, Rachel comes out of her room and stumbles over me. I wake with a start, thinking she's Brad, and punch through my tangle of blankets.

"Sara, it's me, Rachel," she says, holding my arms still.

"I'm sorry. I thought you were..."

"Brad." She finishes my sentence, and I nod. "Come in my room," she whispers.

We sit on her bed, and her shoulders sink low. She buries her head in her hands and drags her fingers through her hair before sitting up with a heavy sigh. "Sara. I didn't mean for this. I'm so confused. I thought Jehovah would take care of this if I relied on Him. If I trusted Him. Maybe He has by using you. But it feels wrong. Doesn't it feel wrong to you?"

"Yes," I say quietly.

"I don't have anyone to talk to. Not my mom, or my old friends. I'm never talking to the Elders again. And Brother Peters won't leave me alone, like I need that too. He wants to court me. He means to marry me," Rachel says. "I'm eighteen. Why would I want to marry him? He's ancient, thirty-five."

"Gross," I say. "Rachel, you can talk to me. I'm sorry I broke your trust. But that secret, that...was all wrong. I messed up. I should've…" I fumble over the words. I hadn't messed up. I had done the right thing.

"No, you didn't mess anything up. You tried," she says as if reading my thoughts. "After all that, with your reproof and everything, you seem different."

"I do?" I ask. Had Momma noticed this too? "In a good way, or bad way?"

"A good way," Rachel says.

I bite my thumbnail and look out the window. "I have changed. It is a good way. The other night, in the kitchen, I meant it, Rachel, what I said. I promise. What we talk about will stay between us," I say, almost pleading. "Rachel, why do you stay? You have a place to go, not like me. I'm stuck, but you…" I stop. Am I stuck?

She looks at me, sadness around the edges of her eyes. "It's not that simple, Sara. I didn't leave on good terms; my family doesn't want me back. Now I'm stuck here, pretending to be something I'm not."

"That's not true. Your family loves you, I saw in those pictures. Your parents are worried," I say. "Could it be you think Jehovah will be angry with you for leaving? That something bad will happen to you?"

She nods. "A little." She wipes the corner of her eye with a tissue.

I put my arm around her. What about Alyce Stephens? Would she take me? Does she even have a place for me? If I go, what will happen to Kaylee and Pearl? I will never see them again, and they will be here with Brad, with no one to protect them. No, I can't leave. I have to stay and pretend to be something I'm not, no matter what.

"Sara, we are like sisters," she says.

Sighing, my eyes moving to look at the closet, and it reminds me, suddenly, that I missed something important tonight. "Can I tell you something? You can't tell anyone," I say.

"I promise. Your secret is safe," she says, and the words sting a little. I hadn't kept her secret safe. But her secret was a bad secret; mine is not.

I push back the edge of the curtain and look out into the moonlight night. "I won the School District art show, first place out of all the 9th graders. I'm moving up to the State competition. Last week was the awards ceremony and I missed it. I couldn't go because Jehovah says following a dream, like being an artist, is taking away from Him."

Dropping the curtain, I turn and face her. Her eyes are filled with tears.

"I don't want to go to Bethel. I don't want to marry Brother Peters. I miss my little brother," she says. "And Brad…" She stops, her words caught in her throat. She doesn't need to explain about Brad. I get it.

I sit on the edge of the bed next to her, staring down at my feet. "We'll figure this out," I say. And I wonder how? Is Alyce Stephens my grandmother? It doesn't matter anyway. I can't leave.

Chapter 25

I keep glancing at the clock, getting more and more nervous with each glance. I'm supposed to meet Gabe at 2:00, it's nearing 1:00, and I still haven't told Momma about needing to go to the library for my science project. It's Sunday, and I was waiting for a time when we were alone, which never happened.

Finally, I find her alone, busy in the kitchen, her head and yellow-gloved hands buried deep inside the fridge, scrubbing away a week's worth of grime. Every Sunday afternoon, after Field Service, she scrubs the kitchen from top to bottom. I never noticed before, but Momma never stills. She only sits when studying about Jehovah or at the Kingdom Hall. Maybe when she's still, doubts about Jehovah creep in.

"Momma, I need to go to the library," I say as I tug out a new bag for the trashcan and replace it.

"What do you mean need?" She stands, pushing her hair off her forehead with the back of her arm.

"It's for science class. I have to do research, and I need a computer and internet," I say, adding another lie to the pile.

"Instead of telling me you're going, you should ask for permission," Momma says like I am a little kid. Momma can't mess this up for me. Play along. "I don't have time to take you either."

"Momma, can I go to the library, please? It's for school, a project," I ask, using the words she needs to hear. "I can ride my bike; you don't need to take me."

Pushing her lips together, she ushers me to the table laden with plastic containers, jars of pickles and salad dressings, and a jug of milk she'd take from the fridge. "I don't like you on those public computers," she sighs as she sinks into the chair. "You know why we can't have a computer or cellphones in this house. They are dangerous. Filled with Satan-serving Apostates who put lies on the internet about Jehovah. All they want to do is take you from Jehovah." She folds her hands in front of the yellow gloves still on, locking her fingers—a signal she won't change her mind.

"What about Brad's laptop? Can I use that? I can sit here at the kitchen table, and you can help me," I ask, even though it's not an option.

She inhales sharply. Her lips move as she silently counts to three. "Why would you ask that? You cannot use your stepfathers' laptop."

I pull a thick binder from my backpack, opening it to the science project Gabe and I chose. "This is what I have to do. All of this, plus research," I run my finger down the page. "I went out in Field Service this morning with Cheri. Yesterday after Meeting, I cleaned the bathrooms at the Kingdom Hall. I've done my study time in the new book you gave me." Another lie—all I did was underline random sentences with pink and yellow highlighters, circling keywords.

She blinks slowly, saying nothing.

"At school, I can only use the computer during study breaks and after school. It's not enough time. I have partners. They'll get a failing grade if I don't do my part," I say. Her expression changes for a split second as she searches the back of her brain for the correct response. I lower my eyes to my lap. "Me making them fail will make Jehovah look bad."

Leaning forward, she flattens her hands on the table and pushes up. "Fine, you can go. I'll be glad when you're out of school; you spend too much time on things of this World. New System school is looking better and better all the time. I wish it weren't so expensive." Her voice trails off.

I'll never go to New System School. Never. That will be like killing me. "I'll be home to help you with dinner." I fling my backpack over my shoulder and get my bike in the garage.

Brad is in the driveway, wiping the hood of his car with a bright yellow chamois. He watches me as I pull my bike down from the hook. Gripping the handlebars, I straddle the bike, meeting his stare, not looking away, not flinching. One of us will look away, and it won't be me.

"Where you going?" His lips curve up into a smile, his eyes dark.

I don't answer. I just stare. I know what you are, I want to say. But I don't.

He runs the chamois across the car door, finally shifting his dark eyes from me.

I ride away, my hair blowing back, my bag bouncing on my back, glad to be free. But this bike thing is getting old, just like the no cell phone and the clothes. I've got to figure this out. The glass doors of the library swoosh open as I enter, the warm air greeting me.

I make my way back to the bank of computers, finding an empty one facing out towards the library. It's almost 2:00; I have enough time to go on to Facebook again. My heart catches in my throat as I log on.

There's another message from Alyce Stephens. Why hadn't I texted her? I feel around in my pack for the hard edges of the phone Rory gave me and add Alyce Stevens to my contact. Only I name her Cheri, in case Momma ever finds the phone. Out of the corner of my eye, I see someone approaching and quickly start to log out of Facebook, my phone still in my hand.

"You're early," I say without looking up.

"Early?" Neena says.

The blood drains from my face. My mouth goes dry. "Oh, I thought you were my study partner.

Her gaze falls, and when I look, I see what she's looking at—the cell phone in my hand. Cold dread washes over me.

"When'd you get that?" She asks.

"Yesterday," I say. I should have texted her. Neena has always thought it dumb that I didn't have a cell.

"Why didn't you call me? Or text? Does your mom know you have it?" She flings her braids over her shoulder and sits in the chair next to me.

I swallow. "No, my mom has no clue. I can't call on it. Text only. I was just putting the numbers in it." I slide the phone over to her. "Put your number in." As she taps away, I glance around for Gabe. "You won't tell anyone, will you?"

"No, I won't. But I don't like secrets. They're never good. I did hear some gossip about you, though." Neena hands me back my phone.

"Gossip? About me?" I ask, trying to sound surprised.

"I heard you were Reproved?" She says, looking right into my eyes like she's searching for something, and I don't blink.

"Since when do you listen to the gossip of the Sisters?" I ask.

"I don't normally, but this was from Cheri," she says, and a chill goes up my spine.

"Cheri??" I ask, my voice squeaking.

"I didn't believe her at first. But then she said she was mentoring you, and then when I saw you out in service today with her... I guess it must be true. You must be in trouble."

"Cheri shouldn't have told you anything. This is between Jehovah and me," I say.

"I thought we were friends," Neena says, and the words sting. More than anything, I want her as my friend, but I will lose her when she finds out I don't believe in Jehovah anymore. Over her shoulder, I see Gabe, his back to us. His head goes back and forth as he looks around the library for me.

"We are friends," I say softly. I have to get her away before Gabe comes over.

"If we're such good friends, then why is Cheri the one telling me about your Reproof?" Why I'm finding out about your phone here in the library?" she asks.

"Discipline is private. I'll be okay. And my phone, I told you, I just got it," I say. Gabe faces us, smiling with relief when he spots me sitting at the bank of computers. "I have to study now. I only have the computer for 30 minutes," I say quickly, putting my fingers on the keyboard.

"Sara," she moves closer. "You don't seem like you're working on your relationship with Jehovah," she says, but I can't tell if she's mad at me or scared of me.

"I am. Really. It's just a phone. I got it so we could text," I say. Does the lie show on my face?

"Just be careful. You're already Reproved. You don't want someone reporting you to the Elders," she snaps and shoulders past Gabe, who looks confused.

I watch her walk away, her yellow skirt swirling around her ankles as she hurries toward the door. I feel a million miles away, floating above myself, looking down as I split in two. Is she my friend, or not? Her last words sound like a threat, or were they just a warning? The old me would say a warning. She's trying to help. The new me is unsure.

"What was that?" Gabe asks.

"It's a long story," I say, my throat tightening.

"You don't have to tell me. That was dumb of me to ask," he says, the weirdness from school gone. "You remember we can't use the internet, right?"

"Yep. Fully aware," I say as I gather my things and log off the computer.

"I want to ask you something before we start our research." His voice cracks. Licking his lips, he glances over my shoulder, then down to his knees.

"What?" I ask, arching a brow.

"Will you go to the dance with me on Friday?" He blurts out.

I slide back into my chair. I can barely think. I can't go with him, my head says. There are a million reasons why I can't. Momma, the Elders...it spins. But there's lightness in my chest, and my stomach flutters–in a good way.

Somehow, I say, "Yes."

He sighs with relief. "For a second I thought you were gonna say no."

I can't believe it. He asked me to a dance. A...*dance.* I press my hands to my cheeks.

How am I going to get out of Family Study?

Chapter 26

Brad is in the kitchen making coffee instead of Momma. He grumbles as he flings open cabinets and throws open drawers.

"Where's Momma?" I ask.

"She's sick, like Kaylee. Their heads have big hurts," Pearl says over a spoonful of Corn Flakes.

"Oh," I slide in next to Pearl and wait until Brad finds his favorite travel mug, fills it with coffee, and leaves. He doesn't say goodbye, have a nice day, nothing. When the door closes behind him, I breathe again.

Rachel ventures downstairs. She says nothing as she pours herself a bowl of cereal and eats it dry, without milk. Pearl starts to say something. Before she can say anything, I say, "I'm walking you to school today. Let's go."

"Fine," she says, her face in its permanent scowl. It's like I never noticed before how unhappy and angry Jehovah makes everyone. Miserable, just like Val said. Did I look like that too?

Pearl and I walk toward her school. She announces proudly, "Momma said next year I don't have to go to this Worldly school. Next year I'm going to the New System school with all the other kids in the Truth."

I look down at her in her dress, her collar closed tight against her neck, and her hair pulled back into a tight ponytail.

The other little girls on the playground wear shorts or jeans, t-shirts with glittery unicorns or flowers, clothes Momma and Jehovah would call immodest or showy.

"You don't like your school?" I ask.

Pearl stops short and folds her arms over her chest. "That's a dumb thing to say. Why would I want to be stuck with all these stupid Worldly kids all day?" Her eyes, dark with anger, cut through me like words.

"Pearl, you shouldn't call people stupid. Jehovah doesn't want that," I say, my voice tinged with sadness.

"You don't know what He wants, that's why you're Reproved," she says, and my stomach somersaults. I want to take her by the shoulders and shake Jehovah out of her, screaming *he's a lie*. But there's no point. She'll only run and tell Momma what I said, and I'll be worse off.

I bite my lip, drop her at the gate, and walk away. I failed again. When I'm far enough away and Pearl can't see, I check my phone to see if Neena texted me. The screen is blank. Nothing. She's still upset. I tap on Rory's number and text:

Thx for the phone.

My fingers shake as I type the words I haven't spoken yet:

A Worldly boy asked me to a school dance

I don't send it. I stare at the words—my secret. The thoughts I'd had about Gabe since sixth grade, I've never shared with anyone. The rollercoaster feeling returns. Should I send it? What will Rory think? Before I can change my mind, I tap the send button and put my phone back in its hiding place. The moment of happiness is replaced with sadness. Neena, the person I want to tell more than anything, won't listen to me. She'll shut me out as if I am poison.

Val is waiting for me outside of school. I try to act happy. I can't seem to force myself to smile.

"What's wrong? You, okay?" She asks.

"I'm tired. It's...hard trying to be two different people." I wipe the tear from the corner of my eye. I don't want to cry, not now, not here in front of Val.

"What do you mean, two people? What's going on with you?" She asks.

"It's complicated," I say.

"I'm here for you Sara. You can tell me anything. We're friends. Right?" she says. The words sound familiar. I'd said them to Rachel. I'd tried to say them to Neena. With Val, it was right. She is a friend. She always has been. I just couldn't see it.

"I figured out that...I decided..." I stumble over my words.

"Take a breath," she says, pulling me to the side, away from the throng of students brushing past us.

Facing her, I will the tears back down. "I'm not in the Truth anymore. I figured out it was a lie."

"Truth?" She wrinkles her brow.

"I don't believe in Jehovah. I don't want to be a Witness anymore," I say.

"Oh," she says. "Sometimes, I don't feel like going to church."

"It's not like that. I can't just not go to Meetings. I can't just say, hey, family and Elders, I don't believe in Jehovah or anything you're teaching me. If anyone finds out, I don't believe and don't want to believe..." How do I explain it to her? "I'll be shunned. I'll be dead to them," I finally say.

Her mouth drops open. "Are you serious? Really? Your mom, your sisters?"

"I'll be kicked out. It will be like I don't exist," I say.

"You exist to me," she says, and I feel the warmth around me like that day in the park.

"Thanks for that. But, but right now, I'm trying to figure it all out.".

Don't do it alone. I'm here for you. I'll help you with anything," she says, putting her hand on my arm.

"You're already doing enough, just being my friend again," I say. "There's something else." I smile wide, my heart doing that fluttery thing. "Gabe asked me to the dance," I blurt out.

"Finally," Val says.

"What do you mean, finally?" I ask.

"Haven't you noticed how weird he's been acting? He tried like three times to ask you," she says. I shake my head, confused.

"Why did I say yes? It's impossible. I can't go," I shrug and lower my head, the tears welling in my eyes again.

"Is that part of what you said about living two lives?" Val asks.

"Yeah. I'm not even allowed to talk to boys unless they are in the Truth. And even then, it has to be with other people around. And school dances," I shake my head. "When I'm ready for dating it means I'm looking for my husband."

"You're kidding, right? That is so wrong. Like, are we in the 1950s?" She rolls her eyes.

"No, I'm not. There's a lot in the Truth that's wrong," I say. I can't say too much. I can't tell her my worst secret.

She leans against the wall, tapping her chin. "If we put our heads together. There's got to be a way we can do this. Can't you tell your mom you're sleeping over somewhere?"

"Maybe. She's been extra watchful lately of me though," I shrug. "Even if I do... I don't have a dress. Everything I have looks like this." I wave my hand down over my navy-blue skirt with the tiny yellow flowers. I hate it, but my other choices are worse.

She loops her arm through mine, "If we can get you to the dance, I have a dress and shoes you can borrow."

"Really?" I ask.

She twists her lips. "Maybe it's not such a good idea. I mean, we're lying to your mom. I don't want you to get in trouble."

Considering everything else that will get me in trouble with Momma and Jehovah, I want to go to this dance. I still can't believe how generous Val is, and I don't want her to worry about me. "I'll figure something out," I say.

The day drags on. All I can think about is Pearl and her anger, Momma going through my things, Alyce Stephens, Neena, and the two pieces of art I'd turned in for the art show. If I win, what will I do? And then there's the dance and Gabe. I can't dance. I don't know how. What about the clothes, the shoes? I'm both excited and nervous.

When it's time for art class, I'm exhausted. Mr. Balentine gives us our exercise for the day—shading—and flicks on music from his old paint-splattered radio. I try to concentrate and follow the directions, but my shading is too dark. The music pounds in my head, and I can't relax. He takes the empty seat next to me and examines my paper.

"That's not like you," he says. And I nod. "Maybe this will cheer you up." He slides a large white envelope to me, my name printed on the front—my awards.

I take it and carefully slit it open. Inside is a gift card for $100.00 to the Kaleidoscope Art Store, a year pass to the Museum of Art, and tuition to their summer art program.

"This is too much," I say, sliding it back to him.

"No, it's exactly right," he says. "You need these things to feed the artist inside you. Those classes they're taught by a good friend of mine. She will help you with your technique and teach you to fine-tune your skills. No one can teach you what you already have: passion." Mr. B. walks away, sliding the envelope back over to me. I tug out a new sheet of paper and start the shading exercise over. This time it's right.

The final bell rings. I am not ready to go home. School is the only place where I can be me. I work my way slowly through the hallway, where not too long ago, I could barely stand to be seen.

I dawdle down the hallway, my phone in my hand. My phone beeps. I glance at it quickly. It's a text from Cheri Wilson, my code name for Alyce Stephens. I want to text her, but what do I say? What do I ask? I shove it into my pocket, look up and freeze. Through the big windows by the doors, I can see Momma waiting for me. She straddles Pearl's too-small bike, its white basket strapped to the handlebars, frayed and falling apart, the bell rusted. She shields her eyes from the sun, scanning the students streaming from the building.

Sucking in a breath, I push through the doors. Around me, there are whispers and nervous giggles. The crowd parts like I'm poison.

Momma spots me and rings the bell. It lets out a sorrowful ping. "Sara, over here," she waves me over.

There's a sharp stabbing pain in my heart and a rumble in my chest, a weird combination of sorrow and hate.

"Why are you here?" I ask.

"You haven't been good with the discipline the Elders gave you. I'm simply making sure there's no more trouble," she smiles, and I deflate.

I wish she would let me breathe. She's so afraid I've left Jehovah and the Truth. She's suffocating me, squeezing the life out of me. If only she didn't believe the lie.

My cell phone vibrates in my pocket. Fear ripples through me. I look to see if Momma heard the faint buzz. But she didn't seem to notice.

"Be right back. I forgot something," I say before she can stop me. I hurry back inside to my locker. Val, at the end of the hallway with Bailey and Zoe, spots me, waves, and starts to come over. I shake my head and shift my eyes to the door behind me. When she sees Momma waiting, a look of confusion washes over her face, then understanding.

I fumble through the combination on my locker and fling the dented metal door open when my phone buzzes again. Using my locker door as a shield, I glance at the messages from Rory lighting up my screen.

A dance? Really? That's great. We need to talk

Can't talk. Mom's here at school to walk me home

Oh no. Sorry. Text me when it's safe.

I switch my phone off and place it deep into my backpack, under the sketchbook Val gave me. Maybe I should leave them here in my locker? No, I need both more than anything. I slam the door shut, turn, and slam into Momma. Her eyes tired, her mouth drooping in the corners. How long had she been there? Had she seen it?

Keep it together. I look up at her, a smile on my face, a bitter taste in my mouth.

"What's taking so long?" She asks.

"Let's go," I tug her toward the door. I look back, and Bailey and I lock eyes for a second. She looks sad.

Momma follows me home on the bike. Its wheels squeak out a rhythm that says, "Jehovah sucks. Jehovah sucks."

And I'm going to the dance on Friday night – no matter what.

Chapter 27

All week, Momma comes every day after school to pick me up. She's watching me. It's as if my secrets, the State Art contest, my phone, and the dance are written in Sharpie on my forehead. And Neena ignores me, too, by not calling or texting me back. Nothing. I couldn't get to school early to work on my art pieces. I rushed through them, doing them during lunch and English class. They're not going to be good enough to win.

My hands shake with fear and excitement as I get ready for my first dance. I lied to Momma about babysitting for Sister Nichol's bible student again. I was surprised she let me go without calling Sister Nichols. I guess keeping a normal appearance to the Sisters is more important than keeping me home.

I grab my study book and roll up a Watchtower magazine, shoving them both into the side pocket of my pack. I make sure the magazine cover, the face of a little girl who'd died because she'd refused a blood transfusion, faces outward.

And if she checks inside, she'll see where I'd highlighted sentences and circled keywords. It looks like I had spent time reading and studying the words of Jehovah for hours, but I hadn't. My phone is safely tucked under a flap in the lining at the bottom. To add to the façade, I line up my highlighters in the front pocket, where the bright caps peek out. Perfect study packet. I've become good at lying to Momma. But then, my whole life has been a lie, one lie after the other.

Val and I have planned out tonight to the second. First, I'll walk from home, heading toward the bus stop around the corner in case anyone is watching. Momma would. Then I'll double back, going to Val's the long way where Momma can't see me from any window in our house. Then, after we change, Val's Mom will take us to the dance. It's easy as long as nothing goes wrong.

Tonight, Momma's hands are full as she prepares a special meal for tomorrow's visit from the Circuit Overseer, Brother Nelson, and his wife. She and the other Sisters have been working all day on making enough lasagna to feed two congregations. On top of all her usual housework, she's doing this and working for Jehovah.

Rachel is helping too. I wish she weren't. She needs to go home to the place that misses and wants her, to her family who loves her.

Pearl's high-pitched voice filters up the stairs. She's talking to Kaylee, something about Armageddon coming soon.

What if Pearl is right? What if tonight is the night Jehovah promised to destroy the world, and I'm at a dance? Worse, a dance I lied about and snuck out for? I reach for my anti-acids by instinct, realizing I haven't used them all week.

Kaylee's laugh trickles up the stairs, and the spell is broken. It's a dance. Satan isn't trying to trick me. The world isn't going to end in a storm of fire from the sky--not tonight, anyway. No cracks are going to open in the earth and swallow me up.

I will be with my friends tonight, and Jehovah, or Satan, can't stop that.

I take a deep breath and head down the stairs.

"Sara, where are you going?" Kaylee cries when she sees me.

"I'm going to babysit," I say.

"You're going now?" Momma glances up at the clock. "Did you do your Study for tomorrow?" Her fingers flutter around her neck.

"If you don't study, Jehovah won't love you. He won't let you into Paradise," Kaylee holds up her upside-down magazine. Her voice is a perfect mimic of Pearl's. I want to take the magazine and fling it far from her.

"I already studied," I shift and show the edge of my magazine and book in the side pocket of my pack. "I plan to study some more after the baby goes to sleep. Do you want to see it?" I offer, wishing she'd let me go. The dance starts in an hour, and I still need to get ready at Val's.

"Well, that's good. How long before this Bible Student comes to a meeting?" Momma picks up a lasagna noodle with a pair of tongs, the steam rising around her face. I shift on my feet.

"She seems close. Next week, or the one after, Sister Nichols said," I say.

"Tomorrow is going to be a wonderful meeting. Brother Nelson is bringing us New Light from Jehovah. It would be nice if she came then." She says it like she's in a dream, like Jehovah bringing new rules is something to get excited about. And I don't matter.

"That would be a blessing to Jehovah. I will ask her," I lie as I slide out the door.

When I get to Val's, she's waiting for me on the porch. She pulls me inside and down a hallway lined with framed pictures of her family.

"You took forever," she says.

I drop my pack to the floor of her room and take the dress she holds out to me. The top is the color of emeralds, and the bottom is a creamy white. I've never owned anything this beautiful, let alone worn it.

"Put it on," Val says.

I slip it on. The dress shimmers in the light, the top clings to my sides, and the skirt hangs above my knee. Not modest in any way. Momma wouldn't approve, Jehovah neither.

I smile.

The sandals I wear are all wrong, too casual, with their flat heels and leather ties around my ankles. Val lends me a pair of her shoes. My feet slide, and I wobble on the narrow heel.

"Wait, those are wrong. Try this pair," she hands me another, the heel high but not so narrow.

"These are better," I say as I walk across the room, a little less wobble.

"You'll get it. Practice walking up and down the hall a few times," Val smiles. And I do. She brings out a pair of earrings for me to wear. I pull my hair back, revealing lobes that have no piercings. She shrugs and gets me a necklace instead. "There, perfect. Now for some makeup."

I cringe.

"It's only going to be a little bit. I promise," Val says.

"Okay," I say. What's wrong with some makeup when I'm already sneaking out to a dance?

After she lightly outlines my eyes with black, Val adds a shimmering shadow to my eyes and finishes with matte pink lipstick.

"You're ready!" She announces.

We pile into the back of her mom's car, my skin tingling with anticipation and a little fear. Will Gabe like my dress? Will I fall in the heels? What about actual dancing?

My phone buzzes in the tiny purse, also a loaner from Val. It's a text from Gabe, a smiley face, and a dancing boy and girl emoji. I smile and show it to Val. We both giggle.

Val and I enter the cafeteria. Its cold gray insides are transformed into a magical place. I stand at the edge, my toes touching the blue line marking the end of the lunch line. Holding my breath, I take in a long, slow look. Chaperones stand at the entrances and are scattered throughout the room. In the far corner, Mr. Balentine is directing a group of students who try to reattach a string of blue and white balloons to a slender white metal frame bent into an arch.

"That's where we get pictures taken," Val waves to Bailey, who waves back with the staple gun, and then aims it at Zoe, who pushes her away. "It's supposed to look like bubbles under the water. Come on," Val urges me forward.

"It's nice," I say softly. There's so much to take in. Small clumps of students huddle around the room, the dance floor empty. Criss-crossing the ceiling and around the edge of the room are thousands of blue and white twinkle lights. LED candles, starfish, and seashells are placed at the center of small round tables on the far side. Long strips of blue and silver streamers shimmer and twist like a metallic wave over the kitchen entrance along the back wall. Over the dance floor, fish cutouts hang from invisible wires, an octopus waves its arms, and a shark swims after a small fish darting away.

Val tugs me. "We need to get one of the good tables, or we'll be stuck along the wall." She drags out *wall*, and I know it's the worst place possible to sit.

We make our way through the tables, stopping at one in the corner. Val drops her sweater onto the back of the chair. "Last dance of ninth grade," she says.

"My first and last," I say, smoothing down my dress.

"You'll have more. There's homecoming, prom," Val smiles, and my stomach falls. There won't be any dances if I'm at New System School. "We're going to need some better ways to get you out."

"Where's Gabe?" I scan the crowd, craning my neck to see around a group of boys standing awkwardly by the entrance.

Mr. Balentine swoops in, his arms out wide. "Go on, gentlemen, don't be afraid. The fish aren't biting." The boys groan and shuffle away. Mr. Balentine spots me. Smiling from ear to ear, he clasps his hands together at his chest. "Sara, you're here. Your entries for the contest are wonderful. The one, 'Rachel,' is beautiful. There's something in her eyes. Like she's lost. I found a charcoal you did early this year. It was on display in the front office, remember?"

The charcoal in the office was one I had done when the Truth was still real to me—not a lie. It was a lone tree in a field. Not my best, but Mr. B. raved about it.

"I remember," I nod.

"Well, I grabbed it and entered it too. You're in three categories. Pencil, charcoal, and pen and ink."

"Really?" I ask. Too many good things are happening now. I feel like, at any moment, the floor will give way. I hear Momma's voice in my head. T*he World can't be trusted, they will always let you down. They'll use you and then throw you away.*

"I told you, you have natural talent," Mr. Balentine smiles.

"I might have something," I say, pushing Momma's voice out."I have something I drew. But it's on a piece of notebook paper. Is that okay?"

Someone calls out to Mr. B. from across the room, "It's perfect. Bring Monday to class," he says and hurries away.

I stare at the twinkle lights until they blur with tiny halos. The words "natural talent, beautiful" float around me. Someone taps me on the shoulder, and I jump.

"It's me," Gabe says.

"Sorry," I say.

"Well, I have someplace to be," Val says and hurries away.

"You look pretty. New dress?" He asks.

I feel the heat rise in my cheeks and hope he can't see the pinking rising on my cheeks in the dim light of the gym. A hush falls over the room as Zoe, in a dress the same color green as mine, taps on the microphone. She welcomes everyone to the dance.

The music starts, and Gabe takes my cold hand and pulls me toward the dance floor. He's holding my hand, what would Neena say? Or Cheri? I block out Jehovah and Satan, not letting them get a hold of my head. Erase Brad, Rachel, and everyone from my head. I only care about what's going on now.

Girls have their arms around the boy's necks, and boys have their hands on the girl's waists. This is wrong, all wrong. They're too close. They're touching. It's too much, too fast. I pull to a stop.

"Maybe a fast song would be better," I say.

"Okay," Gabe smiles. "I don't like this song anyway."

We stand at the edge of the dance floor, my arms hanging at my sides like two dead fish until the music changes and a fast song comes on. One I've heard before.

Gabe looks up at me and jerks his forehead to where the others are dancing. I nod and follow him out, my stomach churning.

At first, I'm not sure what to do with my feet or arms. I glance around and stiffly try to copy what the others are doing. It's not fair. What is wrong with this? Why did Jehovah have to make it wrong? I'm smiling and laughing by the end of the song, and time moves fast, so fast from there. It doesn't feel so wrong now. I wish this would never end.

The music fades and stops.

"Is it over already?" I ask.

"It is," Gabe says. "Ten o'clock."

"So, how was your first dance?" Val swoops in from behind.

"It was nice," I say, looking up to the tiny blue lights, amazed at how afraid I was that Armageddon could happen at any moment. I only wish Momma could have seen me and been happy for me. Or Neena.

Gabe shoves his hands in his pockets. "This was fun."

Bailey and Zoe join the circle. Bailey gives me a thumbs up. "Nice dress," she says.

"Thanks," I say.

"My mom can give you a ride home," Val tells Gabe.

"That'd be great. I'll text my brother not to come to get me," Gabe says, and I blush again, thinking of being so close to him in the car.

Gabe grabs my hand. This time, I don't ask Jehovah to forgive me. It feels good. We turn to go, and there she is – Momma.

I jerk free from Gabe. Val lets out a squeak.

The room spins around me, the voices and laughter fading into the background.

"Sara, what's wrong?" Gabe asks.

"Wow, her mom totally showed up," Bailey says behind me.

Chapter 28

I don't know what's worse, the sudden awkward silence, or the look on Momma's face as she scans the scene around me. Twisting her purse in her hands, the tips of her shoes barely cross the threshold of the gym, as if she's afraid Satan will attack her for being inside. She shakes her head in disapproval at my dress. Her mouth puckered as if she had eaten something sour.

I wrap my arms around myself, suddenly feeling very bare.

"Oh, hi, Mrs. Michaels," Val says, her voice like a bell in the silence.

"Hello," Momma says without looking at Val.

Shame washes over me for not telling Gabe the truth about me. He should have known. But then, I feel him next to me on one side, his sleeve touching my bare arm.

"Hello, Mrs. Michaels. We were just going to give Sara a ride home," he says.

Out of the corner of my eye, I see Bailey's purple hair as she steps up next to Val and Zoe on the other side. All of them unknowingly shielding me from Momma and Jehovah's wrath.

I hadn't expected this. It's nothing like what the Elders preach or what the Governors told me about the Worldly. I have friends…who care about me, no matter what I believe.

Mr. Balentine, oblivious to the thick tension, rushes past and introduces himself. Momma looks at his outstretched hand in distaste.

He raises a brow and drops his hand, wiping his palm on his slacks. "We are so proud of Sara and her recent success."

Momma's jaw tightens, a vein pulses on the side of her head. "What success?" She asks sweetly, looking right at me.

"The District Art Contest, she's moved to the State level. Didn't she tell you?" He looks from me to her. "Oh, did I spoil a surprise?"

"No, she didn't tell me," Momma says, her voice cutting. Her face like stone, her eyes slide to me. She's holding back. Every bone in her body wants to say something about art becoming my religion and how I bring shame to Jehovah, how it's all Worldly.

Mr. Balentine, unaware of Momma's anger and the tension between us, keeps on. "She won first place for Ninth Grade in the entire district. Because of that, she's moved up to the State level. It's amazing. She has such talent. If she keeps this up through high school, she could easily get into an art school."

Momma nods along, smiling, her façade not cracking.

I want to pull Momma away and make it stop, but Mr. Balentine keeps going about me and art. He talks about the free classes at the art museum I'd won over the summer, and Momma's face becomes like stone.

My chest aches. I used to believe like Momma. I could never do enough to please Jehovah. I was never sure I'd make it to Paradise. If I did one wrong thing, He'd forget me forever.

Gabe leans over and whispers, "What's going on?"

"I'm sorry," I whisper back, tears stinging my eyes.

Val grabs my hand and squeezes.

"I'm sorry, we have to go. It's very late, and I have little girls at home who need me," Momma announces, cutting off Mr. Balentine mid-sentence. She grabs me by the elbow, jerking me free from Gabe, Val, and Bailey.

"By all means. I hope you kids had a wonderful time," Mr. Balentine bounces on his toes. "I love these dances. They never get old. We always need parents to chaperone," he winks at Momma, who says nothing. "Okay, then. Nice to meet you."

"We need to go. Now," Momma says through her teeth.

Momma marches across the open quad. Her chin held high, her shoulders back. And I follow, looking back over my shoulder to see the disbelieving looks of my Worldly friends. No--I will not call them Worldly anymore. Just friends.

We pass students who whisper behind their hands, and I am angry. Not at them, but a Jehovah for not letting me live, for destroying everything that brings me happiness. My left shoe comes off, and I stumble forward. Momma stops with a sigh, her arms over her chest. "Maybe if you weren't wearing those prostitute shoes with high heels, you'd be able to walk."

"The heel's not high," I hold up the shoe. "Besides, Val's mother would never let her wear anything like that," I say, slipping the shoe back on. Momma shakes her head, clicking her tongue in disgust. I want to break free and run back inside to the twinkling lights and balloon arch. Biting back tears, I slide into the van.

Who told Momma I was here?

The ride home is a blur. Momma clutches the steering wheel, her lips tight, knuckles white. Upstairs, Rachel's room is dark.

As we pull into the driveway, a dark sedan pulls to the curb behind us. Brother Reed's car.

"You called them already?" My voice shakes. I grind my fist into the vinyl seat, where she can't see.

Her nostrils flare as she stares ahead mutely, her mouth frozen in a straight line.

"But..." I start to say.

"Quiet!" She snarls. "Inside. And don't make a fuss. I don't want the girls woken up." She holds the door open for me, motioning with her head to go into the living room.

The living room is free of the sheets covering the sofa and the lights on low, hiding the shabbiness from the Elders. A sliver of light peeks out from under Brad's study down the hallway. Make him stay in there, I plead.

"Sit down," Momma steers me into the living room. I sit stiff on the edge of the chair, the little purse Val let me borrow tucked into the side. I feel the hard edge of my cellphone and hope I've turned it off.

I want to beg Momma to end this. Tell her there's nothing wrong with what I did. But I can't; I don't. I stay silent. I wish for Rachel. How could I have been happy thirty minutes ago, and now everything is falling apart.

"I don't understand you, Sara," Momma says. She hurries around the room, fluffing a pillow and straightening a lampshade. She wipes nonexistent dust from one of the end tables. "With this one thing," she holds up her index finger, enunciating the number one, "you've destroyed your relationship with Jehovah. She leans forward, her eyes screwed into mine. "You've chosen to worship Satan over the Truth. You will never make it to Paradise."

"It was a dance," I mumble down to my feet like a little kid. A dull pounding starts at the back of my head. "What Brad did is wrong. Why isn't he being punished?"

Momma's face reddens with anger. "This is not about Brad. This is about you. It wasn't *just* a dance. Look at you. You're half-naked. Like a lost sheep, you've fallen for Satan and his tricks." She pulls a sweater from a hook near the door and holds it out an arms-length from her body as if it were dirty. "Your defiance has made you a threat to the spiritual well-being of your sisters. And then Rachel, what you did to her." She rubs her temples as if trying to make this all go away.

I take the sweater and slip it on. "What did I do to Rachel? Where is she? I want to talk to her." My bottom lip starts to shake.

Momma flinches, and her brows go straight. "You don't need to talk to Rachel." She pulls back the edge of the curtain and peers out into the darkness.

"She's my friend," I say. "Why can't I Momma?"

She spins back to me, her face rutted with anger. "She left. Went home. Your doing, of course. You let Satan into our home with your rejection of Jehovah and the discipline the Elders gave you. You certainly learned his tricks and deceit quickly."

I shake my head, covering my face with my hands. She's gone. Free.

It wasn't me who brought Satan into our home. I want to scream. It wasn't me who let the monster Brad stay here. There's a muffled sound of doors slamming and footsteps up the walk.

She steps closer, takes my chin in her hand and squeezes. "You better not make me look foolish in front of the Elders. You will tell them you're sorry and all of this was a big mistake. Do you understand?"

There's a knock on the door, and she lets her hand fall to her side as if she'd been squeezing fruit, not my face, to test for ripeness.

Brad comes out of his room. He looks at me, his eyes landing on my dress, shaking his head with a click of his tongue. I shiver and pull the sweater tighter. Slicking his hair down, he opens the door, and my head sinks to my chest.

"Good evening Brother Michaels," Brother Reed dips his head as he steps in. Behind him, Brother Wilson squeezes into the doorway.

The Elders stand close to Brad and Momma, the light from the crooked lamp casting sinister shadows on the wall. Their heads bobble as they listen to Momma, who shares my failures.

Momma sobs into her hands while Brother Wilson pats her back. "There, there. We're here now. We'll take care of this." He raises his head slowly, his eyes sliding over to me with a look of disapproval.

Goose pimples rise on my arms and legs as I shiver from the cold. Again, I pull my sweater tighter around me but cannot get warm.

They continue to whisper. Brother Reed says Rachel's name. My chest tightens, and my breath seems caught in my throat. They're blaming me for Rachel. They're going to Disfellowship me.

I wish I were anyplace but here. The back door is steps across the room. I could be gone before they noticed. But then Brad will still be here.

Could I really leave? Could I leave everything behind and go?

Upstairs I hear water running, and the hallway light flicks off. My shoulders sag, like my heart. I can't leave. Who will take care of Kaylee and Pearl? Not Momma. It's up to me.

Chapter 29

The Elders shuffle into the living room. Momma must be proud. The room she kept clean for them is finally being used, even if it's not how she intended. The Elders are in our home.

She stands silent with one hand around her waist and the other at her neck. Brad looks at me. His mouth pulled tight. Is he afraid of me?

Brother Wilson's shirt is wrinkled. His pants hang awkwardly, where his belt had missed one of the loops. He wipes the sweat from his doughy cheeks as he moves past Momma. The sofa squeaks as he sits. Letting out a sigh, he smooths his tie over his round belly.

Brother Reed takes the chair across from me, Momma's spot, and looks at me over the tops of his glasses. His eyes rest on my dress. I tug the hem down, but it's pointless; the dress is not long enough. I pull the sweater tighter, its itchy fibers scratching my bare skin underneath.

"I'm sure you've heard about Rachel by now," Brother Wilson says. He pulls his Bible, along with my discipline folder, out of his stiff leather bag.

"Not really," I say, putting my head down like a dutiful Sister.

Brother Reed shakes his head. "She's shifted her focus away from Jehovah. All because she listened to the doubts about the

Truth Satan put in her head. And, you started this chain of events with your Worldly ways and disobedience."

"She didn't. I didn't. Rachel is my friend. My sister," I say. My stomach churns.

"Enough about Rachel. She made her choice. She is no longer our concern or yours." Brother Wilson waves his hand as if he batted away a fly.

Like that, they'd erased Rachel. She's become nothing to them - dead. She's worse than the Worldly. Two weeks ago, she was a good example of a Sister that Momma wanted me to be. She was my shining example of a devoted follower of Jehovah. I cringe. I am going to be like Rachel. Just like her. Erased. Dead to them. I want to cry. Kaylee and Pearl–I'll never get to speak to them again. Color with Kaylee or even argue with Pearl. And Neena, my best friend since forever – never speaking to me, ever.

"We're here for you and your Reproof, and your failure to follow simple biblical instructions from Jehovah," Brother Reed says. He no longer looks like a grandfather to me. His face is pinched and tight.

I twist to look at Momma, pleading with her to make this stop. She moves back and leans against the doorway, the familiar vacant look on her face. "It's best if you leave us in private. This is between Sara and us," Brother Wilson says to Momma and Brad over the top of my head.

"And Jehovah," I whisper under my breath.

"What was that, Sara?" Brother Reed leans in, his nose sharp like the beak of a bird of prey.

"Nothing," I say, hiding the shake in my voice.

Brad takes Momma's hand, and they go down the dark hallway to their room at the back of the house.

Brother Reed rifles through his bag and brings out his Bible and a stack of papers, the edges curled like the hair poking out from his collar. Brother Wilson opens the familiar folder with my name on it. The pounding between my ears turns to pressure as if clamped into a vice. This is going wrong. This isn't what I planned. I need more time.

"Let's get started." Brother Wilson pulls a pen from the yellowed pocket of his shirt.

I try to breathe, but the air is still and heavy. My life has become a web of lies, and now I am trapped in it.

"What was our reason for putting you on Reproof and taking away your privileges?" Brother Reed asks.

"To make me understand how it feels like to be out of Jehovah's love. And being far from Him and not feeling His presence will make me return to Him," I say. I feel as if I'm floating above myself, looking down at a room full of strangers. I want to shake the girl who looks like me and tell her to run.

Brother Wilson twists his lips as he tugs at a blue ribbon hanging from the bottom of his Bible. Flipping it open, he stabs at the page with his finger, the nailbed dirty with grime. "Read this scripture." He passes it over to me.

I don't need to look at his Bible. The verse is instilled in all of Jehovah's followers, starting with the small children. The one we say every day. Momma had it written in a curly script, framed it, and nailed it to the wall beneath her rooster clock.

"Do not be misled. Bad associations spoil useful habits. 1 Corinthians 15:33," I recite. Gabe and Val aren't bad. Rory didn't mislead me. The only people who've mistreated me are those who love Jehovah.

"Do you understand what you've read?" Brother Wilson says down to me as if I were a kindergartener.

"Yes," I say. *Jehovah isn't real. The Elders lie. The Governors lie. I lied.*

"Your mother and stepfather are concerned about you and your spiritual state, and so are we. Tonight's act was one of complete defiance. You have brought shame on Jehovah's name," Brother Reed says.

"Shame?" I shrink down. I saw the look on Gabe's face when my mother showed up. I'd shamed him. I should have told him the truth about me. I should have told Rory too.

"Yes, shame," Brother Wilson nods his head.

Shaming Jehovah's name is why Momma and the Elders told Rachel and me not to report Brad. The World, they said, did not understand Jehovah's ways. The World, they said, would not protect us. It's clear now. I should have gone to the police, not the Elders. Now it's too late, and no one will listen.

"I am sorry. It was one small mistake," I say, my voice level and steady, hoping they don't notice the shake.

Brother Reed licks his lips and lets out a small laugh. "Small mistake? You haven't been following your discipline. Cheri tells me you missed your mentor studies. You lied to your mother, to me, and to Brother Wilson. You attended a Worldly dance. Look at your inappropriate clothing. Sara, your direct disobedience has allowed Satan into your heart and this home."

The words sting, and I want to fight back. But I don't. I must play their game. I can't be Disfellowshipped. I have to lie. It's the only way for me to stay. Everything...everyone I know is here. Disfellowshipped, the thing I've been dreading, the thing I've been trying to keep from happening. I'll never see my family again. Where will I go? The streets? A foster home?

I think fleetingly of Alyce Stephens. Can I trust her? Is she even my Grandmother? I never got to message her back; I should have tried harder.

The room spins. Bile rises into my throat. My chest feels empty as if there were a big hole in me. Every part of me spilled out and puddled at my feet.

"Let me read Jehovah's words," Brother Reed says. *"But now I am writing you to stop keeping company with anyone called a sexually immoral brother or a greedy person or an idolater or a reviler or a drunkard or an extortioner, not even eating with such a man."*

He shuts his bible gently and holds it between his hands as if they were bookends. I can't let them get to me. I am none of these things.

"There was nothing like that going on. I just wanted to dance," I barely whisper as I shrink back in my chair. They must believe me. They can never know about Gabe and how I feel about him. They can't know I don't believe in Jehovah or the Truth.

Brother Reed sighs as if the weight of the world were on his shoulders. "This is the second time we've met to discipline you because of your behavior. You understand what is going on, don't you?"

"Yes," I whisper, my head down and hands folded in my lap. Play the game. Play the game. Don't let them see the real you.

Brother Reed fixes his gaze on the paper in front of him. "Do you have a problem with Jehovah and his Organization here on earth?"

"No," I say.

My hands start to shake, I shove them under my thighs, and my purse falls to the floor with a thud. My breath catching in my throat, I remember my lifeline: I have a way out. Rory. Rory said she'd help me.

A plan begins to unfold as energy surges back into my body. I need more time – but is it too late already?

"Do you understand the Governing Body speaks for Jehovah?" Brother Reed asks, interrupting my thoughts.

"Yes," I say.

Brother Reed clears his throat and then makes a mark on the paper. "This boy you were with, have you let him touch you in inappropriate places?"

The heat rises in my cheeks. I shake my head fast, unable to answer, the words stuck in my throat.

Bother Wilson leans back, and the sofa groans. "And how did you feel about dancing with him?"

"I am ashamed," I mutter, tears leaking out. I'm not crying because I'm ashamed. I'm crying for the humiliation of having to play this game. I cry for the lies I've told to protect everyone. "I'm sorry that I did it. I was wrong."

"Good, a very positive sign," Brother Wilson says, and I look at him, surprised. Positive?

"Sara, you are showing remorse. All you need to do is show repentance and a willingness to seek Jehovah at all costs. We haven't checked all the boxes yet on your discipline form." Brother Reed takes off his glasses and polishes them with his tie.

The world seems to pause. I can Repent. I can keep playing their games; I don't have to leave home.

What do I do?

Brother Wilson smooths down the papers. "We understand it's hard being a teenager in this System of Things. But, with prayer from us, your Elders, and hard work on your part, you can have complete faith Jehovah will take care of you."

Lie. Jehovah doesn't take care of me. He never did and never will. I can never go back.

"Tomorrow is the District Overseer special talk. You don't want to mar the day by having an announcement about you being Disfellowshipped, do you?"   Brother Reed twists his pen. He wants to make the announcement, to pay me back for Rachel.

And then my cell phone starts to buzz.

Chapter 30

Brother Reed looks at me, his eyebrows arched high. My phone rings again, then buzzes. "Sara, are you hiding something? A phone, perhaps?" he asks.

"No, Brother Reed, I wasn't hiding anything. I forgot about it, that's all," I say, trying to sound sincere and not panic.

"I'm quite aware your mother and stepfather don't allow you girls to have cell phones or internet." Brother Wilson says as if he were talking to a small child.

The heat rises to my cheeks. I slip my hand into the purse and pull out the cell phone – my lifeline, my escape.

"Here, you take it." I hold the phone out in my shaking hand. "I'm sorry. Can we pray to Jehovah to forgive me?" I bow my head as Brother Reed takes the phone from my hand. My heart is pounding.

"That's very commendable of you," Brother Reed says.

I must pretend I love Jehovah more than anything else in the world. I've got to go back to being the invisible girl. I have to lie.

"Sara, Jehovah will only listen to your prayer if you are obedient to Him and have faith, of course. You do have faith in Him, don't you?" Brother Reed asks.

"Yes, I do," I say. "More than anything, I want to do what Jehovah requires. I want to live in Paradise on Earth."

"Well then, let's pray." Brother Wilson rubs his hands together, and we bow our heads. "Jehovah, we call on you because you have the Truth. We pray you will rescue our dear Sister Sara. Take away her desires for the World and her lust for the Worldly boy. Remove the doubt about your Truth from her mind. Forgive her where she has shamed your name. Amen."

I say my Amen loud. I stay seated with my head bowed. The words "shame," "lust," and "worldly" smolder inside me, sizzling just below the surface. Brother Reed calls Momma and Brad to come out. The four of them talk in the kitchen. I hear Momma gasp. Brother Reed must have told her about the phone.

The Elders leave, and Brad locks the door behind them. Momma stands over me, her eyes filled with rage. I'm already dead to her. "We'll talk in the morning. You sleep in Rachel's, your room," she corrects. "Away from the girls. I don't want you and your filthy Worldliness around them."

My feet are heavy as I climb the stairs. Momma follows. Just as I am about to ask why, she pushes past me without saying anything, and swings open the door to my old room. It still smells of Rachel. I fight back, the tears stinging my eyes.

"I'll wake you in the morning. You're not to leave this room until I come get you." Momma scowls. She's locking me in. She can't. She wouldn't.

"What if I have to go to the bathroom?" I ask, trying not to sound like I'm pleading.

"Hold it," she shuts the door.

I hear the twist of the lock. The lock is flimsy, and I can easily open it from the inside. But Momma is watching. She is probably at the bottom of the stairs. Keep up the lie. Momma has to believe.

Flopping down on the bed, I fight the feeling of the web pulling tight around me, sucking the life out of me. I can do this. A few more days. School is on Monday. It's my only chance to be away from her watchful eyes.

I fling off the sweater and shimmy out of the dress and into baggy sweatpants and a t-shirt Momma had left on the bed. Sitting on the edge of the bed, I stare out into the darkness at the back of Gabe's house. A light is on in the corner room on the second floor. Gabe's room?

I'm sorry, I whisper to him.

My eyes burn with tears, and I can't stop them.

I can make it. It's two days. All I need is two days.

Chapter 31

Because of the Circuit Overseer and his wife visiting, the Kingdom Hall is full, and people overflow outside. Even those considered "bad" Witnesses are here and on time. I hurry past Sister Winchester and her butterscotch candy. I shoulder through the groups in the entryway, feeling their eyes on me. The chain of gossip about Rachel and me has already made its way through the Sisters. They've already judged me.

I want to scream at them all, tell them the truth about Brad and what he'd done to Rachel. But no one here will care. They will only say I failed, and Rachel failed, to rely on Jehovah to work things out. I am the one who disobeyed the Governing Body. It was me who made Rachel leave the Truth.

I look for Neena. The familiar feeling of losing something close returns, and I feel more out of place and out of my body than before. I don't belong here. Kaylee tugs me to come on.

At the end of the row where my family sits, Momma looks up at me. "There are no seats together today," Momma says. "You'll have to sit in the back."

I drop Kaylee's hand. She looks confused as she slides down the row away from me. I turn and head to the back row, where the *bad* witnesses sit, and collapse into the only seat left—in the back, between an old Brother who smells like bread and dusty books and a gray-haired Sister who clicks her dentures in a nervous tick.

Neena and Cheri move past me, their heads bent together. Neena doesn't even acknowledge me. Something falls from her fingertips onto my lap, a piece of paper folded into a small triangle, like the notes we used to pass during Meetings when we were Pearl's age.

I fumble with the paper and unfold it corner by corner, my chest filling with hope.

I can't believe you went to a school dance! You are far away from Jehovah. I can't be your friend anymore – you will pull me away too. Stay away from my family and me. Don't try to talk to me or text me until you're back with Jehovah.

Tears well up in my eyes, and I wipe them away with my fingertips. Neena, who said she'd always be my friend no matter what, left me.

The congregation stands and sings. I stand too, but I don't sing. When the Circuit Overseer, Brother Nelson, steps up on the stage, we all sit in unison like soldiers. Soldiers something else Jehovah hates. His words evaporate into dust before they get to my ears.

I write in long, flowy letters along the edge of the page of my bible: *the Truth is a lie.* The old Brother next to me looks down and clicks his tongue. He goes to grab my pen, and I jerk it away.

I don't care what he thinks.

Monday morning, my heart races as I dress for school. It's warm outside, but I slip into an olive-green long-sleeved shirt and a denim skirt that reaches my ankles. I shift in the warped mirror. I'm modest. All of me covered except my ankles. I wonder if Momma will find fault.

All weekend, I'd done everything she asked without complaining. And I was never alone all weekend – except when I slept. Even then, Momma checked on me during the night. I ache to get out of the house. My fingers and toes itch to get to school, to see a happy face. I have to talk to Gabe. I have to tell him the truth.

I'll be free soon.

I pad down the stairs. Momma hadn't said I could leave my room yet, but school starts in twenty minutes, and it takes me fifteen to walk.

As I open the back door, Momma says from behind me, "Where do you think you're going?" I jump, and a tiny yelp escapes my lips.

"School," I say.

She shakes her head, and my stomach drops. "You won't be going to school today," Momma says, steering me toward the table. *What*? This can't be happening.

"I have to go," I say.

Her face hardens. "No, you don't. Your eternal life is at risk, and I won't have you bringing Satan into this home anymore. Have you thought about how you've risked the lives of your sisters too?"

I bite the inside of my cheek, fighting the tears. Heat sweeps over my whole body as I scream in my head. *Had she thought about Brad and how he hurt Rachel? How many others had he hurt? How many more are going to hurt?*

"Sit," she tells me, and I fall into the chair, my knees too weak to hold me up any longer.

"I have to finish ninth grade, Momma. I can't just not go to school," I say. What about the State Art Contest? I want to win that. I can't just leave school. And then there are my real friends. I keep those thoughts to myself. They would make Momma mad.

"You will, just not there. Next week, you'll start at the New System school. Brother Wilson pulled some strings and got you in." She clasps her hands together with excitement while my insides roll.

"No," I say. I cover my mouth with my hand.

"Enough," she says, and I jump. There's no use in trying to reason with her. She only cares about Jehovah. "Brad and I agree; Worldly school is over for you now. You've made a big mess of things. This morning's reading seems to be appropriate for you."

She grabs her morning study book and starts to read aloud, and I don't listen. I send myself far away, where I am drawing on a thick sheet of paper, a stick of charcoal pencil between my fingers. I smudge the hard edges; what I wish I could do to Momma.

All week, I am up before breakfast. I get dressed and walk Kaylee and Pearl to school with Momma. Then, return home to endless hours of reading from the Truth book. Over and over. I try to keep my eyes ahead as we pass Val's house; I slow down so she'll see me if she's home. I even think once about writing a note and dropping it at the end of her driveway, where the purple flowers blossom in an old wine barrel.

But I can't risk being seen; Pearl would tell on me for sure. And then, I wouldn't even go on this short walk. Or worse, Brad would take them to school.

At night, I'm sent to my room. Momma locking my door. The lock is changed to one I can't open from the inside.

There's no way out unless I climb out the window and drop two stories to the hard cement of our driveway.

I lay in my bed, envisioning Alyce Stephens. I see her purple dresses, red beads, smile, and the crinkles of happiness around her eyes and mouth. If she's my Grandmother, she *has* to want me. Somehow, I've got to do what I planned. I've got to get to Rory. She'll help me. I'm not afraid anymore of Momma or Jehovah. What can be worse than what she's already done?

Friday around lunchtime, Momma is worn out. After a morning of Field Service and a study with her new bible student, she sits me at the table with the Truth book and a bible. Today, my punishment is to write one chapter of the Truth Leads to Eternal Life book by hand and then a chapter of the bible. Lucky me, she let me choose which chapters to write.

Outside, rain pelts against the windows. Momma grabs her basket of clothes to be ironed and snaps open the ironing board near me. I feel her eyes on me as I begin to write, the iron hissing and spitting as she presses Brad's clothes.

"Am I going to school on Monday?" I ask, trying to sound excited and full of anticipation.

"Yes. It's all arranged. There were some details with the Elders and your reproof, but the school finally decided you could attend," she says.

"Good," I lie.

Then she yawns. "I'm so tired today. Lots of good work out in Field Service," she says. "I am thankful Jehovah will reward me for all my efforts."

"Mmhhh," I say, and keep writing.

She yawns again. She puts the iron down, pulls the plug from the wall, and my heart leaps.

"I'm gonna rest for a minute on the sofa before we pick up the girls. You keep writing. I can see you from where I sit," she warns.

And I can see you, Momma, I think.

My heart pounds in my chest as I hold my pen in my sweaty hand and bow my head over the paper. I keep writing a string of nonsense. *Jehovah is a lie. The Truth is a lie. Brad is a pedophile.* It doesn't matter. When she starts to snore softly, I place my pen down gently. It rolls across the table, and I cringe. I reach the chair beside me, where Momma left her purse.

The rooster clock ticks loudly. I have minutes before it lets out its awful crow and wakes Momma. I hate that clock. I fumble in her purse and find a few dollars in her wallet—bus fare. The bus will be at the Koffee Stop at the same time as the Rooster crows. Momma will be awake, but I'll be gone.

I move to go, freezing when Momma snorts loudly and makes a sound in the back of her throat. She shifts on the sofa. I wait until her snoring starts again and then creep to the front door, opening it slowly so it doesn't let out its familiar squeak. I look back once. Momma's head has flopped back, her mouth wide open. She's out.

"If only you loved me more than Jehovah," I whisper as I shut the door behind me.

Then I run. I run without looking back.

Chapter 32

Stumbling off the bus, I catch myself and race towards Rory's house, just around the corner. I'm almost there.

I check over my shoulder; Momma probably realizes I'm gone by now. I race down the street, not caring that I'm getting soaked by the rain. At Rory's, I press the buzzer and pound on the door. *Please be home. Please, God, let her be home.*

The front curtains move. Rory peeks out. She looks like I've woken her up from a nap. When she sees me, her tiredness becomes concern. The curtains flap back as she hurries to open the door.

"Sara? Are you okay? Come in," she pulls me in.

I rush in and stand in her entryway, dripping.

"Hold on, let me get you a towel." She runs off and comes back with a fluffy blue towel. I dry my hair and do my best with the rest of myself. She takes the blanket from the back of the sofa and wraps me up, telling me to sit, and I do.

"Where's Isabelle?" I ask.

"Miguel took her to the mall. What's going on? Where have you been? I've been texting. I've been very worried about you," her voice cracks.

I suck in a deep breath, and my lower lip quivers. Rory shifts and moves closer to me. She puts her arm around my shoulder and pulls me to her side. She smells like lemon and mint.

"I'm on your side. I won't judge you," she says, and her words undo me.

Tears escape the corner of my eye, and I start to talk. The words spew out of me, and I can't stop. My heart races like it's about to explode out of my chest. I tell her everything, starting from the day Rachel moved in. It bursts out of me; I barely stop for a breath. And then we sit there in silence.

For the first time in a long time, my stomach is still; there is no churning or burning up in my throat. Like that day in the park when I figured out Jehovah was a lie, I feel calm.

Rory sits back, her face pale. "Wow Sara. That's a lot to deal with on your own." She hands me a tissue. "So, what's your plan now?"

I swallow the lump in my throat and dry my face with the tissue. "I'm going to the Police." I say it matter-of-factly, no shame.

She nods.

"Do you think I should talk to Rachel first? Shouldn't she be the one to go?" I ask.

Rory pats my hand. "She should. I'm sure she's scared. And it has to be her choice. But since you're aware of the situation, you can't be silent. You need to go. You have to protect your sisters and other children in the congregation, let alone the community." She runs her hands through her hair. "What else has he done? Who else has he harmed?"

Why did Neena never want to come to our house? I always slept over at her house. Or, the way Cheri only came over when Brad was gone.

"He's hurt others. I'm positive," I say. I bow my head, biting back the tears again. "We should have gone right away."

"Sara don't blame yourself. You did the best you could with what you had. The important thing is you're doing the right thing now — because you understand it's the right thing. You're not doing anything against Jehovah."

"Rachel is going to hate me now."

I lift my head, tears rolling down my cheeks. Rory wipes them away with the tips of her fingers.

"Rachel isn't going to hate you. She may be angry, but you have to do this. You know that."

"Yes." I stand. "I'm ready."

Chapter 33

Rory stands to my right as we stare at our reflections in the Police Station's glass doors. The rain has stopped, and rays of sun shoot out from the clouds behind us. I'm wearing one of Rory's t-shirts and pair of her leggings. The shirt falls to my knees. Momma must be frantic, wondering where I am, wondering who I am telling. I glance over my shoulder, looking for Momma's rusty minivan, surprised it's not here.

"Ready?" Rory squeezes my hand.

I nod. My legs shake as I step forward.

The doors slide open with a whish of air. A woman, not in uniform, sits behind a tall counter, typing on a keyboard.

"What can I do for you?" She asks as we approach.

I stop in my tracks. Rory urges me forward.

"I'm Mrs. Garcey. How can I help you?" The woman asks, her voice even and sweet. She sits back in her chair, and it squeaks loudly.

I stand there, numb, the words caught in my throat. Once I say the words, I won't be able to undo any of it. It was different with Rory.

Mrs. Garcey looks from me to Rory. "Are you her mother?" She asks.

"No, I'm a friend," Rory says. She leans down and takes my hands in hers. "Sara, it's going to be fine."

"Sara," Mrs. Garcey's voice softens. She says my name like we've known each other forever. "Don't be afraid. I'm here to help you. I simply need a little info to get you to the right person."

I answer her questions, my voice shaking with each one. Mrs. Garcey, as if this is nothing new, taps away on her keyboard and squints at the screen, "Looks like you need Sergeant Meeks." She pauses and looks up at the clock. "She's not here."

I drop my head and start to move away.

"Wait, don't go," Mrs. Garcey stands up. "She'll be here in about 10 minutes. I was going to say, pick a chair and wait." She waves her arm at the empty waiting room and its rows of rigid plastic seats.

Rory thanks her and leads me to a chair. I shiver with cold and wrap my arms around my chest. When I'm done here, I won't have a home anymore. *Please, God, help me.*

"Sara, you're a little green. You, okay?" Rory asks. She goes to the vending machine, debates for a moment on what to choose. Finally, waves her phone, pushes a button and is rewarded with a few thuds as the soda drops to the bottom.

A door shuts at the end of the hallway. An officer, her hair pulled back in a tight knot at the base of her neck, her face scrubbed clean so that it shines, walks towards us. She stops, checks the paper she holds, and eyes the two of us.

"Rory? Is that you?" She asks.

"Gina?" Rory says, dropping her hands at her sides. "Are you Officer Meeks?"

Officer Meeks, smiling, nods her head. There is something familiar about her, around the eyes and mouth.

"The last time I saw you, you were Gina Nelson," Rory says, looking back at me. She holds the soda she bought me. "Sara, do you remember Gina?"

And then I realize my prayers have been answered. Officer Meeks is Brother Nelson's daughter. The daughter who no one ever talks about, like she never existed.

"Hi, Sara," Officer Meeks says. "Let's go in the back where we can talk privately." She eyeballs Mrs. Garcey, who quickly looks back to her computer.

Rory and I follow Gina down the long hallway and through an open area of blue cubicles where uniformed and plain-clothed police officers sit. A few look up from their computer screens and phones as we pass. Officer Meeks nods at them. Finally, we stop at the door, Interview Room, printed on the frosted glass.

I pause, my toes on the threshold.

"It's fine. It's just for privacy, nothing else. We can keep the door open," Officer Meeks says.

"I'm okay," I say.

The interview room is not what I imagined. Instead of a dark room with a one-way mirror and a single bulb dangling from the ceiling, it's bright, with a long slender window near the ceiling running the length of the room. There's an overstuffed sofa, matching chairs, and two tall plants in white planters. A small bookcase with comic books and magazines line the other wall. In the middle is a round table with four chairs and a computer.

"I didn't want to talk out there. First, Sara, you can call me Gina. You do remember me, don't you?" Officer Meeks—Gina—asks as she holds a chair for me to sit.

"I think you babysat me once. It was before Pearl was born. I remember you were kind to me. You brought big sticks of chalk, and we drew our silhouettes on the driveway. And then, you went away," I say, the wheels in my head churning. "You went away because you were Disfellowshipped, didn't you?"

Gina rests her elbows on the table and leans over. "I can't believe you remember that. And yes, I went away. I had a problem with one of the Witness boys, and my father, an Elder at the time, wouldn't do anything about it. He told me to rely on Jehovah. Jehovah would take care of it in his own time. The Elders didn't go to the police, claiming it would shame Jehovah. I knew it was wrong, so I went alone and reported it. I couldn't go home after that, but I was able to stay with an aunt in San Francisco. She wasn't a Witness. Then, I was disfellowshipped without the Elders meeting with me or me getting to say anything. Just like that," she snaps her fingers.

She tugs her phone out of her back pocket and scrolls through her pictures. She holds it up for me to see. It's a picture of her when she was a little older than me. Brother and Sister Nelson stand on either side of her, all of them squinting into the sun. It's how I remember her: her long brown hair hanging down to the middle of her back and freckles across her nose and cheeks. And her clothes, always modest, smelled of lavender fabric softener. "This was the last picture I took with my family." Her voice is sad as she puts her phone away.

"Oh," I say, shifting in my seat. I look to Rory, begging her to stay.

"Can I stay in here with her?" Rory asks.

"Of course. This isn't an interrogation; those rooms are on the other side of the building. You can get up and go if you need to," Gina says to me as she flips open the laptop, and Rory takes the seat next to me.

"I'm guessing this has something to do with a Witness?" Gina asks.

"My stepfather," I say, my voice cracking. My cheeks get hot.

"It's going to be okay, Sara. You're doing the right thing," Gina says, and I believe her. "Why don't we start with the basics. Name?"

I stiffen in the chair, and Rory takes my hand. Her butterfly bracelet touches my wrist. "You've got this. Everything is going to be okay," she says.

I look up through the long window, where I can see a patch of blue sky while, at the same time, rain pelts the glass. I take a deep breath and let it out slowly. This feels ok. It feels right. I feel better than when I told Rory.

"I'm ready. I'll tell you everything you need to know."

Chapter 34

When we're all done, my soda is warm, my mouth dry, and the rain has started again. Gina tells me Brad will be picked up and brought in, and CPS will be called to investigate. Sensing my fear, she says, "It's the normal process Sara. In this kind of case, it's what the law requires when children are put at risk or in danger. It's to keep the children safe."

"Momma is going to be mad," I swallow.

"Your Momma is going to be mad no matter what. You did the right thing," Rory assures me.

Gina frowns. "Do you have a place to go? Other family, family who aren't Witnesses?" She knows Momma won't want me back in the house.

"Sara can stay with me. If she wants to," Rory says. My chest clenches. What about Kaylee and Pearl? They don't have anyone. Will they end up in foster care?

"Take a breath, Sara. It's going to be ok. I've seen cases similar to this. I'm not sure, but your sisters may be taken from the home for a bit. You did the right thing. Don't ever doubt that," Gina says. It doesn't take away the tightness in my chest.

"You need a place to stay. Because you can't go back to the Truth," Rory says.

"I know. And I don't want to. But I also don't want to leave Kaylee and Pearl," I sigh.

"I understand. We both understand. If you don't go back, do you have a place, long-term?" Officer Meeks asks.

I look to Rory. "There's a lady I found on Facebook. She says she's my Grandmother. I was in the middle of trying to figure it all out when Momma took my phone."

"We can find out. You have her name, your father's name?" Gina asks. "We'll be able to track her down. But most likely, you'll have to go home today."

"Once Momma finds out what I did, I am probably not going to be able to go home."

"She's more than welcome to stay with me until her Grandmother is found," Rory says. She puts her arm around my shoulder.

"That's certainly an option. Whatever happens, I will make sure your sisters are okay," Gina says.

"What about Brad? When will they get him? And Momma? Is anything going to happen to her?" I feel queasy again.

"Sometime today," Gina says. She looks at her computer screen. "The warrant has already been issued. As for your mother, someone will go to your home, or she'll be asked to come in for questioning."

"So fast?" Rory says.

Gina nods.

"What about Rachel?" I ask.

"I'm going to give her a visit," Gina says, and I feel the blood drain from my face. I shouldn't have spoken for Rachel. She made me promise. "Sara, breathe again. It's going to be okay. It might be a little overwhelming for her and confusing. You've been through the worst part." She shuts her laptop and looks at me, really looks at me, not the way Momma does when I try to talk to her or the way Neena used to when we'd sit up for hours talking—this is different. Gina truly understands. She gets it. She's been in the same place as me before and had the same thoughts as me going through her head. She had her heart torn into pieces.

"You're doing the right thing, Sara. I promise," Rory says. "It's going to work out."

"Thank you for that," I say, even though it doesn't feel that way.

We follow Gina out the way we came, weaving down long hallways until we're at the front entrance again. My body aches as if I'd run a marathon. My stomach gnaws with hunger or maybe fear about what's coming. Gina and Rory exchange words, and then we leave. We race to the car through the pouring rain, both of us drenched by the time we get in.

"You must be hungry," Rory says. "I know I'm famished."

"I am, but…I want to see Rachel. If you'll take me, it might be my last chance," I say.

"I thought you might say that," Rory says. "Let's go."

Rory drives us through a fast-food restaurant where we get burgers and fries. I nibble on my fries and sip at my soda, too nervous to eat. We pull up to Rachel's house and wait outside the pale brick wall, ivy creeping up the sides and along the black iron gate. The house is massive.

"I guess this is it," I say, my hand on the door handle.

"You want me to come with you?" She asks.

"I should go alone. Rachel doesn't know you," I say.

Rory nods as she takes a sip of soda. I push the door open, and a tree branch shakes in the wind, sending a cascade of water over me. I shake it off and hurry to the front door, letting the gate shut gently behind me.

I press the center of the Ring dial, knowing whoever's inside can see me. There's a clamor of little dogs barking. Through the rippled glass, I see a shape, dark and tall. Rachel's dad? I can't tell. The dogs continue barking, and the dark shape doesn't move. I press again; this time, the shape moves, and a garbled voice tells the dogs to be quiet. The door flings open, and Rachel's dad, Mr. Cummings, stares down at me.

"I, uh, came to see Rachel," I say.

"Sara, right? Come on in," he says, looking over my shoulder like maybe I brought my army of Jehovah's people with me.

I step in. The three little white dogs dance around my feet as he shuts the door.

"Rachel told me a lot about you. Of course, we met before," Mr. Cummings says. The dogs, having lost interest in me, wander off.

"Can I see her?" I twist my hands behind my back. What had Rachel said about me? Maybe she doesn't want to see me.

"She's up in her room. She'll be glad to see you. Go on up, third door on the left." He doesn't follow me as I start up the stairs.

A door opens at the end of the hall, and Rachel steps out. She grins when she sees me, like she's both happy and afraid I'm here.

"Come on in," she motions, closing the door behind me. Her room is as I imagined. The walls are painted a pale pink, the color of cherry blossoms. Her bed is covered in layers of pillows and a smooth white spread. There's a narrow desk with her open laptop and a bookcase filled with trophies and books.

She wraps her arms around herself and sits in the chair, the same color as the walls. "Sit," she says. I move stiff-legged to the matching chair across from her and sit on the edge, hoping I don't leave a stain or mark. "I'm glad you came," she says. "I've been worried about you. I didn't have any way to let you know I was leaving."

"I know. It's okay. I came to tell you...I'm sorry," I say.

She tilts her head and raises a brow. "For what? You didn't do anything wrong. If anything, you saved me," she says.

"I could have done more, and Brad should have never," I say. She inhales sharply, and I stop.

Rachel looks to the ground, and then out the window. There's so much more I want to say, but I don't know where to start. My head aches with all the talking I've done today.

"You did what you could Sara," she says.

I shake my head. It's now or never.

"Rachel, did you tell your parents about Brad?" I hope she has. But I know if she had, her parents would have gone to the police right away, and Brad would already be in jail where he belongs.

Still looking out the window, she shakes her head slowly and says, "No. I didn't. Brad told me that if I told anyone, he would hurt Kaylee, Pearl, and you too. He said awful things that scared me." She turns back to face me. Tears stream down her face she wipes them away with the back of her hand. "Sara, I was so scared. I'm still scared. And trapped. I was sure after all I'd done and said to my family, they wouldn't want me back. Elders, your mom, the Sisters, everyone told me my family would hate me for leaving them for Jehovah. They were wrong."

Branches caught in the wind tap at the window. I drop my hands, sliding them under my thighs, so Rachel doesn't see them shake.

"Rachel, I am sure he hurt others, maybe Neena and Cheri," I chew at my thumbnail, then drop my hand into my lap. "I went to the police. I told them about Brad," I say.

She looks up at me wide-eyed, shaking.

"I had to; it was the only way," I plead. "I know I should have asked you first." I bury my face in my hands and start to cry. I hear her pad across the room and know she's angry with me. I should have told her first.

"It's okay," Rachel says, placing a box of tissue on my lap. "You did the right thing. I wish I were as brave as you."

"Really?" I look up at her.

She nods. "Jehovah messed with my head. I should have gone right away, listened to my gut, not the Elders." I wipe my nose with a crumpled tissue as she says, "We can't blame ourselves. It's Brad, the Elders...Jehovah. All of them. We're the victims. I know that now."

I nod, feeling a weight lifted off my chest. I reach into my pocket and pull out the card Officer Meeks gave me.

"Officer Meeks, she's Brother Nelson's daughter. She's helping me—a lot." I say. Rachel takes the card, its edges bent. "You should probably tell your parents. Officer Meeks, Gina, is going to be calling or visiting you," I say as I stand.

"She's Brother Nelson's daughter?" Rachel asks.

I nod. "Yes, and...she gets it. She knows about the lies. She was a victim, too," I say.

Rachel stands and pulls me into a hug. "Thank you, Sara, you've been a good friend." She pulls away and tucks the wet strand of my hair behind my ears. "I know you've sacrificed everything to do this. If you need anything, let me know. Anything at all."

Chapter 35

Four Weeks Later

Brad is in jail. Rachel told Officer Meeks everything, and he's awaiting trial. No one came to bail him out, not even the Elders. I went home. Momma said she wanted me. But she didn't really. Momma only kept me at the house because she wanted to look like a good mother to CPS. Kicking out her fifteen-year-old daughter, who reported her stepfather's abuse, would make her look bad, and then she'd lose Kaylee and Pearl. That would be too much shame for Jehovah to bear.

Momma acted as if I was dead. No surprise there. I was invisible to her like I used to want to be to the World. It was the World that saved me – not Jehovah or the Truth. Those were the lies. Pearl was a professional at ignoring me. But Kaylee couldn't do it, even when she was punished.

Momma switched Kingdom Halls to one on the other side of town, where they don't know her or Brad. It's 45 minutes each way, and sometimes she's late and has to sit in the back row with the other "bad" witnesses. At least, that's what Kaylee tells me. I don't go to the Meetings. I will never set foot in a Kingdom Hall again. Momma had to get a job, like Sister Nichols, to pay rent and buy food. The house costs too much, and they'll be moving soon. I'm not going with them.

Momma doesn't want to bring me anyway; I'm Disfellowshipped. I'd bring shame to her fresh start at a new Kingdom Hall. No one there knows about me or Brad, or Rachel.

The investigators and CPS brought charges up against Momma. To keep Kaylee and Pearl, she must attend parenting classes. Pearl, Kaylee, and I were assigned counseling sessions, not with Elders, but with real counselors. When Momma tried to fight it, saying the Elders knew what was best for the family, CPS disagreed.

Every night, I read my little sisters a bedtime story, one I choose - a book without Jehovah. And they like it. But, because Momma censors the bookshelf, I don't have many choices, so they get Charlotte's Web and the Secret Garden. I wanted to read them books like, "Holes," "When you Reach Me" and "Harry Potter." But, according to Jehovah, those books are full of witchcraft and magic.

I wish I didn't have to leave, but I do. I can't live here, not like this.

Today, after the State Art Show Ceremony, where I won first place in two divisions, I'll be gone.

I twirl in front of the mirror, my new dress swirling around my knees—a gift from Rory. I slip into my new heels with narrow straps around my ankles. Val and I had gone shoe shopping together and gotten pedicures. Momma made a face like sour lemons when she saw the shoes and the blue nail polish on my toes but said nothing. How could she? I was dead to her.

I look around my room one last time; everything is gone. The walls were stripped bare, my bed pushed into the corner, and the fluffy comforter the color of weak lemonade rolled up in the corner. This time it's bare because I choose it, not because of Momma.

My phone buzzes; a text from Val.

Come and see me before you go to the art show.

Ok. Why?

We have a present for you.

We?

You'll see.

A horn honks outside. I look out my window, down at the little silver Honda. Through the glare on the windshield, I see a flash of purple. *She's here.*

I smooth my emerald green (my new favorite color) dress one last time, grab a bag in each hand, and bound down the stairs. Momma sits at the kitchen table, her bible in front of her, boxes with my name crossed off, and "kitchen" written in bold letters stacked against the wall behind her. Kaylee and Pearl wait for me at the bottom of the steps. I bend to hug them, and Momma snaps at them to move away from me.

My heart is crushed when they both listen and back away.

Kaylee's eyes are filled with tears. Pearl has her chin down to her chest. I drop my bags and pull them in for a hug anyway, my neck wet with Kaylee's tears. "I'm always here for you," I whisper and press a small drawing I did of a butterfly into her pocket so Momma can't see. On the back is my phone number. I press a book into Pearl's hands, Charlotte's Web. I'd done the same on the back page—drawn a butterfly with my phone number written along the edge of its wings.

"Bye, Momma," I say, standing over her, my shadow falling over her bible. She doesn't look up at me as her finger follows the scripture. "I'm leaving." Still, she says nothing. I wish it didn't hurt; I wish I could be as numb as she is. But I have to go.

I leave through the front door, shutting it quietly behind me. As I walk down the cracked sidewalk toward the end of the driveway, I look up to see Pearl and Kaylee waving to me from the front window. I ache for Momma to run out the front door and tell me she messed up. Wrap me in a hug and ask me to stay.

She doesn't.

Instead, the front blinds are snapped shut, and I can no longer see the faces of my little sisters.

Alyce, my grandmother, waits for me in the car. As I near, the windows go down with a whir, and she gets out and wraps me in a hug. Her hair smells like I imagined it would: lavender and mint with a hint of pencil shavings. She's an artist like me.

"I'm sorry, my dear. We'll figure something out with your sisters. I promise," she says, looking up to the window. I swallow down the tears. I don't want to cry anymore. Not today.

She'd come through for me. When Momma found Jehovah, she'd disconnected from my father's family and her own. When birthday cards, Christmas presents, and letters came, they were sent back unopened, and then Momma moved. My Grandmother lost track of us until she found me on Facebook.

"I can't believe you just finished ninth grade, and you're getting the award for the State Art competition," Gran says as she takes one of my bags.

I pick up the other. "Me neither," I say, my stomach dipping in a good way, like on the day Mr. Balentine announced in front of the whole school I'd won. "Can we stop at Val's on the way? She has something for me."

Gran pushes her glasses up and starts the car. "Of course, we can. We have plenty of time."

Val, Gabe, and Bailey wait in front of Val's house. Gran pulls to a stop. I rush over to my friends, wishing Neena could be here too, while Gran stands in the porch's shade with Val's mom.

"Nice dress," Bailey says. Today, her hair is bright pink on the left and blue on the right. She wears a head-to-toe black that matches the color of her nails.

"You look pretty, too," I say.

"I wasn't going for pretty. But I'll take it," Bailey laughs.

"I wish you didn't have to go," Val says.

"There's no other way. Not now," I say. I leave off how my mother wouldn't say goodbye.

Gabe grabs my hand and then hugs me. I inhale deeply, smelling him. I don't want to forget his smell or the feel of his arms around me. I don't flinch or ask Jehovah to forgive me. I'm doing nothing wrong.

"I wish you didn't have to go either," he whispers, kissing my cheek. "We were just getting started."

"Me too," I whisper back.

"Michigan is so far away," he pulls back.

"I know. We can talk and text. And we'll always have the dance," I say.

He smiles so his dimple shows and squeezes my hand.

"Here's your present." Val pulls a pink bag topped with white tissue paper from behind her back.

"We all pitched in," Bailey says. "Zoe too. She couldn't be here though."

I pull out the tissue paper, and inside is a new sketchpad, my name embossed on the bottom, a set of charcoals, and a Santa Clara High School t-shirt.

"Okay, the book and charcoals I get, but the t-shirt?" I ask.

"That was my idea. I figured you'd miss us at your new art school, and you could wear that. It'll be like we're with you," Gabe says.

I reach over and hug him. And then Val and Bailey join so I'm wrapped up in them all.

"I'm so excited for you," Val says. "You're going to a school with art, music, and acting."

"I'm jealous," Bailey says. "I'd love to be able to be on stage acting instead of Algebra."

"Gotta go, kiddo," Gran says.

I pause as I get into the car, looking down the street one last time at the ugly coral-colored house, its curtains closed, blinds shuttered to the outside. I suck in a breath, the hole in my chest gone, replaced with something that feels like... promise. Hope.

Everything feels lighter now. The Truth is no longer weighing me down. I've found my truth, one that loves without conditions and judgment, even though it means losing my family and friends. My heart will never stop hurting from that.

"I can't wait to meet my cousins," I say to Gran as a blue butterfly lands on the hood of the car. It opens and closes its wings slowly, soaking up the sun.

"They can't wait to meet you, my dear," she says. She looks at the butterfly. "You know what a blue butterfly means?"

"No, Gran, what?" I grin. Every conversation with her is easy. No heaviness like with Momma. It's genuine.

"It signifies promise and hope." She lifts the sleeve of her sweater, revealing two blue butterflies tattooed on the inside of her wrist.

"Promise and hope," I repeat as the butterfly lifts and hovers near me as if staring into my soul. Then in a blink, it flits away.

"They also say a blue butterfly can be an angel guiding you."

As we drive away, I hold Gran's hand, rubbing my thumb over the tattoo on her wrist, over promise and hope.

"My command is this: Love each other as I have loved you. Greater love has no one than this: to lay down one's life for one's friends."
- John 15:12 and 13 Holy Bible, New International Version

REFERENCES

I tried my best to use actual quotes from the books and magazines published by the Watchtower Bible and Tract Society for the Jehovah's Witnesses. I have used the online library at JW.org, which sometimes differs from the printed material.

From Chapter 1 Opening

"To remain loyal to Jehovah, we need to avoid associating with those who are disloyal to him. We also need to separate ourselves completely from false religion." Truth Book

From: The Enjoy Life Forever!–An Interactive Bible Study Course, Lesson 58 (Summary)

From Chapter 3

"If we want to live eternally in Jehovah's New System we must acknowledge His one true church and its foundation." The Truth that Leads to Everlasting Life, Watchtower Bible and Tract Society

From: The Truth That Leads to Eternal Life. Chapter 13 The True Church and Its Foundation

From Chapter 9

"This world has nothing good to offer you. Those who have gained the most of what it has to offer are among the most unhappy, selfish and burdened people of all. Note how the Bible appraises this world: "Everything in the world—the desire of the flesh and the desire of the eyes and the showy display of one's means of life—does not originate with Jehovah, but originates with the world. Furthermore, the world is passing away and so is its desire, but he that does the will of Jehovah remains forever." Youth Get Saved, The Youth Book.

From: Youth, Get Saved from This Crooked Generation, The Watchtower Announcing Jehovah's Kingdom—1964

From Chapter 16

It is not always easy for us to obey God. We live in a wicked world that is ruled by Satan. He tries to influence people to do what is bad. We also have to fight against our own imperfect thoughts and feelings, since they can lead us to disobey Jehovah..."

From: How to Remain in God's Love Chapter 1

FAQS ABOUT JEHOVAH'S WITNESSES

These are some of the top questions I'm asked about the Jehovah's Witnesses.

Q: Are the Jehovah's Witnesses a cult or an extreme religion?

The Jehovah's Witnesses are a high-control cult. Some assume this group is harmless because of their outward appearance and dedication to God (Jehovah). This is not the case. They believe that the end of the world is coming any day. Jehovah will destroy everything, leaving only his true followers behind to live in a Paradise on Earth. Not a Jehovah's Witness – you won't make it.

A cult, by definition, is a group or movement held together by a shared commitment to a leader or ideology. It has a belief system that answers life's questions and offers a special solution that can only be achieved by listening to and following the leader's rules. It requires a high level of commitment. Below is a list of some of the warning signs of a cult. Jehovah's Witnesses fit all of these.

10 Warning Signs of a Cult from Cult Education

1. Absolute authoritarianism without meaningful accountability.
2. No tolerance for questions or critical inquiry.
3. No meaningful financial disclosure regarding budget, and expenses, such as an independently audited financial statement.
4. Unreasonable fear about the outside world, such as impending catastrophe, evil conspiracies, and persecutions.
5. There is no legitimate reason to leave. Former followers are always wrong in leaving, negative or even evil.

6. Former members often relate the same stories of abuse and reflect a similar pattern of grievances.
7. There are records, books, news articles, or television programs that document the abuses of the group/leader.
8. Followers feel they can never be "good enough."
9. The group/leader is always right.
10. The group/leader is the exclusive means of knowing the "truth" or receiving validation, no other process of discovery is really acceptable or credible.

(https://culteducation.com/warningsigns.html)

Q: *Why don't Jehovah's Witnesses celebrate birthdays?*

Jehovah's Witnesses believe celebrating a person's birth displeases Jehovah. They believe that birthday celebrations originated from the pagan beliefs that evil spirits and influences can attack the celebrants on a person's birthday. The presence of friends and the expression of good wishes help protect the celebrant. They also claim that the early Christians did not celebrate birthdays. There are no examples in the bible of good servants of God celebrating. The only examples of birthdays are bad, John the Baptist losing his head, for example.

https://www.jw.org/en/jehovahs-witnesses/faq/birthdays/

Q: *Are all Jehovah's Witnesses like the ones in this book?*

This book is based on my personal history and the life stories of a few close friends. My family was strict and abusive. While some families are not as severe, Jehovah's Witnesses believe staying separate from the Worldly protects them from Satan's influences. While you may find some that seem to meld into both worlds, chances are the reason is because of fear of fully leaving Jehovah.

The Elders and Governing Body do not regulate each person or family's specific rules, leaving many things up to personal preference. Still, there are rules put in place that all Jehovah's Witnesses must follow.

Here are a few:

- Brothers are not allowed to have beards.
- Sisters cannot pray aloud if a Brother is in the room.
- Attending weekly Meetings is mandatory, and so is preparing by studying the material beforehand. When I was a child, there were three Meetings a week.
- Field Service (going door to door, street corner preaching) is mandatory. It must be recorded on a timesheet and turned in weekly.
- Jehovah's Witnesses dress to glorify Jehovah. Sisters are not allowed to wear slacks or pants; their clothing must be modest. Brothers must wear suits or slacks, a sports coat, and a tie.
- Brothers cannot wear tight-fitting pants. And they are told it is because it attracts unwanted sexual attention from homosexuals.
- Dating is prohibited. If a Brother or Sister is interested in each other, they can court with a chaperone.
- No movies above PG.
- Absolutely no blood transfusions.
- Organ transplants were once forbidden, then allowed, then forbidden – and now allowed.
- No voting.
- No military.
- No saluting of the flag or saying the Pledge of Allegiance.
- Sisters may not teach Brothers. Sisters cannot lead a congregation in prayer or song.
- There is no divorce unless one member commits adultery.
- Homosexuality, gender-neutral, etc., are wrongdoing and not allowed.
- Holidays and National Observances are not to be celebrated (Fourth of July, Thanksgiving, Christmas, Birthdays, etc.)

- Do not say "God Bless You" after someone sneezes.
- No sex before marriage.
- No oral sex – even in marriage.
- No masturbation.

JW.ORG Does Your Style of Dress Glorify God?
JW.ORG When Can I Start Dating
JW.ORG Questions Young People Ask – Answers That Work/Sex and Morals

Q: Do Jehovah's Witness go to college or university?
Seeking higher education is highly discouraged. "Higher education can lead to moral and spiritual dangers." "You will come across educated Jehovah's Witnesses. For the most part, these Witnesses gained their education before converting. A career path must be something that does not get in the way of Jehovah. Many Witnesses take jobs or have their own businesses so they can devote enough time to Jehovah each week. Many work in service industry jobs: house cleaning, night shifts, pool service, etc.

JW.org – JW Education and School

Q: Why don't Jehovah's Witnesses vote or join the military?

Witnesses are to stay separate from the Worldly governments, as they see them as opposed to Jehovah. They follow the laws, except for any that ask them to break what they see as a direct commandment from Jehovah.

Q: When did this cult first start?

The Jehovah's Witnesses' roots go back to the 1870s when a minister named Charles Taze Russel originated the Bible Students. In 1915 when Mr. Russel died, the group was taken over by Joseph Judge Rutherford, and the movement split into several directions. Mr. Rutherford began publishing his magazines and books and created the Watch Tower Bible and Tract Society of Pennsylvania. In the 1930s, the cult was fully developed, and the groundwork for their belief system was laid. Early Jehovah's Witness celebrated holidays.

Q: Is the Two-Witness Rule real?

Yes, this is a rule of the Jehovah's Witnesses. And sadly, it is not one most find out about until it's too late. This rule is not discussed on the Jehovah's Witness website. People studying or learning to become a Jehovah's Witness do not know about it.

The two-witness rule comes from a verse in the bible found in Deuteronomy 19:15.

"No single witness may convict another for any error or any sin that he may commit. On the testimony of two witnesses or on the testimony of three witnesses, the matter should be established.

In the Jehovah's Witness belief system, any wrong committed by one Witness to another requires two or three others' testimony, just as the verse says. The victim must face the person who committed wrongdoing against them in front of two or three Elders. The Elders then use their book, The Shepherd of the Flock, to administer counsel and/or punishment.

Q: Why don't the Jehovah's Witnesses accept Blood Transfusions?

Jehovah's Witnesses will take you back to what is in the bible about this, saying the bible commands not to ingest blood. They take this to mean that blood in any form, whether offered as food or transfusion.

Genesis 9:4. God told Noah: "Only flesh with its soul—its blood—you must not eat." This command applies to all mankind from that time on because all are descendants of Noah.

Leviticus 17:14. "You must not eat the blood of any sort of flesh, because the soul of every sort of flesh is its blood. Anyone eating it will be cut off." God viewed the soul, or life, as being in the blood and belonging to him

Acts 15:20. "Abstain . . . from blood." God gave Christians the same command that he had given to Noah. History shows that early Christians refused to consume whole blood or even to use it for medical reasons.

Jehovah's Witnesses carry medical directive cards noting that no blood will be given in an emergency. Some Elders will go to hospitals, speak with doctors, and ensure that a Witness does not have a transfusion. Or sit in the room with the sick person making sure the family doesn't persuade them to have a transfusion.

JW.org Bible Teachings – Questions about Blood Transfusion

Q: Why do they call their buildings Kingdom Halls? Why do Kingdom Halls have little or no windows?

Jehovah's Witnesses do not want to be any part of Christendom (organized Christian religion), which they believe is Satan's work in this world. To stay separate, they make sure their buildings of worship are plain and do not stand out. Many are built by the hands of volunteers. The insides are unadorned, with religious art. As a child, the Kingdom Halls I went to had folding chairs placed in rows.

Unlike a Christian church or house of faith of any other religion, a person cannot just walk in off the street and attend a service. You will be stopped at the door by a friendly Elder and asked a series of questions – you will not be welcomed as a visitor but be treated more like a threat.

Q: Why do the Jehovah's Witnesses go door to door or stand on street corners?

This is part of the belief that they must preach about Jehovah and Paradise on Earth to everyone. Once every person has heard, then the end will come.

Q: *What happens if someone no longer wants to be a Jehovah's Witness? Can't they stop being one?*

The short answer is no. A person cannot just leave and stop being a Jehovah's Witness. There are options. First, it depends upon how deeply involved a person is. If it is someone who is just studying, then they can leave. However, they will be contacted by the person they were studying with for an extended time. I want to point out that while a person is studying, they don't learn everything about the cult at once. It is a slow process. And no one attends a meeting at the Kingdom Hall until the person studying with them thinks they are ready.

Some Jehovah's Witnesses can leave, put the regimented, dictated life behind them, and move on. But it's tough mentally and emotionally, especially if they leave family and friends behind.

Most are trapped in this life because, for them, it means losing everything they know. It means losing all of their friends, and all of their family and starting over. It means realizing that they had believed a lie and focused their whole life on it. They are scared of the outside world, mistrust others, and many have PTSD, Depression, and Anxiety.

Cult Resources:

Cultwatch: https://www.cultwatch.com/

Freedom of Mind Resource Center: https://freedomofmind.com/

A Little Bit Culty – Podcast: https://alittlebitculty.com/

Help For Jehovah's Witnesses:

AUTHORS NOTE

Thank you for reading my novel, The Truth is a Lie. This novel is based upon actual life events in my life. I have changed the names of the people involved. Some people, except Sara and Gabe, are real people that I combined to simplify the story. Sara and Gabe are all real (names changed, of course).

Sara's story is not uncommon in the world of Jehovah's Witnesses. Sadly, it's one I've heard many times while doing research.

My world turned upside down when my mother became a Jehovah's Witness when I was six. I no longer had any holidays, birthdays, certain books and movies, music, etc. Not only were we in a doomsday cult, but my mother and stepfather were also abusive. I was also cut off from my extended family. I rarely got to spend time with aunts, uncles, or cousins. All of my friends had to be part of the cult. I was allowed to have a few Worldly friends, but I could only see them at school. There were no dances, parties, sleepovers, movies, or talking on the phone – none of the usual things kids do. From six until sixteen, I didn't know this life was not normal. I thought this was how everyone lived except for the TV families.

When I was asked to leave home because I had a Worldly boyfriend, I was thrown into the real world, which I was taught was evil and scary. But, because of the blue butterfly I'd found when I was seven, I knew Jehovah and his Truth were a lie. I kept my mind on the butterfly as much as possible while growing up in an emotionally, physically, sexually, and spiritually abusive home. This story is one that needed to be told. I tell it to protect the other Saras and Rachels out there.

I started this book years ago after attending SCBWI Regional Conference in Los Angeles. I signed up for a class titled "How To Fictionalize Your True Story." I'd already mulled over the idea of writing this book but wanted it in the hands of young adults, the people who were the age I was when I got out. I didn't want to write a memoir. When the third speaker finished her story, I was in tears. I got up and walked out to get some air.

Standing in the hallway of the hotel conference center was a woman. She was getting a breath too. I looked at her name tag and immediately recognized her last name. It was Gabe's last name. A very long, uncommon name. One no one could ever say. But I knew it. When I asked her if she knew Gabe, she looked shocked. But then, she smiled and said Gabe was her cousin.

I took it as a sign! I moved forward and wrote the book!

ACKNOWLEDGMENTS

Big thank you to my family, Andrew Heob, Steven Heob, Benjamin Heob, and Naomi Wongwui, for supporting me through my dream and putting up with my mom quirks. I raised you all to explore life, choose happiness (because, yes, it is a choice), find what brings you joy, ask questions, and love without conditions. I am so proud of all of you—whether you're playing music to a crowd, working a job and doing your best, serving your country, taking time to enjoy nature and the beauty around us, helping your friends and neighbors – choosing love over judgment. It makes my heart swell.

There have been some people who helped me immensely along the way. Thank you to my good friend and hippy Momma, Cara Wilson Granat who encouraged me to pursue my writing career. Without her, these words would never have been written. Thank you to those brave few who read my first drafts and gave me feedback. Thanks to Rose Cooper, Joanna Rowland, Lou Ann Barnett, and Lisa Schmidt for the Sacramento Writer Weekends in Lake Tahoe. They listened while I cried, asked questions, and made me dig deeper. Thanks to my critique partners, some of whom I already mentioned but also include Catherine Arguelles, Shirley Richey, Nikki Shannon Smith, and Traci Van Wagoner. All of these amazing women believed in me! Big shout out to Catherine Arguelles for helping me with my editing!

Thank you to SCBWI North/Central and San Francisco North regions and their volunteers for all the fantastic workshops and conferences they put on. Here I could fine-tune my writing and meet my writing partners. And thank you, too, to Andrea Brown Literary Agency and their Big Sur Writing Workshop, where I received incredible feedback from other writers, editors, and agents. They all told me I had a story to tell.

Also, I want to shout out to all girls with ADHD and/or dyslexia. When I was in school a million years ago, no one knew what ADHD was, let alone dyslexia — they labeled me as stupid, lazy, and a daydreamer. Obviously, in my home life, no one cared to figure out why I was different. But I also had teachers like Mr. Ballentine (he was real) who encouraged me through art. I encourage you, if you have ADHD or have friends who do, to find creative outlets or something you're passionate about and do it. Having ADHD or ADD does not mean you're stupid, lazy, or can't learn—it means you look at the world through a different lens and are AWESOME! ADHD women are changing the world! Dyslexia is not a life-stopper. I can be a challenge at times. If I can overcome these obstacles, anyone can.

Secondly, if you have a friend or relative who is a Jehovah's Witness, be the best friend you can be, like Val. The Vals, Gabes, and the Mr. Balentines of the world gave me hope. If you suspect abuse of any kind, it's okay to report it to a teacher, a principal, or a trusted adult.

ABOUT THE AUTHOR

Sally lives in Orlando, Florida, where she enjoys the local beaches, kayaking in the springs, visiting the local bookstores, and writing. She can often be found writing on her laptop at the local coffee shop or caring for her numerous plant babies. She currently has no pets, but she loves caring for other people's pets, which allows her to visit new places. She loves to listen to true-crime podcasts and watch crime docu-series. Her children are all grown and live in Orlando and Denver.

She is a writing coach, teaching business professionals to write a book in 30 days as well as a mentor. Sally is a member of SCBWI (Society of Children's Book Writers and Illustrators). She loves to teach people how to create with their words and loves to speak to groups about writing, growing up a Jehovah's Witness, or having ADHD.

Sally grew up in the Jehovah's Witness cult and was able to leave at the age of sixteen. After years of recovery and self-discovery, she has been able to help other young people and adults who struggle with leaving and the aftermath.

This picture is me in my early writing days.